W9-ATT-722

THORNGHOST

THORNGHOST

TONE
ALMHJELL

DIAL BOOKS FOR YOUNG READERS

For Torbjørn, first and last

DIAL BOOKS FOR YOUNG READERS
PENGUIN YOUNG READERS GROUP
An imprint of Penguin Random House LLC
375 Hudson Street
New York, NY 10014

Maps and music artwork by Jennifer Thermes

Library of Congress Cataloging-in-Publication Data
Names: Almhjell, Tone, author. Title: Thornghost / Tone Almhjell.
Description: New York : Dial Books for Young Readers, [2016] | Summary: "When strange things start happening in the woods around Niklas's home, he and his lynx sidekick travel to another realm to save their world"— Provided by publisher.
Identifiers: LCCN 2015035420 | ISBN 9780803738973
Subjects: | CYAC: Fantasy. | Magic—Fiction. | BISAC: JUVENILE FICTION / Fantasy & Magic. Classification: LCC PZ7.A4474 Th 2016 | DDC [Fic]—dc23
LC record available at http://lccn.loc.gov/2015035420

Printed in the United States of America

1 3 5 7 9 10 8 6 4 2

Design by Jennifer Kelly
Text set in Minister Std Light

THE TROLLHEIM MOUNTAINS
BUTTERTOP
Mountain Vales
Beach
SORROWDEEP
Rowans
Stone ford
THE SUMMERHILL WOODS
SUMMERCHILD
Path
OLDMEADOW
Oak tree
OAK BRIDGE
N
W
E
S
Ash tree
SCREAMING STONE
MOLYK
Main House
Chapel
Elm
Morello House
Barn
HALLOWFIELD
SUMMERHILL
NETHERFIELD
RIVER ROAD

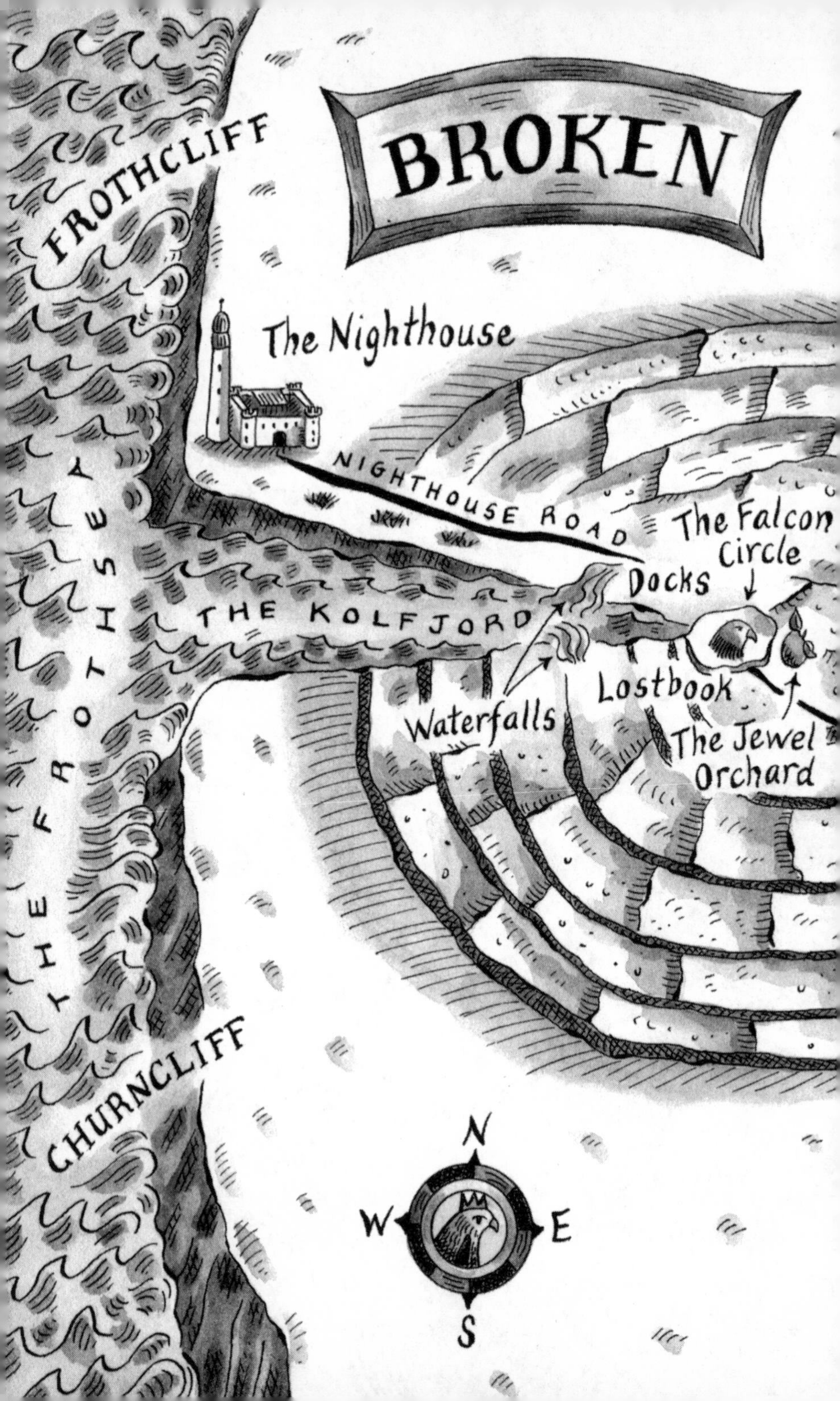
BROKEN
FROTHCLIFF
The Nighthouse
NIGHTHOUSE ROAD
The Falcon Circle
Docks
THE KOLFJORD
THE FROTHING SEA
Lostbook
Waterfalls
The Jewel Orchard
CHURNCLIFF
N
W
E
S

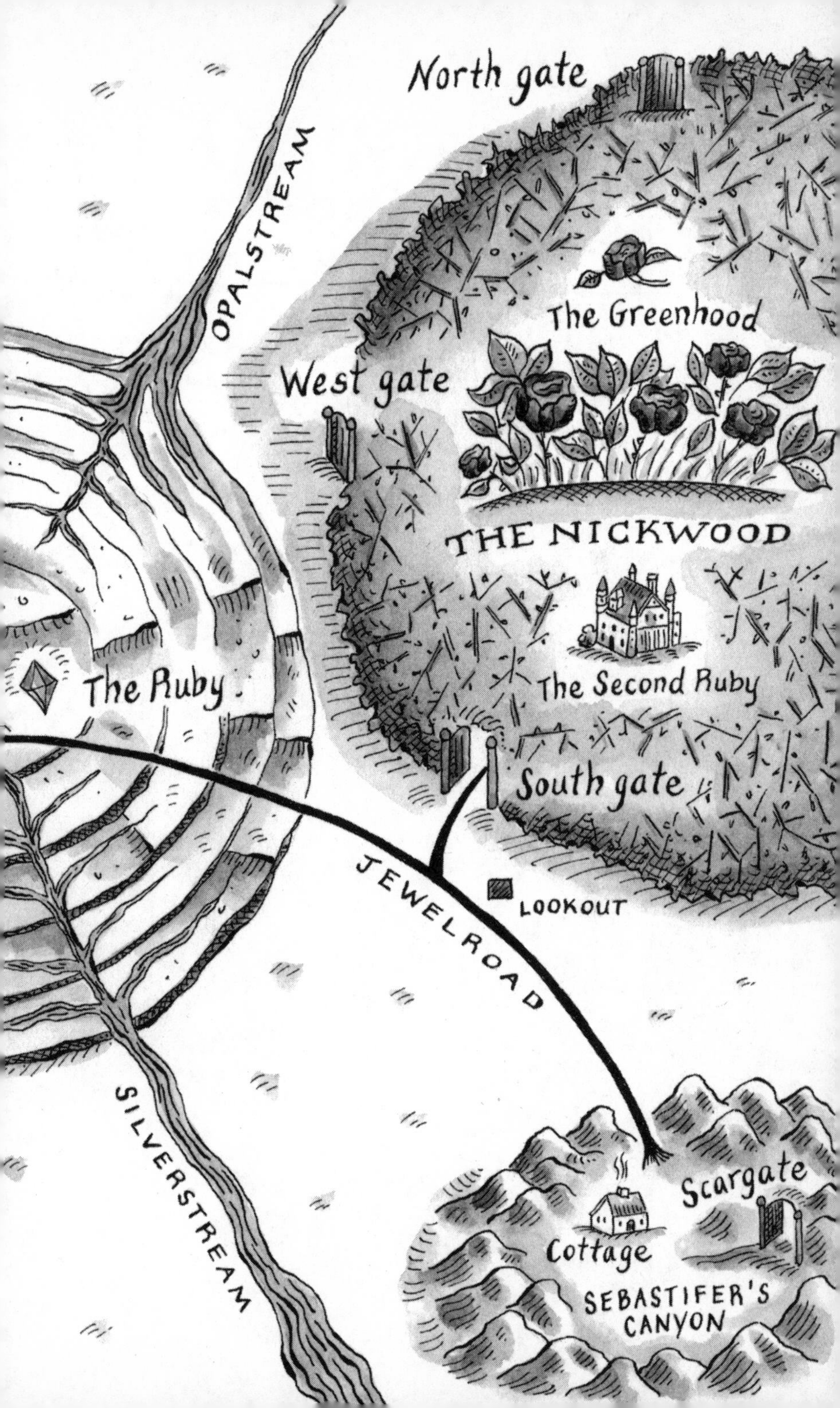
North gate
OPALSTREAM
The Greenhood
West gate
THE NICKWOOD
The Ruby
The Second Ruby
South gate
JEWELROAD
LOOKOUT
Scargate
Cottage
SILVERSTREAM
SEBASTIFER'S
CANYON

When Niklas was four, he said to his mother: "Mom, I have terrible news. There's a skull inside your head!"

He'd told her this in the bird room, below the skeleton mobiles that circled slowly under the rafters. He had been looking in the science books, and he had just figured out that the piles of bones that sat on his mother's desk actually belonged on the inside of living things.

Niklas was twelve now, but he remembered this scene for two reasons. One, because his mother had laughed, and this was his only memory of her laughing. And two, because the next summer, his mother had been buried in the Summerhill graveyard, skull, skeleton, and all.

They were all that remained of her. Her bones, and sometimes, the nightmare.

Chapter One

The apples in the orchard were nothing but sour buds. No point in stealing those.

Niklas Summerhill frowned at the Molyk farmhouse with its paint of patchy lemon yellow. Mr. Molyk probably lurked somewhere behind the windows, watching through his binoculars. He claimed he used them to watch wild birds, when in fact he watched for wild kids.

Not without reason, Niklas had to admit. In all of Willodale, Mr. Molyk was by far his favorite victim.

Usually, Niklas preferred to do his little raids in the evenings, when Willodale filled with deep shadows under the towering mountains. But the rain had only just let up after two days, and he was too itchy after being cooped up to wait any longer. He just had to be careful.

And he had to figure out where to strike, of course. Not the tractor, because that could get expensive. Definitely nothing involving the manure pit. Unless . . . He hated to be predictable, but maybe the boot trick again? Just the thought of Mr. Molyk sticking his feet into sloshy, first-grade muck made Niklas grin. He picked up a small rock, perfect for throwing at the rusty iron roof of the Molyk barn, put it in his pocket, and edged toward the pit.

Down by the river a faint jingling sounded, the source hidden by the orchard. Niklas slipped from tree to tree until he could see the riverbank. Sure enough. The enclosure by the old mink pens held a flock of lambs and the bell sheep Edith, who nipped at the sad grass by the legs of the burnt-out cages. It was mid-August, so the sheep should still be up in the mountain vales getting fat. But Mr. Molyk had brought them down early this year, and that could only mean one thing.

Forget about the boots.

"Come on. We're letting the . . ." He turned over his left shoulder, but quickly closed his mouth. *I'm letting the lambs out,* he corrected himself. Eleven months had passed, but for a moment there, he had forgotten.

She was gone. Always his best friend had hovered there, one step behind, ready to tell him about the flaws in his plan. But Lindelin Rosenquist had left with her mother and father, moved to the city to live in a rotten house on stilts. They claimed they were coming back, but they kept pushing the date for their return. Last he heard, it was another year from now. Niklas rubbed his forehead. No Lin, no one to stop him from taking a risk or two. Besides, what could be wrong with giving the lambs a final taste of freedom?

Staying in the cover of the fence, he unlatched the gate to the enclosure, fetched a couple of sugar cubes out of his pocket, and clicked his tongue softly.

"Here, Edith, pretty, pretty Edith! Want some sugar?"

Edith raised her long, not-so-pretty head, still chewing.

"That's right," Niklas said, holding out his hand. "I've got sugar for you, sugar and green woods!"

Edith came jingling through the gate with all the little ones in tow. As she munched up the treats, Niklas reached into the bell around her neck and twisted the clapper stuck so it wouldn't make any noise. "Keep him off your trail a little bit longer," he said, patting her scruff. Edith sniffed after more sugar, and when there wasn't any, she let Niklas nudge her away from the farm and wandered toward the woods with a line of tail-wagging lambs behind her.

They kept each other company up the hill. The sheep ate glittering tufts of grass, Niklas picked wild strawberries with sweet, cool raindrops. The trail rose hard between the trees, sometimes turning into steps held in place by roots. But neither Edith nor the little ones seemed to mind the climb, and the valley fell quickly away beneath them.

One by one the other neighbor farms came into view. Slanting fields glowing bright in the dark woods, with long, narrow houses tucked at the back of shelves in the plunging mountainside.

Fale with its rows and rows of vegetables, where a fleet-footed thief could snitch a fortune in carrots and plums. Ottem, where only last week Niklas rode the pulley to the top of the granary, but not down again, since Mrs. Ottem insisted on calling a fire truck to come fetch him off the ledge. And Molyk on a strip of sandy ground by the emerald-colored river.

Niklas had chosen it for his favorite target because Mr. Molyk kept lambs that got sent away on trucks at the end of the season. This had been the case since Niklas asked his grandmother where the truck would take them, and got an honest explanation about the fate of most summer lambs. Grandma Alma just shook her head and said, "You should think of something else to do with your life, because you'll make a lousy farmer."

As if he had much of a choice. Who else was there to take over the farm when Uncle Anders got too old? But Niklas would rather be a hero than a farmer, and today, he was rescuing the Molyk lambs. At least for a little while.

For the next three turns, the path wound up through an old rock slide. On that bare patch, he'd be easy to spot, say, with a pair of binoculars. So Niklas made himself some armor from maple leaves strung together on skinny twigs.

"If it will fool trolls, it will fool Mr. Molyk," he told one of the lambs, a little straggler who liked to sniff around a bit before climbing the root steps. She tore off a leaf of sourgrass, looking unimpressed, and Niklas shrugged. "Not my fault you don't know about trolls."

To be fair, not many did. Three summers ago, Lin and Niklas had found an old jar behind Grandma Alma's fishing gear in the loft. The contents didn't seem like much, just a handful of dusty, smelly acorns. But it had a label that said *Troll's Bane,* and when Lin saw that, her eyes had lit up. "This is for hunting trolls," she had said. "In the woods!" Niklas scratched a black spot behind the lamb's ear, and added, "It's our favorite game, you see. Or used to be."

He hadn't been troll hunting since Lin left. No point in that either.

Summerhill lay far enough up the mountainside to stay out of the evening shade, and by the time the path forked, the trees were tipped in gold. Niklas said good-bye to Edith and the lambs and followed the sound of rushing water home.

The Summerchild tumbled down from Buttertop and ran all through the Summerhill lands. "That stream is just like you," Grandma Alma sometimes told him. "Noisy and wild." But Niklas had always thought that the stream was like his mother: just passing through. When he was younger, he used to imagine he heard her voice in the water, singing him lullabies.

The sound of a scratchy engine cut into the splashes, and as Niklas entered the yard, he saw the first sign of trouble: farmer Molyk's truck vanishing down the road like a red-eyed creature retreating into a sea of trees. He'd found out already, then.

Usually Mr. Molyk would just call, shouting until Grandma Alma's phone crackled. Only for some of Niklas's more inspired ideas did he force his old truck halfway up the hill in order to yell at him in person. But Niklas had let the sheep out before without the honor of a red-faced lecture. Something was wrong.

He skipped up the steps and through the front door, and Grandma Alma called him immediately from the bird room.

Something was very wrong.

His grandmother liked to spend her evenings by the black stove in the new room, which wasn't new at all, but a cozy den of old novels, camphor candy, and oil paintings of stormy shores. But tonight she had chosen to wait for him in the easternmost of Summerhill's rooms, in the company of memories.

The room had gotten its name because of Niklas's mother, who had filled it with birds. Not living creatures, but bones and books and sketches. She puzzled the skeletons together with twine and hung them under the rafters. She braided leftover feathers and beaks into long strings that reached from ceiling to floor. They took it all down after she died, but Niklas remembered how the walls used to flutter and click with the draft, how the skeleton birds twirled. Grandma Alma only lectured him there when she wanted to make him squirm.

Before he poked his head in, he put on a mask of innocence. "You need something, Grandma?"

She sat in one of the stern, tall chairs, even though it must make her back ache. In her youth, Grandma Alma had carried so many buckets of water up from the Summerchild that her spine had slowly curled into a question mark. But there was nothing questioning about Grandma Alma's face tonight. "You were in Mr. Molyk's fields, stealing his sheep."

Niklas gave a bow. They had their own way of doing this, like a play they both knew by heart. The neighbors called Niklas the rascal prince, which made Grandma Alma the reigning queen. "Not stealing, Your Majesty! Do you see me carrying any lambs in my pockets? I was just giving them a little taste of—"

Grandma Alma stopped him before he could finish his line. "That was reckless. Reckless and stupid."

Niklas straightened up, still trying to stick to the script. "But I have to prove myself worthy if I'm to inherit the realm."

That ought to earn him a chuckle, followed by a half-hearted scolding. Grandma Alma had once had a town meeting called in her honor to discuss "the slick fingers of that insufferable Miss Summerhill." But that was more than seventy years ago, and Grandma Alma's fingers had grown knuckled and bent, almost too weak to make hot chocolate anymore, let alone do any mischief. They rested now in her lap, clasped and blue in the evening light.

"Niklas, Niklas," she said at last. "Not all pranks are funny, and not all paths are safe. There were hunters in the woods today. Hunters with guns."

"Oh." Niklas felt his mask fall. The hunters could have seen him darting between the trees, all stealthy in his maple armor, and if they got nervous . . . He knew enough to be careful in the hunting season. Except it wasn't hunting season. "What were they after?"

Grandma Alma's voice dropped. "Something has been marauding deer in the woods. Could be a bear. Could be that sneaky lynx. Whatever it is, it's big and out to kill."

Niklas bit his lip. Edith and the lambs were still out there. "I didn't know that. I'm sorry."

"I know you are," Grandma Alma said. "But sorry won't save those poor sheep. Now, I know what you're thinking, and you may not. The hunting party is still out. You could get shot if you go into the woods again tonight, so *you may not.* Do you hear me?"

Niklas nodded. He heard.

Grandma Alma frowned at him with her wet-rimmed eyes. "Sleep," she told him. "Think on your sorry. Tomorrow you may help Mr. Molyk gather his sheep."

Or what is left of them, Niklas thought as he crept up the stairs, all twitchy with regret. He had led a whole flock of lambs and their mother into the maw of a predator.

At the top landing, he sat down by the window to watch the yard. Sure, he had heard. But that didn't mean he was going to listen.

Chapter Two

The night was not black.

Sometime in late spring, all darkness bled out of the Willodale sky and settled in the trees below, leaving everything blue. The white long house, the red barn, the little cottage in the morello garden where Lin and her family used to live: all glowed ghostly pale around the yard. The elm tree stretched inky branches across the grass.

Niklas waited. He didn't worry about Uncle Anders, who had gone to bed early, even for him. But a patch of yellow fell from Grandma Alma's bedroom and onto the grass, and Niklas sat quietly until the light winked out. Then he snuck down the stairs. The hunters may have found the sheep already; he hoped they had. But unlike the hunters, Niklas knew where Edith and the lambs had been heading. He wanted to be sure.

The air felt chill as he slipped under the fence. The

electrical wire was supposed to mark the line between outlying fields and the farm, but Niklas knew better. The fence was not the border.

The true border ran through the screaming stone.

The Summerhill woods were dotted with boulders and rocks fallen from Buttertop. Some were huge, like the very tips of mountains. Others were standing stones that sometimes, when the light slanted in just so, scowled at anyone who passed.

Niklas had scaled each and every one of the bigger stones and leaned against the scowlers. But there was one stone he never touched. A ways up the trail, so close to Summerhill that Niklas could see it from his bedroom, stood the six-foot-tall screaming stone. It had a narrow hole through the middle, and when the wind blew through the slit, it made a sound like a thin wail.

The Willodalers had all sorts of stories to explain why the stone screamed. Most said it keened for the dead, and those doomed to die.

"That's everyone, then." Lin had shrugged, and this was true. But Niklas still kept to the other side of the track when he passed that stone. Lin had asked him why once, but he hadn't told her. He didn't want to invite the nightmare back by talking about it. So he made up a new explanation.

"This . . ." he had said, poking a finger as close to the stone as he could bear. ". . . is the border."

"Which border?" Lin had asked.

"Between the farms and the forest. Between our world and theirs. Right through this troll heart."

"Aha! This is a petrified troll," Lin had said, because she was good with words like that.

"Turned to stone by sunlight," Niklas had said. "Like all the other scowlers. But that's not what killed it. See the hole? That's what troll's bane does. It melts through their flesh. One perfect hit and they're dead."

This night and every night, as Niklas passed the stone, he patted his shirt pocket. Even if they didn't play the game anymore, he always carried some acorns with him into the woods.

From Edith's impatient pace, Niklas guessed she had headed for one of the two perfect spots for grazing on the Buttertop trail. The first was Oldmeadow, a sloping field no more than half a mile up the mountainside. He found it deserted. But he discovered two pebbly piles of dung where the trail curved back into the woods.

That left only one place to look.

Sorrowdeep.

Niklas stared up at the snowcapped peak of Buttertop. To get past it and up into the grassy mountain vales, you had to climb a ragged trail along a lip of cliff, left shattered by the big avalanche almost two hundred years ago. The herds of Willodale rarely went up that path except when their humans made them at the beginning of every summer. But before the trail, on a wide shelf just above the tree line, cradled by slopes of lush mountain grass, lay the black pond of Sorrowdeep.

In the entire valley, it was the place where Niklas least liked to go. Because in those waters lived a darkness that wanted to pull you down. Or so Grandma Alma had told him countless times. It was her favorite scary story. "Stay away from that pond, my boy. It's made of death and sorrow. If you try to swim in it, it will freeze your limbs and still your breath. It will weigh you down with every wrong you've ever done. It will drag you to the bottom and keep you in a cage of regret."

The problem was, sheep didn't care about stories, and neither did predators.

Niklas ducked his head and kept climbing, following the path as it carved its way from ledge to ledge through ever-thinning woods. On the final shelf before Sorrowdeep, the wind came down to meet him, setting the ferns to shivering.

He stopped and wrinkled his nose. The wind carried a faint stench. He left the path and made his way to the end of the ledge, where the Summerchild flew off a cliff. Probably a dead deer, but he should look. If the carcass was in the water, it would poison Summerhill's water supply.

At the top of the waterfall, flat stones formed a dotted line across the stream, like worn-down teeth. Once, before the big avalanche changed the face of Buttertop, the path had crossed over here. But no one used this ford anymore, and the track was nearly lost under roots and dry twigs.

Niklas stepped out on the first stone. The Summerchild rushed past him, misting the air where it fell. He saw no deer, but he heard a rumble, so soft his ears strained to pick it up under the splashing of the stream. He felt it too, a tremor under his feet that brought out goose bumps on his arms.

A howl cut through the mist. Niklas froze, stunned by how strange it sounded. Sharp like the scream of a fox, but so dark it had to come from the throat of a much bigger creature. On the far bank, behind some slender rowans, a single light appeared. Round and big like a flashlight, except there was no beam, and it looked somehow . . . hungry.

Twigs began to snap, the rowan trunks creaked and yielded, and suddenly there were two lights instead of one.

Eyes.

Niklas Summerhill was no coward, but neither was he a complete idiot.

He turned and fled.

Chapter Three

The beast ran faster than him.

Niklas took all the shortcuts he knew, pivoting around the right branches as the path jackknifed down through the woods. The creature behind him was not so limber. For every turn it made, he heard it crash into a tree or thump against a stone. Even so, it gained on him.

When they emerged onto the Oldmeadow, the path looped through the grass in a wide curve with nothing to slow the beast down. Niklas had to think of something, now, or it would catch him.

He veered right and plunged into the thigh-high grass. Nettles licked at his hands as he cut across the field, dodging stones and grooves in the ground. The wind made the grass hiss, bringing the foul smell with it. The bear—it had to be a bear; Niklas couldn't think of any other animal this big and heavy—must be very sick or hurt. He felt a cold tug in his belly. There was nothing more dangerous than a wounded animal.

The beast howled behind him, the same eerie, distorted scream, and so close now. Niklas wanted to look over his shoulder, but he couldn't afford it. The beast came closer for every step. He needed to hide.

They were coming up on the southwest corner of the Oldmeadow, where the path crossed the Summerchild over Oak Bridge.

Niklas knew he wouldn't make it to the bridge. He broke right again, down into the streambed, hurtling into the water. On the far bank, he slammed down on his belly and scrambled under a dense mass of juniper brambles. Dry needles crackled as he crawled in between the bushes.

The beast splashed into the water and stopped. Niklas couldn't see it, but he could smell it, and he could hear it, snorting and wheezing, sniffing at the shrub.

It could smell him, too.

A slithering breath gusted under the juniper. Under the branches, the eyes appeared again, pale green discs, broken into pieces by the twigs. The beast grunted and began pulling the bushes out of the ground, roots and all.

Niklas pushed himself up the bank, squeezing deeper and deeper into the shrub, until he rolled out between two knobby juniper limbs and saw a latticed canopy far above. The oak tree!

He stumbled across the path and clawed his way up the gnarled trunk until he got high enough for the branches to thin. Only then dared he to look down.

A bare wedge of ravaged earth cut into the shrub, reaching almost to the other side. The far bank of the stream was strewn with torn and tossed junipers. But there was no hulking shape, no green eyes. The beast had disappeared.

Niklas tried to keep his gulps of air quiet. This didn't make any sense. A wounded animal would attack; maybe give chase if it felt threatened. But this thing didn't act like a creature crazed by pain. It was hunting him. And bears did not have green eyes that glowed in the dark.

His hands shook too hard to hold on properly, so he slid down a few yards and settled where three branches met to form a chair of sorts. Lin used to call it his throne. He had sat in it hundreds of times because the oak tree was their troll-hunting headquarters.

"Best place to get acorns for the troll's bane," Niklas had pointed out. Oak trees rarely grew this far north, and there were only three in all of Willodale. But that wasn't the only reason they had chosen it. The oak tree had branches that stretched over the stream, and reached out beyond the cliff upon which the tree perched. If you moved around in the canopy, you had as good a view of the Summerhill lands as you'd ever get.

The wind shifted, and hushed voices blew across the

stream from Oldmeadow. Niklas eased out of his throne and moved a notch up the trunk to see better.

The hunting party. They approached quickly along the trail, flashlight beams roving over the grass. "I swear I heard a scream," said a voice, and Niklas winced. Mr. Molyk.

"You're sure it wasn't young Master Summerhill trying to pull our legs?" another voice said. Mrs. Ottem. "He's always lurking around this neck of the woods."

"Well, if it was, maybe I should give him a taste of my peppercorns." Molyk patted his shotgun as he stepped onto Oak Bridge. "He deserves it tonight, that's for sure."

Mrs. Ottem grunted. "It was a shame with his mother, but it's past time everyone stopped coddling him."

"They're just pranks," a third man said, joining them on the bridge. Niklas recognized the voice of one of the Fale brothers.

"Tell that to your wife," Mrs. Ottem said. "It's her plum jam that keeps vanishing."

"Oh, we don't know it's him," Mr. Fale said. "We keep our jam behind locked doors, and Niklas is just a lad. I hardly think—"

"Tell that to my sheep," Mr. Molyk cut him off. "You saw Edith, half-mad with fear, and the lambs, too. We're lucky we got them before they fell off the mountain trail."

Up in the tree, Niklas leaned his forehead against the trunk. The Willodalers didn't get it at all. He might fill their boots with muck when they deserved it, but he would never hurt an animal on purpose. He felt tingly with relief that the sheep were safe. But then Mr. Molyk added, "And that's not even mentioning the last poor wretch. Or was that just a prank, too?"

Niklas's tingles went cold. What had happened to the last poor wretch?

But he didn't find out, because instead Mr. Fale gave a cry. He leaned over the side of the bridge, pointing his flashlight up the stream. The hunters filed down to the water and out of Niklas's line of sight. He heard them arguing over the torn shrubs and whether or not they could have anything to do with the beast. Then they all fell silent.

Niklas craned his neck, but he couldn't see anything. When the hunters started speaking again, the words were harsh hisses that he couldn't make out over the Summerchild. He eased out on a branch that leaned over the stream.

"I'm telling you, it's warped," Mrs. Ottem said.

"No it isn't," Mr. Molyk said. "It's clear as day. It's just too big to be possible."

What were they looking at? Niklas needed to get closer, but the branch he perched on was on the slim side and yielded slightly every time he shifted his weight. He glanced behind himself to gauge how far he could go, and just like that, he forgot all about the hunters' discovery.

There was something in the tree with him.

It sat crouched and tense in his throne, watching him with slanted eyes that were rimmed in black and white.

A lynx.

For a long moment, they stared at each other, boy and cat. Below them, the hunters came clambering up the bank under Niklas's branch. He only had to call out and the men would have both him and the lynx at close range.

But Mr. Molyk spoke first. "If I catch this thing, I'm going to make it pay for my lamb."

The lynx turned away, looking out over the valley. It had paws as big as saucers. Even a male that size would be reckoned as large, but Niklas was sure this one was female. He took in her long whiskers and white chin fur, the elegant curve of the flecked back and the tall tuft that crowned the right ear. The left ear had a split down the middle, a nasty old wound that had robbed her of the tuft.

Huge or no, this could not be the same creature that had chased him. She wouldn't crash into trees on the path. She didn't stink. And though he had no idea how or why, Niklas had the strangest feeling she felt sorry for the lamb.

So he didn't call out. He stayed still until the hunters had passed under them and disappeared down the trail.

When their voices had completely drowned in the Summerchild's noise, Niklas edged farther out on his branch, until it creaked under his weight. If it snapped, he would probably break his neck, but he wanted to put whatever distance he could between and himself and the giant cat. One thing was certain: The lynx had to leave first. Niklas could not climb down until she was gone. He didn't want to be pounced from above.

The lynx didn't make him wait. She slid out of the tree, melting from limb to limb and onto the path without ever snapping a twig or shaking a leaf. Before the woods swallowed her, she turned and looked up at Niklas one last time.

She opened her mouth and a voice came out, slurred and rough, but clear enough to almost send Niklas tumbling from the branch.

"Thhhhank you."

Chapter Four

All the way down from Oak Bridge, Niklas fought to keep his eyes forward. He needed to watch where he stepped, but his back crawled with sneaking horror. He waited for the hunters to cock their rifles, for the smell of the green-eyed creature to catch up with him, for the lynx to attack. Had he imagined that she said those words? He must have, because it was impossible. Maybe it was just a desperate need to be right that she wasn't the killer beast. That she was somehow kind and gentle, even if she was a predator. Uncle Anders's warning churned in his head: *You be careful now. If the cat is big enough, it might consider you prey.*

The cat was big enough, and she could very well be the lynx from this spring. *That sneaky lynx,* as Grandma Alma had put it. His grandmother was still angry about the roast, and she didn't understand when he tried to explain about Lin and Rufus.

Rufus was Lin's pet, a little redback vole that she had rescued in the mountains. Niklas had never had a pet, and he really wanted one. He had asked for a dog a hundred times, but Grandma Alma always answered with a gruff "We don't keep dogs at Summerhill," or "We have animals aplenty." And sure, there was Tobis the cat, who hated kids and preferred the hayloft to humans anyway. There was Dokka, Uncle Anders's horse, who liked only him. There were the milk cows, who let him pat their foreheads, but only if he brought them salt. None of them loved Niklas, not like Rufus loved Lin.

Then the lynx turned up during a spell of heavy snows last March.

They had found her tracks near the edge of the thicket just above the screaming stone. Round four-toed footprints under the biggest ash tree, where she must have perched for a while, or so Uncle Anders reckoned. "That must be one hungry cat to come this close to the house," he had said, shaking his head. So Niklas had an idea. He had taken the Sunday roast and strung it up in the branches.

"You have lost your mind, boy," Grandma Alma had muttered as she served them a dinner of cabbage and potatoes. "Stealing food to feed killers on our doorstep!"

The next morning, the roast was gone. But it was snowing hard, and the tracks were gone, too. Niklas couldn't know for certain who had taken the meat. He believed it was the lynx, but that could be because he wanted it to be her. He just wanted to save her, like Lin had saved Rufus.

He turned the final bend before Summerhill and stopped cold. The last lamb.

She lay draped over the screaming stone, belly down, limbs stretched down the side. The hunters must have put her there to keep the little body away from hungry mouths. There was a spot of black behind her ear, one that he had scratched only hours ago. The little straggler.

She had a single long gash in her side, where some of her pelt had been torn off. What creature did that? The lynx did have big paws and the claws to go with it. But he told himself that the cruel injury fit better with the green-eyed hunter. Not that it mattered to the lamb. Niklas stood beside her for a while, aching with regret. He wanted to lift her down and hug her, but what good would it do? She would still be dead, and his clothes would be stained for Grandma Alma to see in the morning. So he scratched the black spot gently and left her there for the hunters to bring home.

The wind blew the rest of the clouds from the sky, leaving it bleak and bare. It chased down from Sorrowdeep and swept over hill and trail, and as Niklas slunk home to his bed, the screaming stone whistled after him.

Chapter Five

With the nightmares it could go either way.

They could leave him alone or they could poke at him all night. Skeleton birds pecking at his eyes. Dark water rushing in to sweep him away. Giant rocks tumbling down toward the sleeping house. Or worse, much worse. Niklas sometimes thought it had to do with his room, which had windows facing both north, up the mountainside, and south, into the yard. One toward horror and one toward home.

He crept under the covers. *Don't think bad things,* he told himself.

It was no good, of course. Even with his eyes shut, he saw the lamb with the little spot on her neck, and the hungry lantern eyes shining in under the skirts of the juniper. But when he finally gave in and slept, the lamb didn't bother him, and neither did lynx nor beast. Instead the wail from the screaming stone found its way into his ears, curling down his spine, squeezing his ribs good and tight. For the first time in a long while, Niklas dreamt of *her.*

He woke in his bed and turned to the north. The moon lit the sandy path up the slope so it gleamed like a road of bones. He couldn't see her yet, but he knew she would come. The woods knew it, the stream knew it, every sleeping soul in Summerhill knew it.

His heart pounded louder and louder, and when it had him shaking like a drum, she stepped through the gate, wearing a white dress that brushed the ground as she floated up the path. Her face was half turned away, but he could see her high cheekbones and the silver-blond curls.

His mother, going to Sorrowdeep.

At the screaming stone she halted as always. Slowly, surely, she turned, until he could see her gaunt face. She stared straight at him with eyes as black as the pond, silenced by the water that poured from her mouth. But the screaming stone spoke. It wailed and wailed, crying for the dead.

Niklas woke, bolting upright in his bed. The cover dropped to the floor with a whisper. He forced himself to look out the north window at the trail lightening in the gray of dawn.

Empty. It was always empty.

* * * * *

That wasn't at all how his mother died.

The dream must come from Grandma Alma's story, because Niklas had no recollection of his mother even mentioning Sorrowdeep, let alone walking up the trail. By the time he was old enough to remember, she didn't have the strength to trek up the mountainside anyway. Still, he had this nightmare every night from the day his mother died and until Lin and her family moved in.

He sank back on the pillow. His throat felt parched. Uncle Anders had left a glass of water for him right next to the bed, but Niklas didn't touch it. He never could drink water without thinking of the liquid gushing out of his mother's mouth.

Which was stupid, because Erika Summerhill didn't drown. She was eaten up by a sickness that was there before Niklas was born and got much worse after, until there was nothing left of her.

His memories were patchy now. Just scenes, feelings, and colors, like the sunny yellow of the room they shared when he was little. But when his mother couldn't get out of bed anymore, she had moved to the dimness of the room at the other end of the house, where the only sunshine that crept across her covers was red and fading.

Niklas had taken to hiding in the closet across the corridor, tucked behind Grandma Alma's old winter coats. Whenever the door opened, he got a glimpse of rosy light and sad-masked grown-ups who paused on the threshold. One afternoon, Grandma Alma had appeared in the doorway and said, "Erika is leaving now. If someone would like to say good-bye."

Niklas had crawled out from the closet, and peered through the crack. The drapes were pulled back to reveal a bony arm with a white tube stuck to the hand. It looked like it belonged to one of the skeleton birds in the bird room. He thought he heard a whisper then, faint behind the curtain. "Keep him away from me." The fingers twitched, the tube rattled. "I'm dangerous. I'm a Thornghost!"

And Niklas had turned and run, down the stairs and out the door, across the yard and into the woods. That evening, as he sat under the oak tree, he had promised himself: He wouldn't be a coward anymore.

To prove his point, he had stayed until dark and walked home without running. And when the nightmares began, he hadn't once gone crying to Grandma Alma, or anyone.

Chapter Six

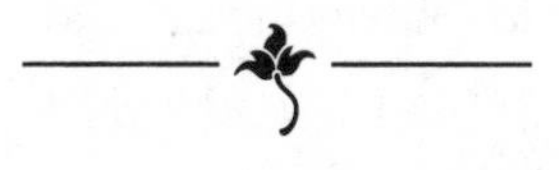

The next morning, Mr. Molyk showed up with two shovels. Niklas followed him down to the hallowfield to dig a hole for the lamb.

The graveyard lay at the eastern edge of the farm, where the Summerchild curved around a meadow of buttercups and headstones.

Back before the big avalanche, Summerhill had been considered the most important farm in Willodale. When the rocks came down and took half the farm, they made this meadow a place of memory for all those that disappeared, and built a small but handsome chapel in the middle to anchor their souls.

But that was many years ago. All that remained of the chapel now was a few winter-gnawed beams that stuck up from a square of tumbling walls. Niklas was instructed to stay away from the ruins so he wouldn't get his head knocked in by a falling stone, and in this case, he actually did as he was told. Mostly he stayed away from the graveyard altogether, because one of the headstones belonged to his mother.

Everyone in the village said it was a shame that Erika had been put to rest there and not by the Willodale church. Many said the hallowfield could hardly be reckoned as hallowed anymore, now that the chapel had fallen into disrepair. Some told Niklas he should be glad that headstone was heavy. "That lady had a dark twist in her head," they muttered, eyebrows arched with pity.

These last ones could always count on their apples mysteriously disappearing in the fall. Gossip-mongers. But Niklas still didn't like visiting his mother's grave. He couldn't bear to look at her name and know that her bones were down there, in the ground. He couldn't bear the thought that the gossip might be true.

Mr. Molyk had no doubt chosen to bury the lamb right outside the graveyard fence to torment him. But Niklas didn't need the graveyard for that. The little lamb was torment enough. She resembled a white rag all mussed and matted. "I'm so sorry this happened to you, little rag," he whispered when Mr. Molyk had his back turned. "I don't even know what your name was."

Mr. Molyk stepped out of the thigh-deep hole. "No name. That's best for these that leave at summer's end. But it was a nasty fate even so."

Uncle Anders said Peder Molyk was a decent man. That he had shut down his father's mink business as soon as he took over the farm, and that he loved his sheep. Niklas had his own opinion on the matter, though, and Mr. Molyk confirmed it when he stuck his shovel in the ground and said, "All right. You can toss her in."

There would be no tossing if Niklas could help it. He lifted the lamb and climbed in with her, laid her down as if she were sleeping, and scratched the ear spot one final time. As he filled the dirt back in, Mr. Molyk watched under heavy lids. "My whole life I've seen lambs come and go. Only once I've seen wounds like these we've had this summer."

"Grandma says it's a bear," Niklas muttered. She had said lynx, too, but he didn't want to give Mr. Molyk any ideas.

"Bears bite and tear," Mr. Molyk said. "They don't slice."

"Then what was it?"

"Good question." The farmer tugged his shovel free of the ground and wandered in amongst the graves. He stopped in front of Erika's headstone. "See you stay out of the woods at night, young Summerhill. For your own sake."

"You said you'd seen this once before," Niklas said, staying put by the fence. "When?"

Molyk turned back to face him. "Twenty-five years ago. Two horses killed at Sorrowdeep."

Horses. A predator would have to be pretty big to take down horses. Niklas squinted. Wouldn't do to look daunted in front of Mr. Molyk of all people. "Did you catch the beast that did it?"

"No. The killings just stopped. Most people agreed the creature, whatever it was, had gone back into the Trollheim Mountains." He fixed Niklas with dark eyes that burned. "There's something I've been wondering about. I've talked to the other farmers in the area. They've all lost livestock this year. All except for you."

Niklas met his gaze. Was he expecting some sort of confession? As if Niklas snuck around at night with a kitchen knife? "We keep a close watch on our flock."

"Any particular reason you didn't send them up to the mountain vales for summer grazing this year? Maybe the fiddler thought the early meadows would be enough for once?"

"We didn't like the look of the trail after the snowmelt," Niklas said, which wasn't entirely true. It was Uncle Anders who didn't like the look of the trail, and Niklas figured it had more to do with Grandma Alma not being able to manage without Uncle Anders if he spent the summer up in the shieling. But that was none of Mr. Molyk's business, and Niklas hated it when people called his uncle the fiddler.

When Uncle Anders was young, he had been a fiddler of renown. He would play at weddings and dances, and he knew most old tunes the valley folk requested. People used to say you could tell the Summerhill cows from others because of the dance in their steps.

But when Niklas's mother passed away, Uncle Anders had put down his violin for good. If people called him the fiddler now, it was just to make fun of how soft-minded he had become, the twin who was left behind, the useless half of a pair.

Mr. Molyk took a step closer. "Here's another strange thing. Up at Oak Bridge last night, we found . . ."

A bird flapped out of the raspberry bushes. Mr. Molyk glanced over his shoulder and cleared his throat. Uncle Anders came trudging down the path with a shovel over his shoulder.

"Done already," Uncle Anders said when he saw the fresh mound.

"I named her Rag," Niklas said.

His uncle nodded, as if he had expected as much. "Better come back up to the house, lad. Your grandmother wants you."

Mr. Molyk watched them leave without another word.

Chapter Seven

It turned out that Grandma Alma wanted Niklas for chopping wood, and fetching potatoes from the cellar, and peeling them after, and cleaning the oven while they boiled. Obviously he wasn't done making amends for letting the sheep out. Niklas didn't mind the work. He felt terrible about the death of Rag, too, so he fetched, chopped, peeled, and scrubbed until his arms ached. He had just come back from emptying a bucket of slop out back, when he heard something strange in the bird room. One sound that was always there had disappeared, replaced by another sound that did not belong.

The missing sound was the birds.

In Willodale, people thought caring for wild birds brought luck, so all farms had feeders. Birdhouses, they called them, because they usually looked like miniature farm buildings. But the Summerhill birdhouse, fastened outside the eastern window of the bird room, was not just a house. It had spires and buttresses, a drawbridge and a tall, domed tower. It was no less than a bird castle, made by an unknown master carver.

All day, the castle teemed with sparrows and finches that nibbled at crumbs and pecked at the panes when they wanted more, so the bird room always rang with chirps and flutters.

But not now. The birds had gone quiet, and instead the sound that did not belong came floating out from behind the closed door.

A violin.

There had been no music in this house since his mother died.

Niklas opened the door carefully so it wouldn't creak. The music streamed through the sunlit room, sweet and melancholy. Outside, the birds sat quietly in their castle, one eye turned.

Uncle Anders stood in the middle of the floor, oblivious to the spilled water and broken glass around his feet. He hugged the black cup of the violin hard, and his usual remote expression had given way to a mask of squeeze-lidded pain. His dark sobs wove through the music as he played.

A coldness turned in Niklas's stomach. He hadn't seen his uncle this distressed in years. After Erika died, this was his usual way, but with time, the sadness had mostly sunk back into his body. It only welled up if something particular caught him in the heart. Could he have heard Mr. Molyk's fiddler remark? Niklas was just about to slip away to get Grandma Alma, when Uncle Anders let his bow sink, opened his eyes, and looked straight at him. "Your mother used to sing you that song."

Niklas froze. Whenever he asked about his mother, he got the same stories, as flat as the small stack of photos that existed of her. If he wanted more, a wall of silence always went up. But here was something new. A crack in that wall. Niklas couldn't help but poke at it, even if it might make his uncle's sadness worse. He tried to put on a bright face. "She did?"

"A lullaby. Made it herself." Uncle Anders played another verse of the slow, twisting tune, watching Niklas closely. "I thought you might remember. She wrote words, too, but I've lost them."

The music seemed too mournful for a lullaby, Niklas thought. Had he heard it before? Was that why his throat felt itchy? He tried to bring the memory out from hiding, but he couldn't. "No, I don't remember. Sorry."

His uncle set the violin gently down on the table and rubbed his cheek. "We made a tape once, but I don't know where she put it, or if it even still exists."

"What is the song about?" Niklas's words rushed out a little too quickly.

"Only Erika could tell you that," Uncle Anders said.

That much Niklas knew already. His mother was all secrets and broken pieces. He had long since given up on fitting them together: The Willodalers' hints about her illness and dark twist. His mother showing him how to string bird bones. His mother dying in her bed. The nightmare.

He tried to swallow, but the itching had gotten worse. The music still turned in his head, no comfort at all. "You always say that. But it's a little too late for that now."

"I suppose that's true." Uncle Anders's gaze seemed heavier than usual. Warmer and more present. His head jerked in an odd mix between a tilt and a nod. "Did she ever tell you about Sebastifer?"

Niklas blinked. If his mother had secrets, his father was the best kept among them. Grandma Alma said no one but Erika knew anything about him, except that he had left the valley before Niklas was born. There were no photos, no stories, no sign that he had ever existed. Not even a name. "Is Sebastifer . . . ? Was he my . . . ?"

"He was her dog."

The surprise almost drowned out the disappointment. "My mother had a dog?"

"When she was your age. She rescued him when he was little. Sebastifer was the result of the Molyk dog and the Ottem dog both escaping at a very inconvenient time. Wasn't exactly a welcome pup, and wasn't staying long, either, if you see what I mean."

Niklas thought he did, and it made him curl his fists.

"Erika wouldn't have it," Uncle Anders said. "She stomped down to the Molyk farm and declared that she was taking the pup to Summerhill." A smirk crinkled his cheeks. "She was only nine, but so determined, even Old Molyk gave in without so much as a word. She carried Sebastifer home in triumph, with me and Peder trailing her up the hill. After that we would follow her anywhere. Not just Sebastifer, but us boys, too."

"You mean you and Peder Molyk?" It had never occurred to Niklas to wonder what his mother was like as a kid, let alone that she could be someone Mr. Molyk would want to follow. She almost sounded like a hero. "You were all *friends?*"

"Oh yes. Peder was the one who told Erika what his father was about to do." Anders plucked the strings of his violin. "Sebastifer was such a good dog. A real mutt, of course, part collie, part retriever. So Erika, being Erika, gave him a jumble of names."

He laughed, and he was right. That name did sound like a joke. Niklas frowned. Except for the time with the skull, his mother never smiled in his memories. The closest she came was a faint quirk of the lip in some of the early photos.

"She didn't used to be so serious, you know." Uncle Anders wiped his nose. "Not before the thing."

"Before she got sick, you mean."

"Oh no, long before that." Uncle Anders's sad mask returned. "When she almost died. The summer we were twelve."

Niklas was too stunned to think of a reply.

But Uncle Anders didn't need prodding anymore. He turned away, toward the path that cut up the mountainside, and when he continued his tale, his voice was half whisper. "We tried to cross Sorrowdeep at night, Peder, Erika, and me. Up to no good as usual. But the boat foundered and we had to swim for shore. I don't know why we didn't notice that Erika had slipped under." Niklas couldn't see his uncle's face now, but his hands trembled. "Sebastifer noticed, though. He dove back in after her and pushed her to the surface, but his paw must have gotten caught in some root or other at the bottom of the pond. By the time Peder and I got Erika out of the water, Sebastifer was already dead."

So that's how it was.

Niklas had always wondered why Grandma Alma told him the story of Sorrowdeep over and over, even before he was old enough for that kind of creepiness. Here was the reason: She wanted him to stay away from the water. But that reason also made the nightmare more real. His mother *had* gone to Sorrowdeep. She *had* died there, or almost. He said, "I thought we didn't keep dogs at Summerhill."

"Erika didn't want another after that. No one could replace Sebastifer, she said. We still honor her wishes."

"Why? Mom's been gone for seven years. She won't know."

At that, his uncle stiffened, and Niklas winced. But it just didn't seem fair that the person who had left him to fend for himself still got to decide he couldn't have a dog.

Uncle Anders turned to him with an odd look; a little hurt, but also scared. His lips quivered as he glanced out the east window, where the birds still watched in silence. "Niklas, have you . . . heard . . . anything lately?"

"What do you mean?" The coldness was back in Niklas's stomach. His uncle did not look well.

"Down by the stream. I've been hearing this . . ." Uncle Anders took a step toward the castle, and a shard crunched under his shoe. His eyebrows flew up, as if he only now noticed the broken glass. The bewildered expression grew into place, and just like that, the crack in the wall of silence closed up. "Oh, look at this mess! My favorite glass and all. I'd better clean it up."

As Niklas went to fetch the broom, his head spun with all the truths about his mother they had withheld from him. She wrote songs. She rescued a dog and kept him for her own. She used to smile, and then she stopped.

She almost drowned in Sorrowdeep.

Chapter Eight

No one spoke much over dinner. Niklas's tongue burned with questions, but he didn't ask them. If Grandma Alma found out that Uncle Anders had told him things, he might clam up for good.

The kitchen clock broke the silence, striking five with brassy confidence. But it was almost seven thirty.

"I thought you fixed that," Grandma Alma said.

Uncle Anders scratched his head. "I thought so, too."

Niklas stood up quickly. "I'm going to the stream to find a stone for Rag's grave."

Grandma Alma pursed her lips, but he headed her off. "I'll be back before dark," he promised.

Of course, he told himself, it never got dark in summer.

He fetched his empty school satchel and added in a measuring tape and a looking glass. He was going to find a stone for Rag's grave eventually, but first he had business in the woods.

Mr. Molyk hadn't gotten around to telling him about the strange thing they found at Oak Bridge, but Niklas had an idea what it might be. Sure enough, on the stream bank, he found it: a footprint, sunk into the dirt that had been sheltered by the junipers. Mr. Molyk had told it true. The print was impossible.

It had a long sole and five toes, like a human foot. But not even Uncle Anders's feet were that big. It measured sixty-seven centimeters from heel to toe, more than two feet. That didn't even include the mark that jutted out between the second and the third toe, where a cut sliced into the ground.

A giant claw mark.

The slash was almost as long as the foot itself. Niklas couldn't think of a single animal that had one huge claw like this. At least he had been right about one thing: This print did not belong to the lynx. He felt a rush of relief. Maybe the rest was true, too.

Thank you.

He looked up into the oak tree. It had filled with black beneath a pink sky. The evening had slipped by fast. Niklas searched for cat eyes among the branches, but saw none. Did the lynx come here often? Was she close now?

He wished he could climb into the tree and watch for

her, but on this particular day it might be best not to argue with Grandma Alma about the meaning of "before dark." More than likely, the hunters would be out again tonight. He put his things in the satchel and headed home.

He made it to the first bend in the trail before he heard the screeches go up. Birds flew out of the woods behind him, black flecks against a bright orange flicker.

Fire.

For a second, Niklas hesitated. How much time would he waste if he ran home to fetch Uncle Anders? Two minutes if he could fly, ten minutes with the way the path looped. But if he could get up there before the fire truly caught, he might be able to put it out. He decided to try. He yelled through the woods, "Help! Uncle Anders! Someone! There's a fire!" Then he turned and ran back up the trail. As he neared the bridge, he filled with horror.

The oak tree was burning.

The flames hadn't reached the canopy yet, but yellow tongues licked up the trunk, reaching higher with every second. How could it be burning? Healthy, green wood like this, alone on the lip of a cliff?

Niklas sprinted past the fire to fill his satchel with water from the Summerchild. He hurried back up the bank and sloshed it against the base of the trunk. The bark sputtered, but it still burned. He fetched satchelful after satchelful, but he couldn't keep the flames from eating their way into the branches.

Niklas didn't stop. The oak tree was his and Lin's, and now it belonged to the lynx, too. He refused to give up on it.

The fire crackled so loudly that Niklas didn't hear the snapping noises until they were close. Uncle Anders at last! Except he should be coming up the trail, not down from the mountain. Niklas peered in between the trees. Someone wove through the underbrush with muted flashlights. The hunting party, then. They must have cut through the woods.

"Mr. Fale! Mrs. Ottem! It's the oak tree! Quick, get over here!" A puff of smoke caught him, and Niklas bent over coughing. "Why are you just standing there?" he croaked. "Come and help me!"

No one came out of the bushes.

"Mr. Molyk?" Niklas rubbed his eyes. "Uncle Anders?"

The rotten stench from last night blasted toward him.

The beast.

This time, he couldn't run. The beast was closer to the trail. It would cut him off no matter which way he tried to bolt. And he couldn't climb into the oak tree. Niklas was caught on a strip of land with nowhere to go.

He dropped the satchel and picked up a fallen branch that had caught fire at one end. The green eyes blinked.

"Oh, you don't like this?" Niklas held the branch like a sword. A host of twigs snapped as the beast moved back. It feared the flames.

Niklas took a step forward. The beast backed farther into the underbrush, until its eyes resembled dim jellyfish in the darkness under the trees.

Sparks whipped past Niklas's face, but he didn't care. He was already on fire, on the inside. "You killed Rag!" he shouted, and pushed on across the path.

Something heavy hit his shoulders and slammed him to the ground. A shape outlined against the blaze from the fire crouched over him, pinning his arms and hips down so he couldn't move. Niklas squirmed and fought, but it did no good. A circle of needle-like teeth opened over his face as the creature snarled.

"Stupid cub! Can't you see that's what it wants?"

Niklas stopped thrashing. The creature had cat eyes, not beast eyes.

The lynx eased off him. "Stand up," she hissed at him. "Get back to the oak!"

Niklas bolted to his feet. The anger had been knocked out of him, and now he felt dizzy. The lynx had taken up position in front of him, right by the burning branch that lay on the ground. Niklas could be mistaken, but it looked like she was barring the way between him and the beast.

In the underbrush, the green eyes narrowed.

The lynx tucked in her stubby tail. "Do you want to die? Back to the oak!"

Niklas stumbled backward until he felt the heat from the fire. The beast let out a piercing double-pitched howl and lunged forward, but the lynx twisted out of the way and leaped across the path with Niklas.

Over them, the entire tree burned. Most of the heat rose upward, but embers dropped down from the canopy and the ground smoldered. "We can't stay here," Niklas coughed.

"We have to." The lynx paced in circles, keeping her distance. "It's the only place it won't go."

"We can fight it off with torches," Niklas said. "It fears the fire."

The lynx flattened her ears. "It started the fire. Threw a rock at the tree and then it burned."

Which must be wrong, of course, because rocks couldn't start fires, and Niklas had seen the beast shrink away from flames himself.

"What it fears is this tree," the lynx said, skipping smoothly to the side to dodge a falling patch of bark. "It won't go near it."

The beast lurked just beyond the forest edge, but Niklas's eyes watered from the smoke, and he couldn't see clearly. "Is it a bear?"

"No bear," the lynx said.

"Then what?"

The lynx bared her teeth. "I don't know. It doesn't belong here."

Niklas squinted. Through the branches he glimpsed massive shoulders, patches of bark. A claw slid out, black and curved like a scythe, and the beast cut the underbrush in one quick sweep. It sneered at them with a mouthful of saw teeth.

Niklas's heart kicked against his ribs. The beast had a *mouth*. A slavering mouth in a face that was too angled and leathery for a human, but which definitely wasn't a muzzle. And it had three ears. The third stuck out from its neck, folding and unfolding.

He felt his limbs go limp.

"What is it?" the lynx growled. "Do you know it?"

He did.

And he understood, now, why the beast had stopped chasing him when he climbed into the tree last night, why it wouldn't cross the path now, why it had left the lamb on the screaming stone of all places. The lynx was right. This creature didn't belong here, or in any other place that was real.

It belonged in a game.

"Yeah." Niklas opened his shirt pocket and scooped out the acorns. "It's a troll."

Chapter Nine

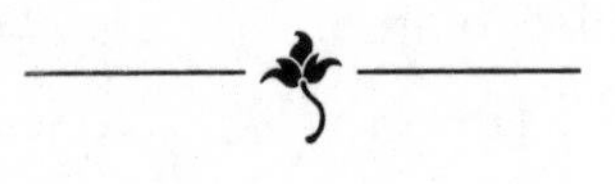

In his defense, Niklas Summerhill had never used troll's bane before. Not for real.

The moment he let go of the acorns, he knew the throw was short. A piece of burning oak crashed to the ground right in front of him, making him snatch his hand back early. But when the sparks cleared, the green eyes had vanished.

The lynx spoke behind him. Niklas felt the hairs rise on his neck. "What did you do?"

"I threw acorns at it. Troll's bane. It kills them." Across the path there was no troll, but no body, either. "Or it's supposed to."

"Like a gun." The lynx began pacing, staying as far away from Niklas as she could get. She looked as if she were caught in a cage. Niklas supposed they *were* caged, inside the protection of the oak tree. Except now the jailer had left. "Do you think it's . . . ?"

"No. Not dead, but you scared it into hiding. Do it again."

Ah right, excellent idea, except he had no more acorns. In the panic, he had thrown them all. He glanced around at the scorched grass. "Do you know the nuts from this tree?"

"Yes. They make the squirrels taste bitter."

"Let's see if we can find some."

Niklas ended up doing the searching, which was hard to do without turning his back on either the spot where the troll had disappeared or the lynx. She watched him silently, gliding out of the way of burning objects until he gave up. The acorns had all burnt, or the bitter squirrels had gotten them.

But he found something else lying in the crook of two roots not far from the tree trunk. A round rock the size of his palm, wrapped in hide. There was a drawing on it: three jagged lines that met at the bottom. He held it up. "Is this the rock you saw the troll toss?"

"Smells like it."

Niklas frowned at the stone. If it started the fire, then maybe . . . He took two quick steps and hurled it into the Summerchild. Immediately the flames in the oak tree died down, as easily as if someone had flipped a switch. Niklas blinked up at the naked branches as his eyesight adjusted. For a moment they were silent and shiny with char.

Then the first crack sounded.

"Look out!" Niklas rolled to the side as a big branch thundered to the ground. All around them, the oak tree's limbs came down in great huffs of ashes, until the trunk itself gave and toppled groaning off the ledge.

Niklas stared at the blackened stump. The fire must have eaten the tree to the core in minutes for it to collapse like that. He was no expert, but it must be far too fast. And the way the fire had died as soon as the leather rock hit the water . . . It was wrong. Unnatural.

Magical.

"It's coming."

That shook him out of it. If there were talking lynxes and trolls, then why not magic? A better question was *why* the troll had burned the tree. "You think the protection of the oak tree is broken?"

The lynx tilted her head in the direction of the path. The green eyes were back.

"We go after the tree," she said.

"Down from the ledge?" Niklas rubbed his forehead. He had perched on the branches above the slope many times. The drop was so steep and littered with boulders that the slightest misstep could set off a slide. "No one can climb down that hill in the dark."

"You can if you want to live," the lynx said, tossing her neck. With two fluid bounds, she leaped off the cliff.

Niklas ran to the edge. The lynx stared up at him from a shelf ten feet down. He cast one last glance back toward the troll, then got down on his belly and went over the edge legs first. The lynx waited until he dangled by his hands before she moved on.

"Follow."

Niklas tried to stay on the lynx's tail, but the four-pawed path she chose among the boulders was hard to copy. More than once she returned to show him the way out of an unstable patch. "Not so slow!"

Behind them, where the top of the hill drew a black semicircle in the sky, a silhouette loomed against the blue of night, eyes glowing like emeralds. It sniffed along the lip of the ledge, but it made no move to climb down after them.

"It's too heavy," the lynx said. "The stones will tumble. The newcomers know. They know the land."

"Newcomers? They?" Niklas couldn't help raising his voice. "How many are there?"

The troll answered with another jarring howl. The lynx flicked her ears back. "Not so loud!"

"Sorry," Niklas whispered.

"Now try to follow. The screaming stone isn't far."

Of course. If that creature really was a troll, and the rules of the game were true, then the other safe place was the farm, on the other side of the screaming stone. "How do you know the trolls can't get past the stone? Have you seen them try?"

"Quiet," the lynx warned. "It's heavy, but it's fast. If it takes the trail, it will be waiting for us on the other side."

They cut a straight, slow line along the dell of the Summerchild. The lynx slipped easily between broken roots and boulders. She looked like she had been magically transported from a jungle with her flecked fur that glowed golden in the tree shadows. When she turned to make sure he kept up, her eyes were lined like an Egyptian queen's.

"Are you the lynx I . . . ?" Niklas cleared his throat. *Saved* seemed too forward. "I mean, did you take the roast I left for you in the ash tree?"

"Old meat," the lynx scoffed. "Disgusting."

"Sorry," Niklas said again, covering a little grin. Now that the troll was behind them, the thrill of hearing her talk jolted his chest. She curled her tongue so carefully around the sounds when she spoke, slurring every *s,* but she still knew the word *disgusting.*

"You asked how many. I've seen two. The three-eared one up there and the clever one with scars. But I stay out of their way when I can."

"Probably wise," Niklas said.

"The forest has changed," the lynx said. "Something is poisoning it. It's not safe anymore. Most of the prey animals have left already. You should leave, too."

Niklas stopped for a moment, trying to find a way down from a mossy boulder the size of a shed. "Why haven't *you* left?"

A quiet sort of hiss, and the lynx replied, "Because you're too rash to watch your back. You can't hide, you can't pounce, and you don't know the first thing about sneaking."

"Hey now." Niklas slid down the stone, knocking his shin against a hazel tree. Being called rash was one thing, but he could sneak well enough. Mr. Molyk and his boots would testify to that. "I know how to handle myself in the wild."

"Do you? Everywhere you've walked, the *trolls,* as you name them, have walked, too. They're hunting you."

Hunting. Niklas thought of the long claw and the saw teeth. After that he kept quiet until they ducked out of the trees by the big ash, only a few yards above the screaming stone. The lynx lifted her lips to taste the air, good ear tall and tense. "Is the troll here?" Niklas whispered as he moved up alongside her.

"No." She edged away from him and jumped onto the lowest branch of the ash. "Go now," she said. "Don't come back."

"What do you mean? Of course I'm coming back."

The lynx beat her tail. "Didn't you hear? They're hunting you, and the oak is gone. There's nowhere safe for you in the forest now."

"But trolls belong in stories and games. They aren't . . ." He cut himself short. He was going to say they weren't real, but with the chill of threat trickling down his back every time he glanced up the trail, that sounded plain foolish.

"They're *mine,*" he said instead. "That thing sticking out

from the troll's neck? He uses it to find people who are trying to hide from him. I know that because I made it up last summer. Just as I made up the border." He nodded at the screaming stone. "So they're *my* problem. Besides, the grown-ups have no idea how to get rid of them. I'm the only one in this valley who does."

Well, except one person, and a stubborn one at that. He glanced down at the main house at the bottom of the hill. Both he and Lin agreed that Grandma Alma must have owned that first jar of troll's bane in the loft, the one that started the game in the first place. He should find a way to ask her tomorrow.

The lynx stared at him, head cocked and white chin tucked in. "But I just told you they'll kill you."

"Good thing I have you to watch my back, then." He smiled up at her. "Can I ask you something? How is it that you can talk?"

She shifted on the branch, making the leaves rustle. "I had hoped you could tell me that."

"No idea," Niklas said. The lynx didn't reply, and he got the feeling he had disappointed her. He added, "But we can try to find out. When did it start?"

"After the last spring storm," she said. "I'd hidden in a cave, so I don't know what happened outside. But something must have, because when I came out from my shelter, the valley looked different to me. Full of . . ."

Her ears twitched at some sound Niklas couldn't catch.

"It is on the trail. You need to go past the stone now, or the killing will happen tonight."

"All right. Just meet me here tomorrow." Niklas bolted out from under the ash tree and past the screaming stone. On the other side, he skidded to a stop. "Wait! I can't go without knowing your name."

The lynx thought for a moment before she said, "I'm the lynx of these woods."

Niklas laughed. "I guess lynxes don't have names. Well, I'll give you one. I'm Niklas, and you're. . . ."

He tilted his head. He didn't know why the lynx could talk, or why she stayed here to protect him. But it made him hurt with happiness. No grown-ups could know about this, not if it meant he would have to share her, or give her up. Not even Grandma Alma.

"You're Secret."

"Stupid cub." The golden fur faded into the darkness of the ash tree. "But I'll keep the name."

Chapter Ten

That night the nightmare changed.

It started as before, the waiting, the coming, the white dress. But this time his mother didn't float. She labored step by jerky step, dragging something heavy up the trail. A rusty cage on a long chain. When she turned by the screaming stone, she raised her arm and pointed up the mountainside, up toward Sorrowdeep, while murky water poured out between her lips.

She looked like she was screaming, too.

Chapter Eleven

When Niklas came downstairs, sun filled the kitchen. Grandma Alma balanced on her toes, straining to fetch her blue mug from the bottom shelf of the cabinet. They would have to move all the cupboards down a foot before long.

Already his grandmother's world had shrunk to just this one floor and maybe the steps outside on a particularly warm and dry day. He hurried over and got the mug for her. "If it isn't the heir to the realm," she said, plucking it out of his hands.

"Good morning." Niklas didn't want to inherit anything if it meant the queen would be gone.

"Is it? I thought it was past noon," Grandma Alma dunked the mug in a pot of dark brown tea. She liked to keep the leaves simmering away on the stove, even though it made the tea so bitter, it was near undrinkable. She also liked to say that anyone with sense in their skull knew to sweeten life with at least three sugar cubes. She stirred the grainy slush. "What's the matter?"

Niklas rubbed his eyes. They still felt puffy from the smoke last night. He wanted to tell Grandma Alma about the fire, but he couldn't, not without admitting he had been out late. "Slept badly," he said into the fridge, where no quick and obvious breakfast appeared, just vegetables, white fish steeping in salt for dinner, and age-old marmalade.

"Hm." She granted him a small smile, the first since their conversation in the bird room. "As a very old lady, I feel I should tell you that grief is a natural part of life. So is guilt. There is no getting around them. But there is one thing that will ease the weight somewhat."

Niklas closed the fridge door. "Making amends?"

"Oh sure, when that's an option." Grandma Alma slurped her tea. "Most often it's not. I was going to say chocolate cake."

Niklas gaped at her. "For breakfast?"

"It's in the tin in the hallway. If anyone would like some."

The chocolate cake waited for him where she had promised, rippled on top and cut into generous squares. Grandma Alma must be feeling very sorry for him when she let him have this for breakfast. Not only did it not fit into her idea of what was good for a growing lad, she only ever made it for special occasions.

She claimed this was because the secret ingredient cost so much, but Niklas and Lin had investigated the cupboards many times without ever finding anything fancy-looking. They suspected she said it to keep the legend strong. It was a well-known tale in Willodale, even among those who had never sampled it, that Alma Summerhill's chocolate cake was the finest of the land.

Niklas made no argument there. In the cool of the hallway the cake had set so he could eat it with his hands, no plate or spoon required, just dense mouthfuls of not-too-dark, frosting-covered magic. It had never tasted better.

He finished six pieces, downed a glass of milk, and as usual, his grandmother was right. It did help a little. He felt almost ready for his first task of the day: acorns. His shirt pocket was all empty, but he had an idea where he could go to get more.

Niklas hadn't been inside Morello House since the Rosenquists left.

He took off his boots and climbed the stairs. Despite the decent summer, the timber walls felt raw against his fingers. The second floor seemed stuffy, as if all the loneliness had drifted up and gathered under the low ceiling.

Lin's room contained nothing but abandoned furniture. The desk where she used to draw her maps, the bed with star constellations on the headboard. But no casket, no papers, and sadly, no acorns. She had taken the troll-hunting gear with her to the city.

It took him a while to find the exception: a piece of paper that had slipped behind Lin's desk. It was an unfinished sketch of a Summerhill map that had been smudged by a teacup before she could finish it. Oak Bridge was marked in green on the map, as were the two other oak trees in the valley, both on the western edge of the Summerhill lands. But those two trees had caught the oak blight last June and had to be chopped down. He hadn't thought much of it back then, but he wondered now if the trolls were behind it. If they could set a tree on fire with nothing but a carved rock, maybe they could give it oak blight, too?

Niklas sat down on the bed. If Lin had been here, he would have climbed the morello tree and knocked on her window last night, to tell her about the impossible things that were going on. Or even signaled from his windowsill, because they did have a code for this: Two blinks meant *danger, troll nearby.*

But she wasn't.

He should call her. The last time they spoke on the phone, everything had been so weird. Lin sounded curt and distant, as if she had all sorts of secrets and worries she wouldn't share with him. Niklas just wasn't very good at phone conversations, or writing, for that matter. It would be different if they could just meet in person.

He had been invited to come visit last winter, had even bought a ticket. But the day he was supposed to leave, Grandma Alma's cold had turned into pneumonia, and

Uncle Anders had to take her to the hospital in Willo-mouth, and Niklas had to stay and take care of the cattle. He had stood at the bottom of the snow-covered nether-field and watched the bus pass by without stopping, as always. The Rosenquists hadn't invited him again.

Still, he should call.

On his way back through the hallway, he passed by Anne Rosenquist's study. The door stood ajar and he peeked in at a tape player and a set of boxes. Lin's mother collected old songs. That was how she and Uncle Anders had become friends all those years ago. She liked recording and playing the old way, so she had thousands of taped songs, all labeled and contained in boxes just like that. Apparently she hadn't taken them all.

Something Uncle Anders had said suddenly struck him. *We made a tape of it, but I don't know where she put it.* Niklas had been too rattled to think clearly, so he had thought Uncle Anders meant Erika. But if anyone made and disposed of a tape, it wouldn't be his mother. It would be Anne.

Niklas sidled through the door and pulled out the three boxes. The first contained loose notes, copied down snippets of the Lindelin ballads. Lin was named for this medieval maiden, who always traveled into great danger and used her wit and magic to save every prince she met.

It suited her well.

He opened the second box and struck gold. Tapes. All of them were dated and labeled with place, musician, and songs.

Except one, which simply said *ERIKA*.

Niklas slapped his forehead. Anne Rosenquist had nearly told him about this tape last summer, while he was waiting for Lin to feed Rufus so they could go troll hunting. Anne had sat with him for a moment, looking out on the morello garden where Uncle Anders was watering the strawberries.

"So, you're Summerknight," she had said, which had annoyed Niklas a little. No one was supposed to know about the code names, least of all a grown-up. Anne must have seen it on one of Lin's maps. He had nodded anyway.

"It sounds like a proper knight's name," she had said. "Your mother would have liked that. She loved heroic songs, especially if they contained death and impossible tasks. Did you know she even wrote one herself?"

She had smiled at him. "I actually have a . . ." And then she had stopped and looked over at Uncle Anders, and Niklas was sure she wished she could take it back. Lin had come out with Rufus concealed in her pocket, and that was the end of that. Later, both he and Lin had tried asking about it, but Anne had brushed them off. The week after, they left for the city.

He bet his entire collection of comic books that she had been about to say "tape." Had she left this here for him?

He shoved it into the player and pushed the button.

At first he heard only muffled voices, fuzzy laughter, a fiddle being tuned.

Then the recorder must have been moved into a better

position, because he heard Uncle Anders say, "You should sing it." He sounded so different. Light, almost crisp. "I'll play, if I can remember the tune."

"Yes, sing it," Anne Rosenquist chimed in. "It ought to be preserved for future generations."

A third voice sounded, echoing from rooms at the very back of Niklas's mind. "It's not worth preserving," said his mother. "It's not traditional."

"Who cares," Anne said. "Every legend begins somewhere. Why not with you?"

Silence followed, and through the scratchy, wheezy filter of the tape, Niklas could almost hear them hold their breaths. Then his mother said, "Because it didn't."

But she sang anyway.

Wake now, little rose,
The night grows dark and old.
Your feet must find the trail tonight,
To Sorrowdeep the cold.

Wait now, little dog,
Your voice will carry through.
The key lies in her hand tonight,
Sebastifer the true.

Stay then, ghost of thorns,
If you can't play the part.

The key will lead you nowhere when
It's locked inside your heart.

The recording ended.

Ghost of thorns. Even if Grandma Alma insisted he had dreamt it, Niklas had always believed that the last word he heard his mother speak was *Thornghost*. That couldn't be a coincidence.

His skin prickled, but he listened to the tape again, then jotted down the lyrics and tucked it away for evidence.

The third box contained a framed photograph, taken in the yard. His mother with her white locks tossed back and an intense, uneasy look in her eyes. The dark twist of the Willodalers' gossip, captured for anyone to see. And next to her a miniature building that Niklas knew well.

The bird castle. Except it wasn't mounted outside the east window, it sat on a workbench beneath the elm tree. The tower lacked its dome, and the drawbridge dangled by its chains, unfastened. But that was about to change, because in her hands Erika held a carving iron and a tiny screwdriver.

His mother had made the castle. She was the unknown master carver.

Niklas pried open the clips behind the frame and removed the cardboard. Anne Rosenquist had written something on the back of the photo.

Erika and her nightmare castle.

Chapter Twelve

A flock of sparrows fluttered up when Niklas turned the east corner of the main house, hauling a stepladder. The birds circled for a bit before settling on the roof to watch.

"Sorry, guys," Niklas said, tugging the ladder into position. "You'll get your place back after. I just need to examine it first."

He had looked at the bird castle plenty of times. He often put crumbs and sunflower seeds inside the parapets of the walls, a task he did by leaning out of the bird room window with a slim, long-handled spade. But he never got truly close that way, and the angle meant he couldn't see the whole castle properly.

From the outside, there was always the danger of falling bird poop. "Don't get any ideas, now," he said up to the sparrows. They shuffled sideways on the eaves, making no promises.

The grass beneath the castle wore a constant, filthy halo of droppings and husks. The castle itself did not, because Uncle Anders cleaned it every week. Niklas had always assumed he did it on Grandma Alma's order. But he realized now it had nothing to do with having the finest birdfeeder in all of Willodale, and everything to do with the person who had created it. Uncle Anders couldn't keep his shirt neat if he tried, but he would not allow so much as a breath of dust on Erika's portraits, or a spot of lichen on her headstone.

Up close, the castle almost took Niklas's breath away. The doors had pinprick keyholes. The pillars were carved with miniature climbing roses. The wraparound balcony at the top of the tower had a toothpick-thin railing, and the drawbridge could be opened and closed with a tiny wrench hidden inside an archway in the courtyard. Niklas turned the handle. Hardly a squeak. Maybe Uncle Anders oiled the hinges, too.

Nightmare castle, the photo had said. There was an unsettling edge to many of the details. The vines that crept up the tower walls bristled with sharp thorns. The roof tiles had ridges that made them look like fingernails. And the tall tower had a ring of windows behind which stood a lone figure.

Niklas squinted through the opening. The figure had

its back turned, but he thought it might be a man with a big cloak. He shifted his grip to see better, and the dome moved under his fingers. With a firm twist, it came off completely, flooding the tower chamber with light.

A chorus of tiny screeches went up from the roof as the sparrows all took to the sky, flapping toward the barn in a chaotic cloud. Niklas took a shaky step down the ladder, heart thudding.

The cloaked man was not a man at all: He had a bird skull for a head. The beak made him look like a plague doctor from Harald Rosenquist's history books. He was not alone. Behind the billowing cloak stood a cage overgrown with roses. Trapped inside that cage was a child.

The skull man reached for the cage with skeletal fingers that had been fitted to the wood. They looked nearly human, but Niklas guessed they had belonged to a field mouse. The child had no features except for shallow dents where the eyes and an open mouth would be.

If his mother had dreamt this, Niklas knew who had given him his talent for nightmares. Sometimes he, too, dreamt of beaked skulls that pecked at his eyes. He thought of the photo and the skittish, pleading expression in his mother's face and suddenly wondered what he looked like when he woke up in the middle of the night. He screwed the tower roof back on, hiding the skull-man and the child.

Instead he examined the castle for more concealed surprises, tugging and pulling every ledge and part. At last he found something, trapped under a round flagstone in the courtyard. It bore a faint mark that resembled a thorn. When he turned it, the flagstone came loose to reveal a tiny dog, curled up like it was sleeping.

Unlike the skull-man and the cage, this figurine could be removed. Niklas lifted it out and held it up in the sunlight. On the bottom, there was a name carved.

Sebastifer.

Chapter Thirteen

Uncle Anders was gone.

Niklas searched everywhere. The loft, the barn, the netherfield, and Dokka's enclosure by the morello garden. He even went down to the graveyard, where Rag's still unmarked grave made a brown scar outside the fence.

He stalked the forest edge above the screaming stone, too, but Secret hadn't come. Maybe she slept the day away somewhere in the shade.

Finally he settled under the yard tree. As elm seeds rustled across the sunbaked dirt and the Summerchild sang in the east, he studied the scribbled notes of the lullaby, the photo of his mother, and the dog figurine. Just like Uncle Anders had said, Sebastifer looked like a true mutt with his floppy ears and curled-up tail. But he was so thin, like he was sick.

It was late in the afternoon when his uncle came walking up the path from the hallowfield. Where had he been hiding? The shrubs around the graveyard were thorny and near impossible to pass through without getting cut. Niklas must have been too quick to look properly.

Uncle Anders stopped in the middle of the yard, gazing up at the strip of clear sky between the snowy mountain-tops. Niklas put his things back in the satchel and got up to join him, but someone beat him to it.

Tobis came sauntering out from behind Morello House, making his way toward Uncle Anders like a cat king inspecting his lands. Uncle Anders stooped down to stroke him, and Tobis rolled over to show his big belly, smirking and wiggling.

"So that's your game today?" said his uncle. "Trying to trick me into rubbing your belly so you can bite my hand? You won't fool me, old friend." He scratched Tobis's head instead until the cat waddled off to the barn to stalk a mouse hole. Uncle Anders chuckled as he watched him go.

His grin looked so different from the sobbing mask he had worn in the bird room yesterday that Niklas leaned back against the elm tree. He couldn't talk to his uncle about this now, not when he was having a good day. There was someone else he should be confronting anyway, and he had wasted a whole afternoon putting it off.

It wouldn't do to be a coward.

He left Uncle Anders in the yard and hurried up the front steps.

* * * * *

He found her in the cupboard, a tiny room that used to be a pantry at the back of the kitchen, but which now served as Grandma Alma's bedchamber since she felt too poorly to climb the stairs anymore.

Under the window, Uncle Anders had fitted a bed. It would be too short for most grown-ups, but for Grandma Alma, it was just right. She lay propped up by thick pillows, papery lids closed over restless eyes.

At the creak of the door, they opened. "There you are. I was just waiting for someone young and able to come wake me."

"At your service." Niklas eased her forward, searching her face as he slipped another pillow behind her back. Grandma Alma never slept during the day. "Are you ill?"

She swatted the words away with weak hands. "No, no. Can't an old queen have a nap?"

"Of course," Niklas said quickly. "Queens can do whatever they like."

He looked away from her swollen knuckles. Above her head hung a yellowed snapshot of his mother balancing Niklas on her lap. He had always hated that photo because he squirmed to get away, like he didn't care that she would be gone in less than a year. But his mother didn't seem to mind. Her calm expression was miles away from the wild stare in the bird castle photo.

Maybe there would never really be a good time for this. He took the photo out of his satchel and held the evidence in the light from the window, watching his grandmother's face turn from tired to sad.

"Where did you find this picture?"

"In Anne's office."

A smile brushed past Grandma Alma's face. "Well, that woman never could leave the past alone, even when she was asked to." She picked the frame out of his hands. "Your mother carved that thing in less than a summer. Day and night, she worked. She hardly stopped to sleep."

"She doesn't look well," Niklas said.

"I tried to tell her she needed to rest, that her lungs weren't strong enough for that kind of fervor. She wouldn't listen." Grandma Alma ran a trembling finger over his mother's curls. "You're very much like her, you know."

"What do you mean?" A worm of worry stirred in his belly. He smoothed down his hair where it stuck up in the front, as dark as his mother's was pale.

"I mean in most ways that matter. Bull stubborn, the both of you, can't be talked out of anything. Take the castle, for instance. Before she died, Erika suddenly got it into her head that we had to remove all the beautiful things she had carved, including this."

"Why?"

"I'm not sure." Grandma Alma put the photo on her nightstand, facedown. "I said you were alike, and you were, to begin with. But your mother changed. She had an accident when she was your age."

"At Sorrowdeep."

Grandma Alma frowned, and Niklas added, "You're always telling me to stay away from the pond. I thought that must be why."

"You thought right, then. That accident was hard on all of us. Afterward, the nightmares began. Dead birds and evil fogs and I don't know what. My guess is she had another dream about this castle and tried to work it out of her head. She did that sometimes. The dreams got stronger toward the end when she couldn't carve. I think her mind . . . slipped a little."

Niklas swallowed. "But you put the castle back up when she died?"

"It seemed such a harmless thing, when we kept to her wishes in all other matters." Grandma Alma's eyes filled with tears. "Even when the instructions seemed a little cruel. It is only natural for a young man to ask about his mother, but she wanted you to know as little as possible."

Niklas bit his lip. It was her, his mother, all along. The secrecy and half-told stories had been her wish. "She didn't want me to know her?"

Grandma Alma sighed. "I don't know why she wanted it so, my boy. But I don't believe she would have asked this of us if she didn't think it very important."

She pushed the photo toward him. "Well done for finding this, but now I must tell you to let the story rest. I know you won't want to, but . . ."

"What about Sebastifer?"

"Sebastifer?" Grandma Alma folded her hands. "I don't know what you're talking about."

A hard knot weighed Niklas's chest down. He could have said that he already knew, that Uncle Anders had told him, but something in the set of her mouth stopped him. Instead, he placed the figurine of the dog on top of the photo. "I found this in the castle. It says *Sebastifer* on the bottom."

She stared at the dog, lower lids tight. "Strange."

Very calmly, Niklas said, "One more thing. The afternoon Mom died, when you said I could come and say good-bye. I remember her saying that I should stay away from her, that she was dangerous. That she was a *Thornghost.* But you said I had just imagined it. Are you sure about that?"

After, as he sat on the steps and let the sun warm him up, he realized that he didn't ask because he wanted the truth, or because Grandma Alma's gentle patting of his arm would reassure him.

He asked because he now knew exactly what she looked like when she lied. And his mother's last words had been no dream.

Chapter Fourteen

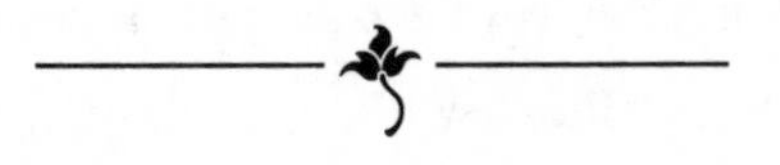

Secret?" Niklas stood under the ash tree all fidgety with worry. Dusk had eased up from the river, pushing the red-gold sunset all the way to the snowcaps above. Time for nocturnal creatures of the woods to stir, but still no lynx turned up at the border. What if she had left now that she had warned him about the trolls? Or what if the troll had gotten her? He climbed deeper into the thicket. "Secret? Are you here?"

She dropped out of the ash and landed behind him.

Niklas whirled around. "Finally!"

But Secret didn't seem quite so thrilled to see him. "I told you not to cross the border. But since you don't listen, you can see for yourself. Under the worm ferns by the screaming stone."

Stubby tail whipping, she climbed back up into the ash to wait.

Not Niklas's favorite thing, coming so close to the screaming stone, especially after last night's nightmare. But he couldn't let Secret see that, so he brushed aside the green fronds. In a crescent around the stone, half-buried in the spongy moss, there were animal skulls. Small ones that might belong to squirrels, big ones that could be deer. They had all been carved with a rectangle sliced in half by a slanted line. Though the mark had a different shape, it didn't take a master riddle solver to recognize the style from the leather stone last night. Troll magic.

"They put these here?"

"They both came while you slept. The nasty one with scars put those into the ground. I think she's trying to destroy the stone." Secret looked straight at Niklas. "Are you scared enough now?"

Niklas didn't reply. It had occurred to him that maybe he was in over his head. Last night the oak tree had burst into flames at the touch of one of the troll marks. He had no idea if these skulls had the power to break the border. "Did you see her cross the path?"

"No," Secret said. "But she said they would return, *after*."

"After what?"

"I don't know. Did you find more acorns?"

"I didn't. But I found . . ." Niklas hesitated. Usually, he didn't discuss his mother with anyone. Secret flicked her good ear toward him to say she was listening. And maybe it was because she didn't stare at him with pity the way everyone always did, or because she just waited instead of filling the silence to cover the awkwardness. But he found himself telling her everything he had discovered that day.

As he explained about the song, the photo, the castle, how everyone had kept the truth from him after she had died, Secret sat in the tall worm grass and groomed herself, never looking in his direction. When he was done, she didn't offer any of the poor-orphan phrases. She said, "My mother also died. Killed by hunters."

Her paw came up to clean the split ear. Suddenly Niklas saw how the tear looked way too smooth to have been made by teeth. It was a gun wound. No wonder Secret looked so lost up in the tree the night of Rag's death. "They almost got you, too?"

Secret yawned, which Niklas thought was cat-speak for a shrug. She turned to him to say something, but instead she jumped to her feet, crouched low on her hind legs, ear tuft trembling.

"What is it?" Niklas searched the tree line for green eyes. "Are the trolls coming?"

But Secret's ears didn't point toward the mountain trail. They pointed toward the farm. "Music, I think you call it. In the bone field by the stream."

"You mean the graveyard?" Niklas strained to hear it. The hallowfield was just inside the gate and down a short hill, but still the Summerchild almost drowned out the noise. It took him a moment to pick out the sad, lilting tune of his mother's lullaby over the rushing stream. "It must be Uncle Anders playing again." Niklas winced. "I'm worried about him. When my mother died, he got so sad, it made him sick. He's been all better for years, but lately he's thinking about her."

"He speaks the same word over and over: Erika." Secret whipped around to study him. "What does it mean, this word?"

"It's my mother's name." Niklas swallowed. "I have to see if Uncle Anders needs help."

"You're scared," Secret said. It wasn't a question. "More than when I showed you the skulls. Why?"

"Hey now," he said quickly. "I don't do scared." Even he could feel the smile he tried wasn't a very good rascal-face. Secret just stared at him without stirring a whisker. He adjusted the shoulder strap of his satchel. "I get nightmares sometimes. About her, coming from that field. They're just dreams . . ." He trailed off. Just dreams, yes. But the normal rules didn't apply in Summerhill. Not anymore.

Secret looked away for a moment. "Then I'll come."

"Not a good idea," Niklas said. "What if Uncle Anders sees you? Or the hunters come?"

But she tossed her head and slipped forward.

At the fence, she turned and flicked her tail at him.

"I know," Niklas muttered, hurrying after. "Not so slow."

* * * * *

They found the hallowfield pooled with darkness, out of reach from the last rays of the sun. The naked roof beams of the chapel jutted up like folded hands. Secret had called it the bone field, but in fact it was mostly empty. Most of the headstones belonged to people who died in the great avalanche, but their bodies lay somewhere under the mountain. The only grave with bones in it was the one marked *Erika Summerhill*.

The notes of the Thornghost song floated through the air, but Niklas couldn't see Uncle Anders.

"The music comes from the ground," Secret said. When Niklas stiffened, she added, "Not from under the headstones. There's a cave below the house."

Niklas had never heard of any cave below the chapel.

They edged around to the east side of the chapel, where the wall had tumbled so they could see inside the ruin like a stage. Secret was right, there was a cave beneath the house. Or a cellar. Light seeped up between the floorboards together with the music and Uncle Anders's muffled voice. He wasn't singing. He was holding a conversation.

"Please don't come back. Please don't be angry," he pleaded.

Niklas's skin prickled. "Is someone else down there with him?"

"No," Secret said. "Or, if so, they are silent."

The music died, then the light. Moments later, Uncle Anders rose out of the floor like a wraith, clutching his violin in one hand and a bucket in the other. His back seemed stooped as he closed a hatch in the floor, pushed an old pew over the opening, and shuffled out of the chapel without noticing he was being watched. "A nice cup of tea," he muttered, wiping his nose with the back of his hand. "That's what is needed now." His face was gray and tired, but the dark mood seemed to have lightened for now.

So Niklas let him trudge back toward the house and the tea without stopping him. When he had disappeared up the hill, Niklas snuck into the chapel and undid Uncle Anders's covering up. The hatch groaned when he lifted it. Cellars below chapels were called crypts, he seemed to remember. And crypts were for the dead.

"I'll wait here," Secret said from the shrubs behind him.

"You're not coming?" Niklas heard his voice go squeaky and cleared his throat. "I thought you said no one was down there."

"No one is," she said, turning her ear low. "But to me human houses are like cages."

"Oh." Niklas tried hard not to think about the cage his mother had carried in his last nightmare. "I can understand that. I'll go then." A ladder led down to the crypt. He tested it for sturdiness once, twice. Secret didn't comment, but she tilted her head as if there was something she didn't quite understand.

Niklas plastered a smile on his face. "I'm going. I'm just waiting for my eyes to get used to the darkness." He gave her a brief nod and climbed down.

He had expected the cellar to reek of mildew, but instead it smelled sweet like dry wood. A small lantern sat on the bottom rung of the ladder. He lit it.

"Secret," he called out softly as the light crept into the corners of the crypt. "You should see this! There are creatures down here!"

Positioned along the walls, there were carved statues.

On one side there were animals. Wolves howling at the sky, horses rearing up to strike. On the other side, there were monsters, skeleton birds fitted with tarp for wings, like the creature inside the nightmare castle. All his mother's work.

How had she fit the blocks through the hatch? Maybe she had added the outstretched limbs afterward. Niklas could picture her moving between these creatures, filling the crypt with wood chips, face screwed up with madness.

At the farthest end of the cellar stood a cloaked figure. This statue was smaller, more straight-backed, and turned toward the wall. Niklas's pulse whooshed in his head, louder than the Summerchild. But he had to look.

He walked to the end of the crypt on watery legs. Holding his breath, he turned the statue by its shoulders. It came around smoothly, grazing him with its outstretched arms.

It was a girl his age. The carver had made no effort to catch her in a pretty moment, but with the gathered mouth under the stubborn curls, she looked exactly like herself.

"Mom," Niklas whispered.

Chapter Fifteen

Please don't come back, Uncle Anders had said. *Please don't be angry.*

Secret eased onto the chapel floor above. She moved so silently, but the boards creaked beneath her paws, loud enough to drown out Niklas's heartbeat. "Cub? What is wrong?"

He had to force the words out of his mouth. "I found my mother. Or not her, but her statue."

The floor creaked again, and Secret's front paws stepped gingerly down the ladder, letting her dip her head just low enough to look into the crypt. She watched him stand there with the lantern, then said, "I can see how you're her cub."

"You can?" Niklas had studied every photo of his mother's face, looking for signs of himself, and found none.

"Not when you're the boy of the farm, running around

with your friend. But when you walk the woods alone. When no one is watching."

"You mean no one except Secret, the stalker lynx," Niklas said, but the joke didn't sit right. He didn't want to look like this statue, all worried and lost.

The statue dripped with water, which Niklas guessed came from Uncle Anders's bucket. It had washed away the dust, bringing out the colors in her eyes and lips, before gathering in a puddle on the floor. Her eyelashes still carried drops.

"Uncle Anders keeps all my mother's things clean," Niklas said. "But I don't think he's been doing it here, at least not until tonight. All the other statues are grimy, and there's still dirt in some of the folds of her cloak, see?"

Secret sneezed in the dusty air and pulled back up through the hatch. But she hovered near the entrance. "Then why start now?"

"I don't know." Niklas bit his lip. "But he plays his violin, which he hasn't touched since she died. He told me he hears things . . . Maybe the magic taint is affecting him, too."

He couldn't bear to meet the dead eyes of the statue anymore, so he turned and walked around the cellar. In the corner by the ladder, there was a piece of tarp that hadn't been fastened to a bird statue. He pulled it aside and found a casket.

"You've been right all along, Secret," he snorted. "I *am* stupid."

He had always assumed the jar of acorns he and Lin had found in the loft must have belonged to Grandma Alma, since it was tucked behind her fishing gear. But the arm that had been carved on the casket lid was definitely Erika's handiwork, and it was definitely a troll. The troll hunt had been her game.

It seemed he and his mother were more alike than even Grandma Alma had guessed.

The troll's claw stuck out between the knuckles, poking up from the lid, and the arm bore another one of the brutal marks, a four-pointed star. There was a finicky latch of moving parts, but the wood had bent and Niklas had to use force to get the lid off. A gust of bitter almonds stung his nose. This casket had not been opened for a long time. He lifted the contents carefully out onto the floor, describing them to Secret. There were carving tools, small pots of paint that had long since dried out, and a metal flask with a label he had seen before.

"Troll's bane." He unscrewed the flask and tipped it gently. A fine powder poured out. He grimaced. "Or it used to be. It's turned to dust."

Don't think about turning to dust, he reminded himself. *Not here.* He screwed the lid back on. "I guess it's better than nothing."

Next he found a leather-bound notebook. The first page said *Book of Troll Runes.*

Niklas leafed through it with shivering fingers. No

wonder he couldn't remember inventing magic for the trolls. He hadn't, and neither had Lin. It was Erika's doing.

"My mother didn't much mind being creepy," he told Secret. "Listen to this: 'All troll magic comes from pain. They carve their runes in living things, in skin and bones and teeth.'"

Each page had an illustration of a troll rune with crude lines and sharp angles, and a title. "I found the one from the oak tree rock." He held a page with a jagged three-line mark to the lantern light. "It means *burn*. And here's the divided rectangle with one black and one blank section."

"What does that mean?"

"*Break*." Niklas grimaced. "Or destroy. Let's hope it doesn't work."

The last page did not describe a rune. It was a brief note, almost like a journal entry. The ink strokes were hard.

> *I have to stop.*
>
> *Two horses dead at Sorrowdeep, both slashed and rune-marked. If not for the troll hunt, none of this would have happened.*
>
> *Every night I hear Sebastifer. Sometimes he barks. Other times he howls. Twice I've heard him whimper like he is giving up.*
>
> *Anders says it's not real. But the nightmares erase the lines between truth and story, and I can't see them anymore. I only see the troll*

witch and the cage and the black water rising up to drown me.

Anders says I shouldn't talk like that. Maybe he's right. But I also think I'm right that my games are dangerous. I'm dangerous. So I'm going to lock this in the box and I'm going to stop.

~~The Knight of Thorns~~ The Ghost of Thorns
Erika Summerhill

Niklas closed his eyes. Mr. Molyk had talked about another wave of killings twenty-five years ago. The summer his mother was twelve. Two horses had died at Sorrowdeep that year, and according to this, his mother had been convinced she was to blame. That she was dangerous.

Maybe Niklas was dangerous, too.

"Cub."

Niklas's hair stood on end. Secret had silently come halfway down the ladder, and from the flat edge in her voice, he knew something was very wrong.

He made himself open his eyes, but he couldn't believe them.

The statue was lowering her arms. A moment ago they had been stretched out in front of her, fingers flexed and crooked. But now they were sinking slowly toward the floor, making a faint scraping noise as they came to rest against her thighs.

Please don't come back.

Niklas's lungs seemed empty of air. "Mom?"

"Careful." Secret shifted uneasily on the ladder.

But other than the arms, Niklas could see no change. He stepped just within reach of the statue, leaned forward and touched her cheek. It felt hard and unalive. Now he noticed the lines where her arms met her shoulders. They were hinged. The water had probably loosened them. "It's okay," he said. "She's not alive, she just . . ."

Wait.

On the statue's chest, which had been hidden in the shadows between her arms, something blinked in the lantern light. A medallion. It was carved with the same thorn that had marked the loose flagstone in the nightmare castle, and like the flagstone, it could be twisted. With a click, wood sprang back against his hand to reveal a dog under the lid. Niklas pressed it. To the left and below the medallion a concealed door swung open where the statue's heart should be.

"There is something wedged inside," he said.

Didn't the Thornghost song say something about a key locked inside a heart?

But it wasn't a key. Instead his fingers found a long, thin object. He eased it out.

A twig.

He held it up to the lantern. The twig was still flexible, or he wouldn't have been able to pry it out, but it seemed shrunken like cured meat. Three curved thorns stuck out from the black bark. "It's a briar."

Secret's nose wrinkled. "It smells like old blood."

"Oh?" Niklas tested the thorn with the tip of his finger. Sharp enough to draw blood without even pushing. "I guess that explains it."

"Why go through all this trouble to hide a twig?"

"I don't think it was meant to be found. Remember, she wanted everything about her to be forgotten."

"That's what I mean. Why put it down here?"

"I don't know." Niklas put the twig in his satchel along with the notebook and the acorn flask. "But she must have hidden the twig extra well for a reason."

A desperate, high-pitched screech cut the air. It came from the direction of the yard, and for a moment, Niklas thought the border had been breached. He turned to Secret. "Is it the trolls?"

Secret shook her head. "It's the little fat cat. He's in trouble."

Chapter Sixteen

Tobis had scratched his way into the elm tree and clung to a high branch. His entire fur stood on end, but from the hard swishes of his tail, he didn't look too injured.

Niklas and Secret huddled below the barn bridge. While they were in the crypt, night had come to the farm. A fat moon hung between the mountain peaks. "Tobis," Niklas called softly, but as soon as he spoke, the cat gave a loud, warning yowl.

"He won't come down as long as I'm around," Secret said. "But I don't think I'm the reason he's up there. Something is going on here. I hear the horse inside the barn, too. She's scared."

She nodded at the main house. There were no lamps lit, and the front door yawned wide. "Does your uncle usually leave the door open like that?"

"Never," Niklas said. "It lets in flies." He looked around,

found a milk churn sitting on the bridge. "I have to make sure he's okay. You keep watch. If you need to warn me, knock down the milk churn."

The door to the bird room stood ajar, letting out a slim wedge of blue. Niklas walked slowly to the doorway. Moonlight shimmered across the walls. Outside the east window, the tower of his mother's castle poked up like a tusk. "Hello?" Niklas took a step into the room so he could see all the corners. "Is someone here?"

At first he thought there was no reply. But then he heard it, behind the desk. No words, just strange little tinkles. The hairs rose on his arms. He pulled the long-handled spade he used for the bird castle down from the wall and edged around the desk.

He didn't quite know what he had expected to find, but it wasn't this. He lowered the shovel. "What are you doing?"

Uncle Anders didn't answer. He lay on the floor, clutching his violin like a baby, shivering so hard his beard scratched the strings and made them whimper and mewl. Niklas reached for his arm, but his uncle curled together like a wounded animal.

"Uncle Anders? What's wrong?" Niklas patted him on the shoulder. "Please, what's going on?"

Only then did his uncle look up, and his face was pulled into a mask of despair made more terrifying because it didn't shift. "It wasn't her fault," he gargled out between stiff lips. "It wasn't any of our faults. We didn't mean for anyone to die."

"Who do you mean?" Niklas's tongue felt numb. "Are you talking about Sebastifer?"

"The boat was leaky, we knew that. But we had always managed to bail the water out before. We were just so much heavier with the cage."

"The cage," Niklas said.

Tears streaked Uncle Anders's cheeks. "I told her it wasn't her fault. Peder did, too. We were just trying to help. But she wouldn't listen!" He grabbed Niklas by the shirtsleeve. "The bad dream is back. I hear her voice in the stream. She's coming back!"

"Who?" Niklas heard his voice crack. *"Who is coming back?"*

Uncle Anders didn't look, but he lifted his arm and pointed out the north window, toward the inky mountainside and the white slash of the Oldmeadow path.

Out in the yard sounded the cold metal thunder of a milk churn falling down.

And Niklas knew that she would come.

She stepped through the gate, keeping her face half turned as she floated up the path, hidden behind a curtain of silver curls. At the screaming stone she halted as always. Her white dress hung heavy from her frame. Slowly, surely, she turned, until he could see her face.

Erika.

But not the Erika of his nightmares, not the bone-thin mother. The young Erika of the stubborn mouth and strong hands.

She raised her arm, fingers stretched out down the hill, staring straight toward the bird room window with pond-black eyes. Straight at Niklas, who leaned against the window, breath held and hands shaking. He couldn't look away. She cocked her head, waiting for something. For him?

"What do you want from me?" Niklas's breath made a very small cloud on the pane. It was just a whisper, not even loud enough for Uncle Anders to hear from where he lay curled up on the floor. But Erika still answered.

Her arm swung around like a compass arrow, until it pointed up the mountainside, toward the broken face of Buttertop that hovered above the treeline.

Toward Sorrowdeep.

She held his gaze, still waiting.

"No," he said.

A spot appeared on Erika's chest where her heart would be. She put her hands over it, but black liquid welled out between her fingers, spilling down her nightgown.

Somewhere in the house sounded a scream and a crash of shattering glass.

On instinct, Niklas's head jerked in the direction of the crash. But in the corner of his eye, he saw Erika change.

He turned back, watching in horror as the darkness in her chest spread. It covered her entire body now, turning it into water that loomed over the trail like a cresting wave. Then she dissolved and splashed to the ground.

The water drained into the moss and trickled down the trail, until the only sign of the nightmare was a spattering across the face of the screaming stone.

Chapter Seventeen

Grandma Alma lay on the kitchen floor next to the kettle. Her long white locks spread over her face, and her nightgown was splotched with tea. Niklas threw himself to the floor beside her and lifted her hair aside. "Grandma! Are you all right?"

"Niklas?" She stared at him.

He helped her sit up. "What happened?"

"I was making tea." Her eyes flicked to the north window and the trail, then to Uncle Anders, who hovered on the threshold, puffy-faced with tears. "I must have fallen asleep somehow, because I thought I saw . . ." She licked her lips in confusion. "It was an old night fright, that's all."

They all crammed into her bedroom. Even Tobis came out of the tree to curl up at her feet, glaring at anyone who came near. As they fussed about, fetching painkillers and the last of the chocolate cake and extra blankets, Grandma Alma settled back against the pillows, limp and pale. "Dreaming while standing on my own two legs," she mumbled. "It doesn't make sense."

No, Niklas thought. *It did not.* But then, she hadn't been dreaming. Erika really had walked up the trail. *An old night fright,* his grandmother had called it. *The bad dream is back,* his uncle had said. It sounded like they also were familiar with Niklas's nightmare.

Uncle Anders sat in a chair sipping his tea with solemn gratitude. Unlike Grandma Alma, he hadn't seen the nightmare, and Niklas hadn't told him what happened on the trail. He didn't want to ask either of them any questions until they had recovered.

Outside in the yard, he heard a soft bark. Niklas peered out into the elm tree and saw a pair of purple eyes up among the leaves. He felt almost dizzy with relief. Secret was out there, watching over them.

He took Grandma Alma's empty mug. "I'll just make you a fresh cup," he said, and slipped out into the night.

Secret stretched out along a branch with a view of the bedchamber window and the barn bridge. Niklas set the mug down and climbed up next to her. "Are you okay?"

Secret swished her tail. "It wasn't interested in me. It just walked straight past me up the hill from the bone field."

It. Niklas shuddered.

"Your grandmother is unhurt?"

He pulled his shoulders up. "On the outside. But both she and Uncle Anders are pretty shaken up. My mother . . . I mean, *it* . . . came from the hallowfield?"

"Yes, but not out of the ground, I think," Secret said. "It didn't smell like dirt."

"It looked at me," Niklas said. "I asked what it wanted, and I could have sworn it heard me. It pointed up the mountainside."

"Toward Sorrowdeep?"

"I think so. What else could it be?"

But why? Twenty-five years ago Sebastifer had died there, and later two horses had been killed. The line from the journal entry played over and over in Niklas's head. *My games are dangerous.* Mr. Molyk said the attacks—troll attacks, most likely—had suddenly stopped back then. Maybe his mother's decision to end the game had helped? But Niklas hadn't even played the troll hunt since Lin left. There was no game to end, no book to lock up, not so much as a jar of acorns to destroy. And now the nightmare was real, too? He couldn't control his dreams, much as he would like to.

Through the golden squares of the window, he could see Uncle Anders holding Grandma Alma's hand. It was hard to tell who was comforting whom. "We have to fix this, Secret," he said. "This magic taint, we have to find out where it comes from. It must have a source. Can you track it somehow?"

Secret thought for a moment. "I sniffed the stains where the nightmare fell apart, but they just smelled like wet roots and stones. Like the stream."

"Like the Summerchild?" Niklas frowned. Didn't Uncle Anders say he heard Erika's voice in the stream? The troll first showed up near the old ford, then near Oak Bridge. And the nightmare had turned into liquid. There was only one magical creature that didn't seem connected with water: a certain talking lynx who was just now licking her paws.

He sat up straight. "Secret, when you sheltered from that spring storm, what did you do?"

"I hid in a cave near Buttertop. It's deep, mostly empty, and it has—"

"Water." Niklas could hardly keep his voice down. "I think we got it wrong. Willodale didn't change while you were in there. You did."

Secret crinkled her nose. "I don't understand."

"Think about it. All the strange things that have happened have one thing in common: Water. I think you changed when you drank in that cave."

As Niklas explained his theory, Secret's tail began to thump against the branch. "The only water inside the cave is a spring," she said. "It's where the Summerchild begins."

Niklas whistled softly. "If I'm right, that means the

entire stream is tainted by magic. All of Summerhill's water supply."

He curled his fist. "You have to show me where that cave is. We have to find a way to un-taint the spring. Although we should wait until tomorrow so the trolls will be hiding from the sun."

"The sun won't help us," Secret said. "Look."

Heavy clouds rolled up Willodale. It would be a foggy and wet morning. The trolls would be a danger no matter when they left. "Well, that settles it." Niklas swung his legs down from the branch. They felt light and ready for danger. "We'll go now, before the rain makes the path slippery."

When he returned inside, Grandma Alma slept silently and Uncle Anders snored in his chair. Niklas wondered if he should wake them and tell them what was happening. But they would never let him leave. They would call for help, and the Willodalers would have even more reasons to call his uncle crazy. Actually, they'd call everyone at Summerhill crazy, and he bet none of them would listen to theories about a magic taint in the water.

He left a note on the nightstand instead.

I'll be back soon. Don't let anyone go
into the woods. Don't drink the water,
not even in tea. N.

"You take care of them," he whispered to Tobis, and closed the door.

He ate two cheese sandwiches and stuffed another into his satchel. He also brought a flask of apple juice, his flashlight, a folding knife, and the things he had taken from the chapel crypt: the bottle of acorn dust, his mother's book of troll runes, and the shriveled twig he had found inside her heart.

Last of all, he added the dog figurine from the castle. They were going up to Sorrowdeep tonight, and Sebastifer had saved his mother there. Maybe he would do it again.

For a moment he weighed Uncle Anders's phone in his hand. There was no reception up the mountainside, so there was no point in bringing it. But he needed to make a call.

His fingers shook as he dialed the number.

Lin didn't answer. Of course she didn't, it was past midnight. Niklas still tried two more times before he gave up and wrote her a message. He hoped it would make sense to her, but no one else.

"If this message were a flashlight, it would blink twice. I'll try to fix this, but if I can't, at least you know what's going on. Be careful. Bring acorns. Bye."

He left a lamp on in the kitchen, not so much for his sleeping family, but so it would shine for him up the hill.

Chapter Eighteen

Even on the most brilliant of days, Sorrowdeep showed black, studded with water lilies and disturbed only by fish that slid between the stems. Tonight, under the gathering clouds, it looked like a hole into nothing.

Niklas turned away from the water and found Secret watching him.

The lynx sat beside him, closer, he thought, than she had done before. If he stretched out his arm, he could almost reach her. She nodded at the broken face of Buttertop across the lake. "Do you see that cut in the rock?"

Niklas's night vision couldn't match Secret's, but he thought he saw a line of black snaking down the mountain wall. "The tall one in the middle?"

"That's the entrance to the cave."

Niklas felt his eyebrows rise. He had thought the cave would be farther up the trail to Buttertop, somewhere along the lip of the avalanche. The pond lapped against the sheer wall, except for a narrow beach below the cut. It would be impossible to reach it by dry land. He managed a brittle laugh. "I didn't know we would have to swim. I should have brought a towel."

"I only ever use the cave when the lake is frozen," Secret said. "But we don't have to swim. There's a boat over there."

A finger of rock poked into the pond, and on the other side bobbed a tiny rowing boat. Just the thought of crossing Sorrowdeep in that little husk made Niklas's belly churn. Images pushed their way into his head. Children swimming for their lives. Horses dead on the shore, cut by runes. A green-eyed monster rising from the water to grab Rag by the leg, while Edith and the other lambs scattered in panic. "Could the trolls be down there?"

"No. Their smell is stronger than any creature I've met. I would know if they were close."

"I wonder where they are tonight? Full moon, a storm coming in. You'd think they'd be on the prowl." He hesitated. "Do you smell any wet roots?"

"You mean the nightmare? No again. Sorrowdeep smells like always. Still water and silt."

Even so, Niklas couldn't help thinking of the nightmare pointing, commanding him to come here. He had told it no, but here he was, all the same. "All right," he said. "But if you can bear it, you should come in the boat with me. Just in case."

He took out the Sebastifer figurine and put it in his shirt pocket, near his heart. Somehow he trusted the dog to mean him well.

They climbed into the boat and pushed out between the water lilies. Secret crouched down on the bottom boards, ears turned out and tail tucked in. She must be very scared, but she didn't complain. Niklas decided to stop complaining, too. It wouldn't do to be a coward.

He dug the oars into the lake. Rings reached out over the surface.

Mostly he saw his own reflection in the water. But sometimes he thought he glimpsed things in the deep; hair that wafted in the currents, a nightgown billowing like a sail snagged on the bottom. Pale bones. *They're not hers,* he reminded himself. *No matter what Sorrowdeep wants me to believe, her bones are in the hallowfield.*

As the first raindrops plinked down around them, they crunched against the pebble beach. Niklas pulled the boat up on shore, almost nauseous with relief.

But Secret shook her fur out and stared into the darkness of the cave, nostrils flaring.

"Still no troll stench?"

"Nothing." Her good ear stood tall. "And not as much as the scratch of a bat."

"That's great." Niklas patted the Sebastifer figurine in his pocket. "Bats are annoying."

"Yes," Secret said. "But I don't like that they're gone."

The cave floor felt odd under their feet, spongy and gnarled. Niklas suspected it had been forest floor once, before the avalanche. Secret insisted on going first so the flashlight wouldn't ruin her vision. "Do you know what we are looking for, cub?"

"Not really." Niklas stepped around a sharp outcrop in the wall. Secret's so-called cave was more of a tunnel so far.

"But you know how to get rid of a magic taint," Secret said. "Or you wouldn't come up here on a troll night with no plan and no acorns."

Niklas grinned. That was something Lin could have said. "Let's get there, and we'll see what we'll see. When a dead deer poisons the stream, you need to get it out of the water. I figure it works the same way with magic."

Secret slipped under a huge splinter where a tree had once been crushed. The wood was so rotten, it came apart under Niklas's fingers.

Secret returned to sniff it. "Something is wrong. I don't know what it is. Nothing smells off, but there's this not-sound. It bounces wrong off the walls." She gave a soft growl. "I will go ahead and check."

"And I'm supposed to wait here? On a troll night with no acorns?" Niklas crossed his arms.

She turned back to glare at him. "I can't see as well with your flashlight making all the wrong things bright. And I can't hear anything over your clumsy tread."

"Rubbish. I'm stealthy as a cat," Niklas said. He was

only half joking, too. But he slid his satchel off his shoulder and leaned against the wall. "Fine, I'll wait. But don't do anything without me."

Secret melted into the darkness without a sound.

Niklas shone his flashlight on the wall, from rock to wood to dead roots. How stable was this tunnel anyway? After the great avalanche, they never got the dead out for fear of disturbing the masses, but that was a long time ago. Secret had been here many times, so she should know if it was safe. Except something had her creeped out. What if it was her lynx sense telling her that the roof was about to collapse?

And that's when he pointed the flashlight at the skull.

He bolted to his feet. Two yards above him, someone had wedged a dead bird's head into a crack in the wall. The skull was carved with two jagged lines that crossed like an X.

A troll rune.

So they *were* here. He got his mother's notebook out of his bag and leafed through the pages with one hand, holding the flashlight with the other. Two crossing lines . . . meant *hide*.

There was something up there the trolls didn't want anyone to see.

He shone the light after Secret, but decided not to yell. She might not be the only one to hear.

Instead he put his flashlight in his mouth and climbed up to investigate.

He found nothing out of the ordinary around the skull, so whatever it hid, it hid well. He thought the lines of the rune had been first painted, then carved into the bone. The black liquid was smudged and worn, as if it had been rubbed or touched many times.

Niklas put the tip of his finger on the rune.

The X lit up red.

Immediately, the troll stench fell upon him like a smothering blanket.

He lost his grip and tumbled backward, dropping hard to the ground. The flashlight fell, too. The glass cracked, but the light didn't go out. It shone on the tunnel wall where a gap had opened to form a giant doorway.

In that doorway, baring all his saw teeth, stood the three-eared troll.

Chapter Nineteen

Niklas wanted to run, but the troll scooped him off the floor before he could even get to his feet. He wedged Niklas's head under his arm and dragged him through the doorway and deeper into the mountain. Niklas kicked and clawed and yelled for help, but the troll arm around his neck might as well be a metal collar.

"Rafsa will be pleased now." The troll's voice sounded garbled, as if his tongue took up too much space in his mouth. "Big night just got bigger!"

As they turned a sharp bend, Niklas managed to cast a glance behind him, to see if Secret had returned. But there was only his satchel lying deserted on the floor, in the dying beam of his flashlight. His heart and thoughts raced, too fast and painful. Maybe Secret couldn't hear his screams. Maybe the rune still worked for anyone who hadn't touched it, and she would return to an empty tunnel with his abandoned things. He was in deep muck now. The floor changed. The spongy remains of the old avalanche gave way to unyielding rock. Piles of naked sticks rolled under Niklas's feet, more and more, until they emerged into a large, smoky cave, lit by a fire pit in the middle.

Oh, the muck just got deeper.

Secret had been off with her number. There were more than two trolls. Five of them sat gathered around the pit, sliding their claws in and out.

But that wasn't the worst of it.

All along the cave wall, stalactites hung from the ceiling, like icicles made of rock. Except for six that had cracked open, they were wrapped with rune-marked leather.

Niklas remembered this rune. A square with an eye inside meant *awake*.

There were faces trapped inside the stalactites. Big ears and bared teeth and blind eyes, and many, many claws. A hundred more trolls waiting to be released from the stone.

A troll walked among the hanging pillars, fastening a hide here, tracing the line of a nose there. She didn't look like the others. She wore a mail of bones strung together, but the rest of her was ruined skin. Burn marks and tattooed troll runes, covered in more scars and more runes. Her hairless skull had fresh burns and blisters.

"Rafsa!" The three-eared troll roared above the din of the cave. "Look what I found in the tunnel!"

All heads whipped around, and after a moment of slack-jawed staring, a raucous cheer broke out. Rafsa took her time crossing the floor, while her grin grew wider and wider and the fire-pit trolls grew louder and louder. When she stopped in front of him, Niklas could hardly hear her cry, "The boy-enemy!"

She held up her hand and waited for the noise to die down. It had a tattoo of a four-pointed star, like the troll from Erika's casket.

"How good of you to show up," Rafsa said. "I thought we would have to tear this forest apart to get our hands on you. But here you are, just in time for the awakening."

Rafsa bent down to speak into Niklas's face. The stench was like a clammy towel over his mouth and nose. "We have waited long for this moment, for the magic to grow strong enough to bring our brood out of the rock. Third-Ear came first, weeks ago. The magic was still thin then, but he wanted so badly to come and hunt you in the woods, he broke free on his own. That's how much he hates you."

Third-Ear tightened his grip around Niklas's neck.

Rafsa pointed at the stalactites. "Five more of us awakened last night, and no trouble at all. The magic runs thick and true. So tonight we'll bring them all out. An army to run through the valley and take back what's ours." Her finger came around, scratching at Niklas's cheek. "More hunters will come to the woods to look for you, I wager, but they don't know the first thing about bane. We'll hack them to pieces while they fumble with their guns!"

"They'll figure out how to stop you," Niklas blurted out. "I'm not the only one who knows about . . . Knows how to . . ." He shut his mouth.

"He means the girl-enemy," Third-Ear said.

The brood erupted in screams. "The girl-enemy! Where is the girl-enemy? We want to cut her heart out!"

A small, cold seed stirred in Niklas's gut. He was grateful for every mile between Willodale and the city. Then Rafsa said something that made the cold burst into freezing vines inside him. "Don't you worry about the girl-enemy. She loves this little brat. When we kill him, she'll come home."

She would. Especially after the message he had left her.

Third-Ear dragged Niklas to the fire pit and dropped him. His belly didn't exactly calm down when he discovered that the pile of sticks and stones next to it wasn't sticks and stones at all, but bones and skulls. Sheep skulls, deer skulls, smaller ones that might belong to birds.

Rafsa grinned. "They were all trapped here when the mountain fell. Died painful deaths, which is why they work for my magic." She plucked a bone from the pile and let it rest in her hand, picking at a fracture. "This one I think is human. One of your ancestors, maybe? Do you want him back?"

She tossed the bone at Niklas. He flinched when it clattered to the floor.

"Oh, a scared little boy! Fancies himself the prince, but look at him now!" Rafsa leaned close again. Niklas bit his lip to keep the nausea under control. "The last time I walked these woods, I was alone. All I got for my hunting was two measly horses."

"You're the one who killed the horses at Sorrowdeep!"

"It was as far as I got before I had to leave. This time I've come for good. This time I know how to make myself an army." Her leer dropped quickly off her face, replaced by a scowl that pulled her burn scars tight. "But after twenty-five years of waiting, what do I find? A stone that stands between us troll-kin and what is rightfully ours. If we're to take the valley, we need to bring down the border magic. But old bones and teeth won't do it, and neither will a fresh kill. I've tried."

She meant Rag, innocent little Rag in the hands of these murderers. Niklas looked away. He didn't want her to see how much it bothered him.

"But you—our boy-enemy—you made up the border. So I think your skin will work better!" Rafsa slid her claw out and held it up. "Bring the ink!"

A bulge-eyed troll rushed over with a bowl of black, thick liquid. The three-eared troll pulled up the sleeve of Niklas's shirt and held him so he couldn't move. Rafsa dipped the tip of her claw in the liquid and began to draw a rune on the inside of his arm. A rectangle with one black and one blank section, sliced in half by a slanted line.

Break.

Sweat slid down his neck. He looked around for an escape, but saw only greedy, hungry trolls. Secret made no sign of showing, but that was just as well. Even if she had figured out how to see past the *hide* rune, there was no way she could fight a whole pack of trolls. They would only kill her, too. He had to think of something fast, something other than acorns, something better than fighting. If Lin were here, she would tell him to use his best weapon: words.

"Stop!" he yelled, hoping an idea would drop into his head. "You can't kill me. You'd . . . disappear!"

The tip of Rafsa's claw hovered right above Niklas's arm. She didn't reply, but she peered at him through tight lids that couldn't hide the glint of uncertainty.

He pressed on. "Like you said, I made the border, and I made the troll hunt. You can't exist without me." He suspected this was not even remotely close to the truth, especially since Rafsa was his mother's creation and not his. But he brought out what he hoped was his most superior smirk. "Sorry."

"Not true, not true!" screeched the bulge-eyed one.

Rafsa licked her cracked lips. "Might be true. Might not. Can't risk it now."

Boos and hisses filled the cave, but Rafsa roared until all the others went quiet.

"I said, can't risk it *now.*" She put her claw against Niklas's cheek, eyes glittering. "Don't worry, broodlings. I'll ask the king. He'll know, he has his books. He has his dark roses. And if the boy-enemy is lying . . ." She let her claw sink into Niklas's skin so a drop of blood trickled down. "You know I like my little games."

She knocked him over the head.

Chapter Twenty

When he woke up, Niklas found himself stuffed in a cell: a shallow scoop in the mountain wall closed off with a net that gleamed in the darkness. He sat up, touching his forehead where a bump had risen. There were no trolls around, only a faint red glare that flickered down the worm of a tunnel. But he could hear the occasional whoop and howl. They must have started their celebration.

If only he hadn't taken off his satchel, he could have used his knife to cut through the net. Actually, if he hadn't taken off his satchel, that nasty Rafsa would probably have taken all his things. Hopefully they were too busy to bother looking for lost items—or lost lynxes. He wondered if Secret was searching for him, or if she was waiting by the concealed doorway. Or worse, if something had happened to her.

Somewhere in the distance, a wet gargle changed into

a scream. Niklas got to his feet. He had to bend his neck to stand up, but he still felt less vulnerable. The trolls screeched and yelled all the time, but there was a different quality to that scream. It sounded panicked. Then another howl went up, and another. What was happening in the troll cave?

Suddenly a smudge of darkness dropped past the net and landed on the floor with a thump. His satchel. "Quiet," said a voice above him. "We have to be quick."

Secret landed silently beside the satchel. She looked none the worse for wear.

"You found me! How did you . . . ?"

"I said, quiet. Don't touch the net." She used her teeth to open the satchel and pick out the flask of troll's bane. Taking care to avoid the shiny rope, she pushed the flask into the cell. "Use this. Make a hole."

Niklas pulled out the stopper and carefully poured powdered acorns over the knots. The rope hissed and stung his nose, as if the flask contained a strong acid.

"It's made with troll hemp," Secret said. "I heard them gloat about it. It can't be cut by blade, and if you touch it, the binder will know."

When the smoke cleared, the bane had burned a hole in the net, just big enough for Niklas to ease through. But the flask was empty. He shook it, dismayed. "But this is all the troll's bane we have! I thought I was careful!"

Secret's eyes showed purple in the dimness. "Hurry."

The ruckus in the cave reached them in rising waves. "What's going on out there?" Niklas whispered. "Is it the awakening? Are the trolls coming out of their stalactites?"

Secret didn't look at him. "No."

Holding his breath, Niklas slipped through the hole and slung on his satchel. Secret didn't waste another moment. "This way."

She slunk down the corridor. Torch light showed through an opening on their right, but they continued straight ahead, until the tunnel ended in another cave with a fire pit in the middle, tens of carcasses strung up under the roof, and stacks of crude bowls. A big, half-empty cauldron of stew simmered over the fire. It smelled almost as disgusting as the trolls themselves.

"You found their kitchen," Niklas said. "Did you know these tunnels already?"

"They weren't here before. The taint must have made them." Secret pushed the bolt shut on the heavy door.

Niklas let out a sigh of relief. "Now will you tell me what's happening?"

"What's happening is that we're out of acorns," Secret said, glancing at the cauldron.

Niklas faltered. He *had* been careful with the troll's bane. There just wasn't much left in the flask. "You put the bane in their stew?"

"There were guards and I needed to distract them." Secret flattened her ears along her skull. "I've never tried fighting with poison before. I didn't know it would work quite so well."

He had no idea what would happen if a troll ate bane. Gruesome death, most likely. But Rafsa was clever. Maybe she would figure it out before it got them all. "How many ate it?"

Secret lashed her tail. "All of them."

Maybe not.

Niklas stared at the bubbling stew. A fresh scream sounded from the big cave, muffled by the door, but still enough to make his hair stand on end.

Secret tilted her head. "You don't like the killing. But it had to be done."

"I know that." And he did. The trolls wanted to kill him and Lin and everyone in this valley. They didn't belong here. Still, this hero thing was messier than he had thought.

"Then not so slow," said Secret. "We have a bigger problem than the trolls. It's this way."

Chapter Twenty-One

In the old avalanche tunnel, the flashlight still lay on the ground, extinguished. Secret stepped over it. Though they had both crossed back over the threshold to the troll tunnels, the entrance still remained open. It seemed touching the rune once was enough to see through its magic for good.

"How did you find the doorway," Niklas said. "The rune can't have been visible in the dark."

"When I returned, the troll had already dragged you off. His smell was concealed, but yours wasn't. So I sniffed around until I found your cheese-sandwich fingerprints high up on the wall. Whiskers work as well as fingers, it seems."

"You never thought I had left? Gone home to Summerhill with my tail between my legs?"

"You're too stubborn for that," Secret said. "Besides,

the boat was still there. I knew you wouldn't swim across the lake."

She was right about that. "But did you get to the spring? Did you find the source of the taint?"

Secret's ruff twitched. "I think so. Like I said, we have a problem. I'm not sure your plan is going to work."

"Why not?"

"Because it's not something you can lift out of the water."

They continued on into the avalanche. Without his flashlight, Niklas had to rely on his hands and Secret's curt instructions to find the way. "Crooked root at left shin. Three steps, then wobbly stone."

"You really know your way around this tunnel." Niklas fumbled at the wall.

"This was our den," Secret said. "I was born here. When my mother was shot, I hid here. Every time there is a snowstorm, I shelter here. So yes. I know it." She padded on in silence for a while, then added, "I was starving already, before the storm last spring. I wouldn't have survived without the meat you gave me."

Niklas was stunned. His plan had seemed so far-fetched back then: Give the lynx food, save her life. Make her like him, like Rufus loved Lin. Yet somehow, it had worked. "Then it was worth the scolding Grandma Alma gave me. She still hasn't forgotten, you know. Sometimes she makes me cabbage and potatoes and claims it's what I like to eat for dinner."

Secret wheezed at the back of her throat. "Cabbage and potatoes. Your grandmother is a hard woman."

It began as a faint murmur, but as they pressed deeper into the mountain, the sound of water grew to a steady rush. The air in the tunnel changed, too. Niklas wondered at first if his nose had been damaged by the troll stench, because to him, it smelled like flowers. But then he bumped against the wall and felt something sinewy and sharp scratch his shoulder.

"Is this . . . ?" His fingertips struck a silky, cool object that gave off a sweet scent. Suddenly it flashed under his fingers, and for a bright second, the tunnel became visible. Sure enough, the object was a pale, perfect rose. "It is! How can a rose grow here in the darkness? And why does it flash?"

"I don't know," Secret said. "But it gets worse."

The tunnel widened to a cave. It wasn't very big, but after the cramped corridor, it seemed like a ballroom. It was decked out like one, too. All the walls were overgrown with thorny branches that wove into a dense tapestry, tied with fresh shoots and dotted with white roses. Now and again the thorns twinkled.

"*This* was your den? What are you, lynx royalty?"

"It didn't look like this back then," Secret said. "It was just a cave with a spring in it."

The water spilled out through an opening halfway up

the cave wall, gathered briefly in a small pool, and escaped on the other side, hurrying under the mountain to become the Summerchild. The opening looked like another grand doorway. It was taller than Niklas, pointed like an archway, and lined with more shrub.

"The roses weren't here before, then?"

"No." A little below the threshold and just to the side, a half-moon ledge stuck out of the wall. Secret jumped onto it. The ledge could barely hold all of her, but from the comfortable way she tucked her tail in and settled down, Niklas guessed it was a favorite spot from when she was little. "And neither was the doorway. It was just a crack in the rock, nice to drink from." She sniffed the green skin of a vine. "Last spring I did notice a small twig poking out, but it looked old and dead. I guessed it was just a piece of the avalanche that had drifted here with the water. I never thought it could be alive."

Niklas pushed at a branch. This one was thicker than his thigh. "You think the roses cause the taint?"

"The roses or the doorway. Or both. They have this strange *smell* . . ."

Niklas couldn't smell anything other than pretty flowers, but he trusted Secret's nose. "Well, you're right. This isn't something we can simply lift out of the water."

He climbed up to examine the archway. "Maybe we can follow the shrub back to its roots. If we sever them, the rest of the plant should wither."

The rosebush delved into the mountain as far as he could see between the vines that trailed down from the roof. The flashing light traveled along the tunnel like a slowly beating pulse.

"With the shrub shoring it up, it won't cave," Niklas said. Thorns stuck out from every branch, some small and vicious, some as big as knives. But with a bit of care, he thought it would be possible to find a path between them. He nodded encouragement at Secret, the way he would nod at Lin if they were lost. "Come on. Let's see if we can find the roots."

He climbed up into the opening. The beginnings of the Summerchild flowed toward him along the stone floor, no more than a streamlet of shallow eddies. At least there were no thorns in the water.

Behind him, Secret gave a low whine. She lingered in the opening, front paws planted in the water where it slipped out through the archway, while her back paws still remained on the half-moon ledge. Her ears turned down and out, one tufted and perfect, the other torn and limp. "Cub," she said. "I feel so strange."

Without her calm dignity and hunter crouch, she looked much smaller. A wild animal out of her depth, so different from the brave Secret who watched his back and rescued him from trolls. Niklas swallowed. He hadn't thought of this until now, which made him the world's biggest idiot. The trolls wouldn't be the only magic to go away if they got rid of the taint. "Wait," he said. "If we stop this . . . you'll go back to . . ."

Secret shook her head. "I'll be the lynx of these woods again. You'll be the boy of the farm. And we'll both go back to our ways."

Of course, Niklas's way was being alone all the time. He glanced around at the roses, tried a smile. "Maybe we don't have to get rid of them now. After all, we already took care of Rafsa and her brood."

Secret hadn't taken her eyes off him. "But not the nightmare."

Niklas nodded. She was right. He knew that, even if the cold filled his stomach again. He covered up the chill as best he could. "You know what? It won't happen like that." He took two steps back toward her, pulled a sinewy branch out of her way. "Because we know each other a little by now. For instance, I've learned that if you turn very quiet, something is wrong. And that if you squint and look away, you're pleased."

She looked away, squinting. "And I've learned that if your smile turns wide instead of lopsided, you're lying."

Niklas laughed. "See? So what if you can't speak? Lin and Rufus are friends, and he never said a word in his life. I promise you, when the taint is gone, you and I are going to raid Mr. Molyk's apple orchard together."

"Hard to raid anything when you don't know how to sneak." With a shiver, Secret jumped into the tunnel.

When she slipped past the branch he held for her, she nudged his hand with her nose. "But maybe you'll learn that, too."

Apart from knocking him to the ground at Oak Bridge, it was the first time she had touched him. Her nose felt scratchy and warm, and it melted every bit of cold away.

Niklas yearned to see the sky. As the Summerchild dwindled to a trickle under their feet, the passage narrowed, and the thorns closed in on them from every direction.

A darker kind of vine wove through the rosy branches, snaking in and out like barbed wire in a flower wreath. These vines didn't flash and they didn't bear flowers. They had a shriveled appearance, as if they were sick. But their thorns, brown and curved like claws, were sharp enough.

Niklas used his satchel to push aside a tangle of vines, hoping to find the roots. Instead he found a weave of branches that barred their way. Some of them were of the withered kind, but most carried rosebuds.

"Do you think this is the end of the tunnel?" Niklas tested the weave with the tip of his boot. It yielded only a little, and he couldn't see through to the other side. The sound of water had disappeared completely.

Secret had also been very quiet since the cave. She just lifted her lips to taste the air, then shook her head. The breeze blowing through the bony strands of rosebush seemed fresh enough. But whether the passage continued or not, Niklas and Secret couldn't go on.

Suddenly the silence broke.

"Who is there?"

Niklas whipped around. The voice came from nowhere and everywhere, and it had a strange double pitch. Secret crouched low, ready to attack, but she circled as if she couldn't find her target.

"Who is it?"

One of the rose branches stirred. It coiled free of the wall, creeping along Niklas's leg, scratching his pants with its thorns. Another lifted toward Secret.

"Who?"

With a snarl Secret batted at the vines, striking them aside. But others took their place immediately. Niklas cried out as one of them sank a thorn into his arm, deep enough to draw blood.

All around them, the rosebuds sprang open, spreading their petals like focusing lenses.

"Not her."

"Not the trespasser."

"Not the burned one."

It wasn't a double-pitched voice, Niklas realized, but two voices, one thunderous and very old-sounding, the other whispering sweet. They had been speaking as one, but now they spoke to each other.

"It's a child," said the whispering voice.

"Yes," the other voice boomed. *"A child and his cat, come to brave the crossing."*

A long hiss swept through the tunnel, and the dense weave pulled aside to reveal two thick branches that barred the way in a great cross. One was thick and gnarled, but the bark still bore fresh green thorns and pale flowers; the other branch was choked with dark vine and looked brown and leathery.

"He has not been invited." The shriveled branch didn't move, but Niklas still felt that the whispering voice controlled it somehow. *"He does not have a key."*

"He has a key," the thunderous voice replied. *"A forgotten one. A late one."*

"But it does not belong to him." Niklas didn't like the whispering voice. There was a nasty undertone to its too-sweet murmurs.

"No, it belonged to someone else, someone . . ." The old voice sounded confused, as if it struggled to remember. And after a pause: *"But he has a right to it."*

"The boy is just as weak," said the nasty voice. *"Taste him again and see."*

"Yes," agreed the booming voice. *"Taste him."*

The tendril pricked Niklas's arm a second time. The thorn drank the blood drop, and soon after, the nearest rose gained a red smudge on its white petals.

"Fear." The shriveled branch creaked. *"Fear in this one,*

gray as old bones, heavy as a cage. He tries to cover it with bravery, but it eats at his core. He is not worthy."

All the roses opened very wide.

"Are you scared, boy?" As the old voice asked the question, the thorny vine prodded Niklas, as if to underline that an answer was required. He had an uncomfortable feeling he was being tested. "No," he said. His chest felt so tight, he had to squeeze the words out. "I'm not."

Secret said nothing, but her tail lashed.

"You seem to think it's a bad thing to be scared, when in fact there is so very much of which to be afraid." The old voice sounded disappointed. *"You might not have been chosen, if there was choosing to do. But there is not, now. Well, you can run and you can steal and you can lie through your teeth. Perhaps there is still . . ."*

The dark vines snared tighter. The thorns on the nasty branch grew longer, like the troll claws. *"You forget the rule. No Twistroses will pass!"*

Around them, many thorns followed suit, flexing and growing. Dark webbing appeared in the bark like veins, and the tendrils snared around Niklas's legs and arms, pulling tight. He clenched his teeth and tried to wrestle loose, but the tendrils were too strong.

Secret shook her confusion and sprang into action. She bit at the vines, even if the thorns must sting her mouth terribly. But not even she could break their grip.

"Stop!" The old branch gave another long, slow creak. *"He is not a Twistrose. He is just a boy with a dead key. He will not challenge the rule or ruin the plan. We will let him pass."*

One by one, the thorns retracted and the tendrils dropped to the ground, leaving Niklas coughing, but free. Finally the old branch moved to the side, scraping along the rocky tunnel floor, drawing a line of splinters and dust. Behind it, the opening had widened again, showing a short stretch of tunnel, and then stars.

Only the nasty branch still barred their way.

"Let him pass," said the old voice.

"Let *us* pass," Niklas said. "We won't do any harm."

The nasty branch didn't move. "No," it said. "Kill them."

Niklas whispered in his smallest voice, one he hoped would only be audible to a lynx. "I don't think this piece of shrubbery quite agrees with itself. You go left, I'll go right?"

Secret's good ear turned ever so slightly toward Niklas.

"Now," he said, and dove for freedom.

Chapter Twenty-two

They tumbled out of the tunnel. The dark vines lashed after them, but Niklas fell flat on his belly, and he heard them whip through the air over his head. He crawled away from the opening, hands and feet slipping through fine, cool sand, until the lashing stopped.

He sat up, rubbing his arm where the vine had cut into Rafsa's half-finished rune. Immediately, his hopes of hacking off the roots were dashed. Outside of the tunnel opening, there were no roots and no roses. The vines had retracted into another doorway in the barren mountain wall, weaving it shut so only a softly pulsing light escaped through the thorns.

Secret sat on the ground next to him, blinking.

"Are you all right?" Niklas reached out to touch her, but at the last moment he remembered himself and let his hand hover.

"I won't bite." Secret smiled. "I think."

Now it was Niklas's turn to blink. He hadn't seen her smile before. The corners of her mouth curled up extravagantly like a waxed mustache.

"Not so slack-jawed, cub." She turned away from him and lifted her paw to scratch her mangled ear. But she set her foot carefully back in the sand. "Maybe instead tell me where you have taken us."

Niklas turned to see what she saw, and slowly let his hand settle on Secret's shoulder.

He had absolutely no idea.

Niklas had climbed Buttertop many times with Lin and Uncle Anders. At the end of every August, when it was time to bring the cattle home from summer grazing, they combed the shallow, windswept mountain vales of the Trollheim in search of the flock. Those valleys did not look like this.

It wasn't just the dark sand or the patches of coarse, silvery grass. The mountain itself seemed unfamiliar, cragged and sharp, with facets that shone like glass. It cradled the tiny valley on three sides, and the fourth opened to the night sky.

Myriads of stars spread across the heaven like gem-studded dust. In Willodale, the night would be too light to show stars for weeks still.

"I don't know. I think it must be somewhere *else.*" Niklas got to his feet, his hand still buried in Secret's fur. It felt rough against his fingers, keeping him on the ground when the stars tried to pull him up, strange and impossible. His heart pounded with the danger of it.

Hooowooooo.

The sound didn't come from the tunnel, it came from somewhere in the canyon. Secret wound tight like a coil.

A creature appeared against the sky, so quickly, it seemed to blink into existence from one moment to the next. In the near-darkness it was hard to tell, but Niklas thought it wore a great cloak that shifted and swelled. But he could make out the creature's head, which gleamed in the starlight. It was the skull of a giant bird.

"What is that?" Secret whimpered.

"A nightmare," Niklas said. His throat felt dry. "It's the creature from the bird castle." And from the chapel crypt, and from his own dreams.

The taint was here, too.

The skeleton skipped to the side. Where it had stood, another followed, and more, until six of them lined up in a half circle, barring the way out from the canyon. Their beaks curved slim and sharp, and the wind threaded through their eye sockets, making an eerie hooting scream.

Hoooooowooooo.

Niklas and Secret had nowhere to go but back to the canyon wall. They moved slowly, feet treading the soft sand, hardly daring to breathe.

The creatures kicked off from the ground. As they took

flight, the black cloth spread out, showing their bodies underneath. They were all bones, unbound by ligaments and muscles, but still linked, like his mother's marionettes in the bird room. The bones glowed with pale light as the flying bird skeletons circled overhead, claws stark and ready, blotting out the stars above the canyon.

Niklas half stumbled over a stone. One of the birds dove for him. He wrenched to the side a heartbeat before the beak sliced the air where his head had been. Then the creature wheeled back up into the air.

He pressed his back against the rock. "Now what?"

"Can't run," Secret growled beside him as another bird dipped down. "So we fight."

With a snarl, she launched herself at the skeleton. She tore a piece of cloth off the wing, but the creature kept attacking, and now the others followed, wings flapping and beaks slashing. Secret became a sinewy streak of claws and teeth. She was almost as fast as the creatures, but not quite, and there were six of them. Her battle scream wrung high into a yelp when one of them stabbed at her.

They seemed to have forgotten Niklas. His only weapon, the pocketknife, lay tucked away in his satchel. He fumbled under the lid until he found it, clutching it hard in his sweaty palm. He had never fought anyone in his life, let alone used a weapon.

But when Secret screamed again and a wound opened

up in her flank, he let out a roar of his own and sprang forward.

His knife skittered along a bone. He toppled, rolled, and ended up flat on his back. The skeleton bird towered above him, no more than a yard away, but it didn't strike. The air whistled in its eye sockets as it moved its head from side to side. As if it was searching for him.

It didn't know where he was.

His old nightmare flashed through his head. The birds had pecked at him until he couldn't see anymore. Were these birds *blind?*

Niklas grasped at the ground. His hand came away with a handful of small rocks. He sent them flying along the canyon floor. As soon as they plinked down, the bird whipped around and flapped off, hacking at the sand where the rocks had landed.

It worked! Niklas didn't call out to Secret; he couldn't. But he picked up another handful of bigger rocks and threw them, one by one, as far away from Secret as he could manage. Two of her attackers peeled away to check. Then another. Then the last.

Secret turned to look at him, panting hard. Niklas put his finger over his lips, hoping she would understand the signal. She must have, because she calmed her breathing.

The birds had gone back to circling now, waiting for their prey to make a noise and reveal themselves. But Secret proved she was a master at sneaking, gliding along like the tiniest whisper in the sand. Niklas covered his heavier tread with carefully timed stone-throwing as they made their way through the canyon.

Out of the darkness grew a building. A small cottage nestled in a large crack at the foot of the canyon mouth. The shutters were closed and the door had fallen off its hinges. Suddenly the breeze shifted, and Secret opened her nostrils wide. She turned to him. Niklas nodded. He could smell it, too.

Wood smoke. The cottage was not abandoned.

But they had to pass by it to get out of the canyon, so they kept going. A weathered picket fence guarded what might once have been a vegetable patch. The dirt still lay gathered in grooves, but nothing grew there.

Secret froze.

Another skeleton bird had appeared in the cottage doorway. It flowed onto the porch, shoulders hunched, head swiveling back and forth. When it looked in the direction of Secret and Niklas, it stiffened. Niklas thought he saw something glint inside the hollow skull eyes.

This one was not blind.

The creature raised the tip of a cloak wing to an object on its chest: a round disc with glittering spikes. An amulet. It flashed red.

The hooting sound rose to a scream at the bottom of the canyon, where all the other skeleton birds moved as one. They came hurtling through the air, straight for Secret and Niklas, and now they seemed to know exactly where to find them.

Niklas barely had time to start running before he lay pinned on the ground with claws over his throat, looking up at a long beak. He lifted his hands, but they were empty. The pocketknife must have slipped out of his grip when he fell. His fingernails did nothing against the cold bones of the bird's foot. He heard Secret growl, but she was far off to his left. They couldn't help each other.

The bird drew its beak back to strike.

Suddenly the air sang around them. Burning streaks hit the ground with a thunk. The skeleton bird stood straight. Its skull had changed color. Instead of the silver glow, yellow and red flickered along the edges. Another bolt of fire struck it in the shoulder, and it stepped back.

Niklas rolled over and bolted to his feet. Two burning arrows stuck out of the creature's wing, and more sailed through the air.

Along the left top of the canyon, two black silhouettes had appeared against the night sky. They shot so fast it seemed like they were letting loose a firestorm of missiles, striking the skeleton birds, striking the ground, nearly striking Secret so she skittered to the side.

Niklas rushed over to her, keeping his head low. She trembled all over. "Hunters!"

"We have to take cover!" He pushed her shoulder hard. To his relief, she let herself be jolted into motion. They sprinted toward the canyon opening. In a few steps, they left the reeling nightmare birds behind, but still the missiles kept coming. "They're shooting at us, too," Secret snarled.

Niklas broke to the side, guiding her into the naked rows of the vegetable garden. "They're not. Look."

A burning arrow rammed into the beam of the cottage porch, where the final skeleton bird stood watching. It followed the arrow's path back to the bowmen on the canyon edge. Then it gathered its cloak tight, stepped off the far end of porch, and melted into the darkness.

Niklas poked his head up from between the rows to see where it went. Secret put a paw between Niklas's shoulders and pressed him into the dirt. "Keep down."

The whole canyon glowed with flames now. The skeleton birds flailed in panic. One had caught fire and flew off like a blazing meteorite.

It didn't take many more arrows for the others to follow, cloaks fluttering with speed.

The night filled with the quiet, crackling sound of arrow shafts burning. At the top of the canyon, above the cottage and across from the bowmen, Niklas thought he saw the last skeleton bird, outlined against the stars. It waited for a moment, then disappeared.

A voice came from above. "All right, idiots. Stay where you are."

Chapter Twenty-three

We're going to do exactly as they say?" Everything in Secret's posture read disagreement: the restless twitchy tail, the outward-pointing ears and dipped neck.

"They stopped shooting as soon as our attackers fled, right?" Niklas patted her shoulder. "But they may start again if we try to run. I'm sure they mean us no harm."

In truth, he didn't feel sure at all. But he had dragged Secret into this mess, so he had to rely on his usual plan in sticky situations: smile and look confident that he knew the way home.

The archers climbed down an invisible path in the cut-glass canyon wall. As they neared the light from the burning arrows, their shapes gained color and form.

Secret tucked in her tail. "Stay calm," Niklas murmured, though he felt rather nervous himself.

Because the bowmen were not men at all. They were

animals of strange proportions: a giant squirrel and a gray striped ferret, both walking on two legs as if they had never done anything else. They filed down the path, dressed in black vests and with bows at the ready, firelight painting their faces grim.

"You were right, Kepler," the squirrel said, tilting her head. "It *is* a boy."

"Of course it is," said the ferret. "I may be shortsighted, but I'm always right. That's why they call me the wandering encyclopedia."

The squirrel rolled her beady eyes.

"They don't actually call me that," the ferret said. "However, I do like a nice, juicy piece of information. So tell me, who are you, and what are you doing here?"

Niklas glanced from one to the other. Both the ferret and the squirrel were slightly taller than him. He cleared his throat. "I'm Niklas."

The two animals turned to Secret. She glowered at them, concentrating her withering stare on the ferret, who, for all his slouch and smirk, seemed to be in charge.

"Her name is Secret," Niklas said.

The ferret gave a baffled shake of his head. "What is your business up here? I know it's a fine night, but most people don't go gallivanting deep into Nightmare territory just because the stars are out."

Niklas's head spun. Nightmare territory? Did these creatures know about his dreams?

Beside him Secret seemed much more disturbed by the human-like animals than any monsters plucked from his head. Every time one of them used their front paws as hands, she looked one whisker shy of panicking. He took a step forward, putting himself in the middle. "We didn't mean to trespass."

The ferret narrowed his eyes. "Trespassing with a *key,* then?"

Niklas waited to see if this was another joke, but no one laughed. "I'm not sure what you mean," he said, using his best voice of innocence, with a dose of now-be-reasonable layered in. "I don't have a key."

Except the voices in the tunnel had also said something like that. *He is just a boy with a dead key.* The ferret and the squirrel exchanged glances, and Niklas could tell they figured he was lying.

"Why doesn't your Wilder speak?" asked the squirrel, nodding at Secret. "Is she mute?"

"Sorry, my what?"

"Your lynx. Your Wilder."

Niklas snorted. "Secret's not mine. She's her own."

The ferret turned to Secret. "Where are you from, lady fair? I bet you're not from Wichtiburg, and you're certainly no Legenwalder with those garish colors."

Secret bared her teeth at him. "Watch it, half-rat, or I'll tear your pinchy head off."

"Garish tongue, too." The ferret grinned. "I think I like you."

Secret tensed, but Niklas put his hand on her shoulder before she could attack. This wouldn't do. "Listen," he said. "We're not your enemies. Let us go, and we'll get out of your hair."

"Let you go where, exactly," the squirrel said, nodding at the canyon opening. "You wouldn't find a safe place for leagues, and you wouldn't last two minutes out there."

The ferret elbowed the squirrel in the side. "She means to tell you her name is Castine and she's very pleased to meet you." Castine fidgeted with her bow, lifting her lips in a not very friendly smile.

"And I'm Kepler," Kepler continued, unfazed. "Now. We may be rather closed off from proper civilization around here, but we are still enlightened citizens. We know you must be here on a secret mission." He paused. "It's fair if you won't share, but we are here in Nightmare territory together, fortunately for you, I might add. So why don't we call a truce?"

Niklas turned to Secret, who showed no signs of standing down. He nodded anyway. "Sure."

"Excellent," said the ferret. He let air out through his small, sharp teeth. "You're lucky we heard the skullbeak screams and even luckier it's still dark. Those creatures are mostly blind in darkness, but they never miss in daylight. One hit and they crack you open like an egg." He glanced up at the sky. "We should go before they show up again."

"Show up?" Niklas said. "The flames didn't kill them, then?"

Castine rolled her eyes again.

Kepler shrugged. "The annoying thing about skullbeaks is that they're already dead. You can shatter a bone, or slice off a leg if you hit a joint. But you can't kill them. The best you can hope for is to cripple them for a while."

"Our real problem is the rest of the flock," Castine said. "Skullbeaks have a hive mind. They're connected. They know instantly when their mates have been attacked, and more always come."

"So that's why," Niklas said to Secret. "When the final skullbeak spotted us, the others knew where to find us."

Kepler and Castine exchanged looks again. "Spotted you," said Kepler quietly. "You mean to say *it could see you?*"

It felt like the air in the canyon had gone electric.

"I'm pretty sure it did," Niklas said. "It stood there on the porch, looking straight at us. We weren't moving, so it can't have heard us. And I know it didn't catch our scent, because the wind had shifted, so we were downwind. Don't you agree, Secret?"

Secret didn't answer. She stared hard at the newcomers. Her hackles were up and her tail whipped, and the others were no better. Castine snatched an arrow from her quiver and nocked it.

Kepler stepped close to the squirrel. "I thought you said it was a stray arrow."

She turned in a circle to scan the canyon. "I took the shot because I thought I saw movement on the porch. I wasn't sure, and I certainly had no idea it was *him*. What was he doing out here? With only six skullbeaks for a guard?" She lowered her bow when she couldn't find a target. "They're lying. They must be."

"We're not lying." Secret growled. "But you both smell like cowards."

Kepler touched his hand briefly to his chest. "You might too, lady fair, if you had any idea what you were dealing with."

"Tell us then!" Niklas didn't like the direction this was taking. "What are we dealing with?"

"The Sparrow King." Castine spat into the sand, and Niklas thought her voice sounded choked when she said, "The Sparrow King was here, right under my nose, and I didn't even fire at him twice."

Kepler insisted they had to risk a peek inside the cottage, even if the skullbeaks must be on their way. "I can go in alone," he told Castine. "If you would rather stay here and watch over our new friends."

Watch over, he said, but Niklas knew he meant just watch. Secret kept eyeing the canyon opening, and Niklas guessed she wanted to make a run for it. But he had seen the other animals shoot. Any attempt at running would end with an arrow in the back, he was sure of it. He shook his head in what he hoped was a discreet manner.

"As if you'd even know if something was different in there," Castine said. "I should be the one to look."

So they all shuffled awkwardly onto the porch, while their rescuers tried to keep Secret and Niklas at point blank. Castine snapped the arrow that still lodged in the beam and tossed it to the side. "No need to burn the place down," she said.

Secret hesitated outside the door. She had never yet set foot inside a proper building, and Niklas remembered how much it had cost her just to stick her head inside the crypt. But while he tried to think of an excuse for not coming inside, Secret melted across the threshold, taking care to place herself between Niklas and the others while they searched the cottage.

The smile was not the only new thing, then.

The little house had only one room. The air smelled of dirt and time. A threadbare quilt covered the bed in the corner, faded and dressed in dust. Wooden figurines filled the windowsills, the result of long hours of whittling. In the corner there was a rocking chair and a little stove where a dying fire glowed behind the blackened door. The source of the smoke they had smelled.

"Those are new." Castine's tail bristled as she edged over to the stove. On a table next to the rocking chair there was a beautiful crystal glass and a bottle. She read the label on the bottle. "Emerald River," she muttered. She uncorked it, releasing a pale green shimmer. "It's starmead! Real starmead!"

Kepler whistled. "Fine loot for a dump like this."

"Don't you dare speak ill of this place, fresher." Castine wrinkled her snout at him.

Kepler lifted his hands to say he wasn't. "I think our new friends told it true, though. Someone was in here just now, warming themselves on the fire, getting ready to drink starmead from a crystal glass. But skullbeaks are empty shells. They don't drink. He eased a backpack off his shoulder and stuffed the glass and the bottle into it.

"I still can't believe it was him," Castine said. "Out here? Without his army? Does that sound like the Sparrow King to you?"

Suddenly Niklas remembered something Rafsa had said to him in the troll cave. *I will ask the king. He has his books, he has his dark roses.* Maybe this Sparrow King was in cahoots with the trolls. He was about to raise his voice, but Kepler beat him to it.

"Well, we do know it can't have been the owner of the cottage, poor guy. He wasn't exactly the sophisticated kind, living out here alone."

"I told you, don't mock him," Castine said. "I know he's only a story to you, but he was my friend. There was never a more loyal soul than Sebastifer the true."

Niklas turned his back to them so they wouldn't see his

face. His hair stood on end. Was there even a tiny chance someone else bore that name? The answer waited for him in the windowsill. The carved figurines cast snaking shadows across the floorboards. He picked one up.

It was clunky and crude, not even close to his mother's exquisite work. Still, he could tell what the figurine was supposed to be: a human girl with long, curly hair.

It was her. All the figurines were her.

"Careful." Castine spoke behind him. Niklas took a moment to put on his prince mask and turned around to face the squirrel. Secret watched them both very quietly. He could tell she was ready to leap between them.

Castine hefted her bow all casually. "Some say wood carries the soul."

"How so?" Niklas smiled and smiled while he tried to put the figurine back. But he didn't trust his hand not to shake, so he stuck it in his pocket.

"You might become like *her.*" Castine glanced at his arm. "The most hated coward this side of the mountains."

Niklas stared after her as she walked toward the door.

"Trust me," the squirrel said over her shoulder. "You don't want to become another Erika Summerhill."

Chapter Twenty-four

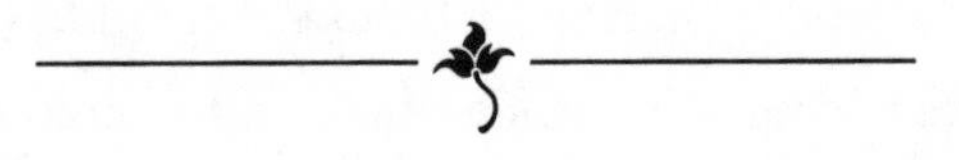

The gorge opened up around them, falling back into the ground until only the hillside remained. The starry sky widened like a great sail, cut off in the distance by more mountains. Around them a shifting wind whispered and moaned, and Niklas felt exposed, or worse, like something horrible was about to happen. He could tell from Secret's stance that she agreed.

Kepler and Castine whispered briefly between themselves. Then Kepler took the point while Castine brought up the rear, keeping her distance. Enough, Niklas thought, to get them both with an arrow before they could spring on her. Good thing she didn't know his last name.

"That was close," he murmured to Secret, trusting that the wind would snatch away his words. "I almost told them where we came from."

"There is something wrong in this place," she said. "We need to escape."

"Not a good idea." Niklas nodded at the bow slung on Kepler's back. "Not yet. We'll need better gear if we're going to get rid of those roses."

That wasn't the whole truth. His head still churned with questions he couldn't ask. How could Sebastifer have lived in that cottage? And why did Castine hate his mother? What could she have done to these creatures? All his life, Niklas had blamed everyone else for not talking about her, but he hadn't asked, either, because he didn't want the nightmares to come. Now that the mystery opened like secret doors within secret doors, he couldn't stop. He had to know more. "What did they say before?"

"The squirrel doesn't trust us, so no surprise there," Secret murmured. "The ferret says he likes our mugs, whatever that means. They've agreed on taking us to someone named Odar, who will decide our fate."

"Right," Niklas whispered back. "Obviously we want to do all the fate-deciding ourselves. But let's go with them for now."

Secret's tail whipped. "Not so stupid, cub. You heard what the squirrel said, in the cottage."

"I did. So I'm not going to tell them who I am."

Secret turned her ears out, but she didn't argue anymore.

They hit a road of flat, smooth stones and followed it

along the spine of a crest. From the silty lightening of the sky behind them, Niklas guessed they were walking westward. If there were skullbeaks or other monsters in the gloom, he saw no sign of them.

Dawn crept over the moor, and the hues of the landscape came to life. Tiny violet flowers that softened the heather, shades of blue moss, and slick green stones in rivulets that trickled down from snowcapped peaks. As they descended the mountain, more and more ruins dotted the hillside. Gap-toothed fences and roads reclaimed by grass, but also houses staring after them with burnt-out eyes.

Niklas caught up with Kepler. "What happened here?"

"Nightmares," Kepler said. The morning light picked out the details of his striped fur, and now Niklas saw that the ferret had scars on his face and arms. Not burn scars like Rafsa's, but cuts, most old and some new. Castine had them, too, especially on her legs and face. "These farms were the outskirts of what used to be the realm of Jewelgard," Kepler said. "But now it's just known as Broken."

"Is that where you're taking us? I thought there weren't any safe places for leagues."

"No safe places you would *find,*" Kepler said with a little smirk. "Not the same thing. And anyway, it depends on your definition of safe."

Before the morning sun cleared the peaks, they left the road and the open view and turned to the mountain again, on a winding, rocky path flanked by tall walls on both sides.

The sky grew bright, then deep blue above them. Secret kept licking at her gash every few steps. Niklas suspected she was getting tired. His head hurt, too, from Rafsa's punch. By the time Kepler lifted his arm and called them to a stop, he felt dazed with hunger.

He looked around, confused. As far as he could tell, there was nothing different about this particular stretch of glassy rock and dark walls. "We're here?"

"Nearly. Castine is going to scout before the last bit." As soon as the squirrel had disappeared along the trail, Kepler took off his backpack and slumped against the stone. He put the bow in his lap, but didn't seem too concerned about keeping the arrows close.

Niklas sat down and brought out the sandwich. Secret just grimaced when he offered her some, but Kepler's face lit up in wonder. "Is that really cheese? Where did you get that?"

"I brought it from home," Niklas said. The ferret looked so starry-eyed that Niklas gave him the whole thing. Kepler ate it with glee. When he had finished, he brushed crumbs out of his whiskers with a happy sigh. "Thank you. I'd almost forgotten about cheese."

He fished an object out from his vest and twirled it between his fingers until it spun into a blur. A medallion. It was smaller than the one the Sparrow King carried, and made from wood instead of spiky glass.

"So this Sparrow King," Niklas said. "Is he a nightmare, too?"

"He is the king of Nightmares." Kepler caught the medallion in his hand and kissed it. "Also the not-so-rightful ruler of Broken. It would be an understatement to say we'd like to get our hands on him." He slipped the medallion inside his shirt. "Of course, being heroes and all, we're content to have saved you instead."

"We didn't need to be saved," Secret said, tufted ear tall and imperious.

The ferret smiled, delighted that she had spoken. "I've read about you lynxes. You have incredible eyesight, don't you? Want to see something while we wait?"

Secret swished her tail. "What?"

"I'm only guessing," Kepler said. "But I'd say the reason you're here." He leaned his bow against the wall and climbed up the side of the cleft, finding slits and cracks for his fingers and toes. "Don't worry, your boy can come."

Niklas took off his boots to follow. Secret swished her tail again, but he pretended not to notice. He wanted to see this reason. So Secret soared past him instead, to a slim ledge halfway up the wall. They peeked over the top, into a distant valley pooled with haze and golden sunlight.

"That's Jewelgard." Kepler tilted his head. "Or it used to be, before the Breaking. That's what we call the war when the Nightmares took the valley." He pointed eastward. "The trolls came from the mountains behind us."

"Trolls," Niklas said. So there were trolls on this side of the tunnel, too. Maybe he should have expected it, from

Rafsa's comment about the king, but he still wished it wasn't so.

"Oh yes. They're one of the most common kind of Nightmare," Kepler said. "Jewelgard was rich and peaceful, mostly scholars and gardeners. They didn't stand a chance. The trolls came by the hundreds, united under a new strong leader." He pointed across the valley. "There. Do you see it, Secret? On the far side of the valley, by the sea."

Niklas saw only blue mist, but Secret said, "I see it. The tip of a human tower."

"That's right. If you ever need a looting mate, let me know." Kepler winked at her. "It's not human, though. The Nighthouse is the Sparrow King's stronghold." He turned to Niklas. "I know your mission is secret, but . . . Am I right? Is that why you have come? To help us?"

"No." Niklas winced at Kepler's disappointed face. "Our home valley is in trouble. We just came to look for roses."

"Roses." Kepler cleared his throat. "You're in luck, then."

"Get down from there!" Castine had returned and glared up at them from the path. "It's daylight, or haven't you noticed? Skullbeaks could spot you through that slit."

They did as she said, but Kepler shrugged. "I thought they should at least get a glimpse of the garden."

Castine tossed her head. "Just go. The path is clear."

As Kepler stepped into a groove in the rock, Niklas thought that the ferret's back looked more bent than before.

At the end of the cleft, they learned what Kepler meant by his luck comment.

They found roses, all right, and more than they were looking for.

A giant wall of thorns and flowers towered above them, dwarfing even the shrub in the mountain tunnel. Niklas had to tilt his head back to see the top. It was a rose fortress.

Castine touched her hand to a thorn the size of a saber. The petals on the nearest rose turned red. With a whisper, the hedge opened, making a doorway for Castine, exactly the shape of the one in the Summerchild cave. There could be no doubt that this was the same kind of rose. As if to confirm Niklas's thought, golden flashes began to drift along the branches.

Niklas touched Secret's back and whispered, "I guess this one would take some pretty large garden shears."

"It will only prick you a little, so no need to worry." Kepler leaned in. "But I wouldn't mention those garden shears if I were you."

"That was just a joke," Niklas hurried to say. "I meant that this is the biggest rosebush I ever saw."

"Rosebush?" Castine laughed. "This isn't a rosebush. It's the Rosa Torquata."

"The Rosa Tor-what now?"

"Torquata," Kepler said. "*Twisted* in Latin. Our home, or host, or guard, or prison, depending on your outlook. One thing is certain: We would be dead without it." He placed his pink palm against a thorn. "It can tell who we are by tasting our blood. If you were a Nightmare it wouldn't allow you to pass."

Another rose turned red, and a new gate appeared in front of Kepler.

The golden lights reflected in Secret's black pupils as she turned to Niklas. If the Rosa Torquata could tell who they were, would it also have half a mind to kill them, like the one last night? But Niklas couldn't see any of the dark, strangly vines. He took that as a good sign.

"Seems polite enough," he told Secret, hoping she would understand. "Very fresh and, uh, healthy." He held out his hand. Secret looked uncertain, but she raised a paw. Unlike the hungry roses in the tunnel, this shrub didn't stab at them, so they had to press against the thorns. A sharp sting, and two more roses turned red.

The hedge shivered for a moment. Then it created a portal for them, weaving its thorns into a handsome pattern. The lemony sweet scent of ripe roses wafted out to welcome them.

Niklas let his breath out.

Secret kept close to the ground, but she followed Niklas through the wall.

The roses continued as far as he could see: Massive stems and jagged branches crisscrossed. Thorns jutted out of every limb, like razor-sharp daggers, while bony roots puckered the ground. "Welcome to the Nickwood," Kepler said, licking a fresh, thin cut on his arm. "Try not to fall."

Castine watched Niklas and Secret gaze around, a smile playing in the corner of her mouth. "The Rosa isn't just a shrub. It isn't even just these woods. It grows under every mountain and below every valley, connecting every corner of the world in one giant root system. It is everywhere."

Niklas nodded, trying to look calm on the surface. All the roses, all the thorns, even the ones in the Summerchild cave: They all belonged to one and the same enormous plant. That could only mean one thing.

Garden shears would never do.

Chapter Twenty-five

Don't stumble, Kepler had warned them, and Niklas did his very best to follow the advice. He was so busy not cutting himself on thorns that he didn't notice the village until after it had sprouted up around them. Kepler smiled. "Our grand capital."

Castine chuckled, and Niklas could see why. *Camp* was a better word for the small gathering of shelters in the green, dappled light.

The shelters were made from what the Rosa had to offer: twig platforms connected with woven ladders, panels made snug with crushed flowers, leaves for roof tiles, and prickly branches for beams.

More human-like animals appeared as they passed by. Niklas saw badgers, rabbits, foxes, and mice. They wore wooden medallions and tattered clothes in faded black, but some had added embroideries in reds, blues, and pinks. None of which covered up the fact that their fur was full of nicks and scars.

It seemed the Rosa was a difficult host.

The villagers gawked at Niklas and Secret. A few touched their medallions, eyes shining with something Niklas thought might be hope or sorrow, or maybe both. But most looked skeptical. One fox even spat on the ground.

"Not so friendly," Secret mumbled, sticking close to Niklas.

Kepler walked tall beside them. "We don't get many freshers around here," he said. "I'm the last one, and that was four years ago now." He smiled at the fox. "See you for supper, Gidea?"

The fox gave Niklas a pointed look. "You tell Odar he has lost his mind." She closed the door to her hut.

"We don't get many children, either, with or without *keys*." Kepler tugged at his vest. "Some of these people have been here since the Breaking. They're a little wary, that's all."

"They have a right to be," Castine said.

The rosebush gave way to form a bell-shaped dome over a small meadow. High above, the canopy of dark green leaves trailed boughs of white roses. They snowed petals down on the building that sat in the middle of the clearing.

The house was a giant patchwork. It had two floors of

piled stones and planks in different colors. Cornices and turrets stuck out with no thought for symmetry. Cracked pillars and balconies fought for room beneath tall, carved gables and chimneys that blew out wisps of smoke. Above the front door hung a much-glued wooden sign that said *The Second Ruby*.

Niklas had to laugh. "How can you have an *inn* inside a fortress of a rosebush?"

"This is the only place where the Rosa will allow us to light a fire," Kepler said. "Everyone comes here to heat their tea stones and fill their bellies of an evening. But in addition to serving as dining hall, the Second Ruby is built to keep our memories. All the bits and pieces were rescued from the rubble of Jewelgard."

Kepler ducked under a knuckle of roots to pick up a basket of yellow, swirly-topped mushrooms. "You'd better go in first, Castine."

Castine clicked her tongue. "You think Odar is going to believe the mushroom story now? Haven't you considered our guests can actually talk?" But she still took the basket and disappeared through the massive turquoise front door of the inn.

"Sit if you want," Kepler said. "You must be tired."

Niklas sank down on the front steps next to him, but Secret wouldn't settle down. She paced the swath of grass between Niklas and the handful of villagers who peeked out from the edge of the clearing. They didn't seem too concerned that a giant lynx prowled in front of their snouts.

"You're all friends here, then?" Niklas asked. "Rabbits and foxes, cats and mice?"

"Oh, there are differences," Kepler replied. "Petlings and Wilders is the most important distinction, between animals who are tame and those who are less so." He shot Secret and her whipping tail a glance. "Before the Breaking, there used to be clans and guilds and factions, too, but none of that matters here. We're all that's left of Jewelgard: forty-one scarred souls who hide here among the roses."

Niklas met the gaze of a tall field mouse. Her eyes widened before she ducked behind some leaves.

"They'll come around," Kepler said. "It's not really you they fear."

"It's not?" *Was it someone else, then? Another human? Maybe his mother? What could she have done?* Niklas wanted to ask so badly, his tongue itched.

"No. So you don't have to worry either, lady fair," Kepler said, confident that Secret would hear it. "They would never hurt a human child."

"Is that so?" Secret made an extra-wide turn at the corner of the steps, pointing her ear for Niklas to come look. Of all things he found half a fountain sticking out from the side of the inn. It worked, too, spouting water from three statues of children.

Three *beheaded* children.

Their heads had been replaced by those of animals carved from wood: a weasel, a raccoon, and a whinnying horse.

Niklas turned to Kepler, not sure if he should run very fast or laugh at the ferret's mortified expression. "Cheery decorating."

"Uh, yes, we're a cheery lot." Kepler scratched his chin. "That looks bad, doesn't it. We didn't lop their heads off, the Nightmares did that, but since we had lugged the other parts all the way from the ruins, we thought we might as well use the fountain for our own heroes."

At that moment, Castine stuck her head around the corner, and Kepler nodded.

"We can go inside now," Kepler said. "Listen. Could you not discuss our little adventure in the canyon with Odar or any of the other villagers? Tell them that we bumped into each other at the edge of the woods."

Secret flattened her ears. "Why?"

"We've had a bit of trouble lately, so no one is allowed to leave the Nickwood without Odar's permission." Kepler sighed. "I promise you, Castine and I are only trying to do good. But you must do what you feel is right."

Niklas put his hand against Secret's chest to stop the pacing. "Let's decide later," he whispered. "Are you up to it? I know you don't like houses, but it didn't end so well the last time we split up."

He watched Secret glance up at the blue door. The Second Ruby wasn't very big, as public houses went, but with all its mismatched, jutting parts, it still looked imposing. She shook her neck fur. "You are crazy to trust these people. You're even crazier if you think I'm letting you go in there alone with the head-loppers."

Chapter Twenty-six

The Second Ruby's common room had a bar and a long table, but otherwise it looked more like the workshop of a museum than an inn. All shelves and tables were crammed with precious objects that needed mending. Cracked vases and jade cats with snapped tails fought for room with lidless chests of trinkets and tiles. The smell, however, did belong in an inn. It reminded Niklas of the Willodale tavern where Uncle Anders sometimes bought them dinner if Grandma Alma felt poorly: spilled beer, corners left to grow musty, and hearty, slow-thickened food.

Logs made of bundled twigs burned in the fireplace in the far corner of the room, and though daylight pooled under the windows, it was dark beneath the rafters. They could only see the faces of the animals gathered around the long table in the glow from wax-bogged chandeliers.

Next to Castine sat a small, black cat with spectacles

and a green shawl over her vest, and at the end of the table loomed a huge raccoon with sharp eyes in his scoundrel's mask. He held a steaming cooking pot in his paws.

Kepler bowed. "No apple cake today, Odar?"

"No," the raccoon said. "And you know it. I see you've brought company."

"Yes. This is Secret, and her boy, Niklas. We found them sniffing around near the north gate."

The raccoon put the kettle on the table. "Well, the young cat here is our dear Too, and I am Odar." He gave Niklas and Secret a good, long looking-over. "Usually, all Brokeners eat at purpledusk, at the sound of the bell. But this evening we'll make an exception and eat early, just the six of us. Come. Sit. There is stew that now has mushrooms in it, thanks to the hard work of Kepler and Castine."

Niklas drifted closer to the table, lured by the delicious smell of spices, and found a seat next to Kepler at the end of the bench. He hadn't eaten since the night before, and as soon as the others lifted their forks, peering at him over their plates, he tucked in faster than he could chew. "This is really good," he said with his mouth full.

"It's the caraway," Odar said. "My specialty."

Secret didn't care for the smell of caraway. She stood uneasily behind Niklas, wrinkling her nose.

"Something the matter?" The raccoon watched Secret intently. "Dinner's not to your liking?"

"Cooked, slimy plants," said Secret. "I can't eat that."

She sent Castine a look, and Niklas knew her confusion. Secret usually ate squirrels, bitter ones or not.

"No?" Odar ladled a small helping of stew into a wide, shallow bowl and placed it in front of Secret. She grimaced as brown liquid oozed out around chunks of golden root vegetables. But soon the hunger got the better of her, and she bent down and nibbled at a flute mushroom. A small whimper sounded at the back of her throat, and moments later, her bowl was empty.

Odar waited until she had finished before he commented. "Your tastes have changed. It's part of the awakening. You'll find there are many unexpected things you can do and even want to do now."

"Such as walking on two legs," said Kepler.

"And drinking mead," said Castine, draining her cup.

"And wearing warm clothes when it's cold outside," said Too. When the black cat saw Secret's expression, she added, "Of course, you don't have to, but most of us do."

Odar grunted. "I have seen enough. You really are completely new. Something must have gone very wrong for a fresh fresher to be sent out alone to meet the Twistrose. Where are you from? The nearest safe town is weeks away, and I didn't know any of the other Realms had called for a Twistrose. We sure haven't."

There was that word again, the one the nasty voice and old voice had quarreled about in the tunnel. Niklas put on his most reasonable smile and said, "Mr. Odar, I wish

I knew what you are talking about, but I don't. What is a Twistrose?"

"A Twistrose is a human child. A visitor, if you will, invited by means of a special *key.*"

He waited for Niklas to say something, but Castine did it for him. "He claims he doesn't have one."

Odar turned to Secret. "Who sent you all this way alone, Secret? How did you cross the Nightmare mountains?"

"And where did you pick up Niklas?" asked Kepler. "Was it around these parts?"

Secret turned her ears out. She wasn't doing well with all the questions. "I didn't pick him up anywhere. We came here together."

"That's right," Niklas said. He stood up. He had no idea what was going on here, so he decided to go with the simplest and easiest kind of lie: half the truth. "We found a shrub-infested hole in the mountain, walked through it, and ended up here. We just need to borrow some tools to clear out those roots, and we'll go home again."

A thick silence unfolded.

"I consider myself something of an expert on lies," Odar said at last. "And I believe the two of you are telling the truth right now, if not all of it. It's impossible, but here you are, with neither invitation nor key, where you should not be. On the other side of the wall. In *our* world."

Niklas set his cup on the table, weighing his words. But despite years of practice with Grandma Alma, he didn't quite know how to frame this question. "You mean to say this is not *our* world?"

The raccoon chuckled. "Well, I'll be scratched. I never thought I of all people would be giving a Twistrose his welcome speech." He got to his feet to tower over them, big, gray chest puffed out. "No, lad. This isn't your world. This is the Realms of Dream and Thorn. Our world is made from the imagination of human children. Games and stories, nightmares and horrors, hopes and wishes, they all belong here. Which is why the folk that live here are animals who once shared a bond of friendship with a human child. When we died in your world, we woke up here to live a second life because our children loved us and grieve for us."

He lifted his cup. "Here's to you for that."

Niklas searched their solemn faces. They were not kidding. Too even had tears in her eyes as she drank the toast.

"Are you also saying you're all dead?" Niklas rubbed his forehead. "But you live here because you were friends with a human child. Best friends."

He would have figured it for nonsense, if it weren't for Sebastifer. It actually made sense. After he drowned in Sorrowdeep, Sebastifer had come here and stayed in the cottage and whittled images of Erika, and somehow his mother had heard his barks through the mountain. At least that's what she wrote in her notebook.

Niklas didn't quite trust his legs, so he sat down on the bench again.

"Mine was a boy named Magnus," said Too. "He read me the best books."

"My Marti had the best twigs in her hair," said Kepler, kissing his medallion with a look of triumph. Suddenly they all talked at the same time, arguing about whose child could spit the farthest or told the best ghost stories.

All except Odar, who poured himself another cup of mead. "We're all forgetting the most important thing," he said. Niklas thought there was a dangerous glint in his eyes. "There's a boy here who claims he is no Twistrose and has no key, and who just happened to show up in Sebastifer's canyon while the Sparrow King was there."

The others fell quiet again. No need to wonder whether to keep Kepler's secret, then, because someone else had already told. Kepler glared at Castine, who hung her head with shame. "He can tell when I lie," she muttered.

"You're a bigger idiot than I had imagined, Kepler." Odar's voice was so soft, but his smile wasn't. "That canyon is deep in Nightmare territory."

"Secret and Niklas would be dead if we hadn't been there." Kepler pushed his chin up. "We rescued them from skullbeaks."

Odar cocked his head. "With what? Your front teeth?"

"Castine made us bows," Kepler said. "We're getting quite good at using them."

The raccoon slammed his fist on the table so both the stew and his belly wobbled. "Don't you have any sense between the whiskers? You traipse about on the moor playing at bows and arrows? I said no one must leave the Nickwood! Or have you forgotten what happened to the others? Four of us dead in a few months, Kepler. I thought the deaths would have made more of an impression on you, since you always claim to be fighting for the good of all Brokeners."

Too slid halfway off her seat, ready to hide under the table, and Castine had somehow managed to slip out of the room. But Kepler didn't back off. "First of all, we don't *traipse.*" His voice was tight with anger. "We're risking our lives, and yes, it's for the good of all Brokeners. We heard something big was going down in Sebastifer's canyon, so we went. Second of all, we brought home evidence that will help us figure out what it was." He emptied his backpack and put the bottle and the glass on the table. "And third of all, we brought home a Twistrose, the first Twistrose to come here since Jewelgard was still the glittering vale, the gem of the west coast, the most beautiful city in this world." He swallowed hard. "I say it doesn't matter who called him, because he's *here.*" He turned to Niklas.

Niklas nodded in what he hoped was a neutral manner.

Odar stared at them for a long moment before he sat down, frowning at the green bottle. Niklas felt Too sag with relief beside him. "You will tell me everything that happened, every detail of it, whether you think it important or no. But later. The rest of the Brokeners will be here for supper soon. Niklas, Secret, go upstairs and stay there. Clean up and sleep."

"Upstairs?" Kepler couldn't keep a squeak out of his voice. "We're not going to present the Twistrose to the other Brokeners?"

"We don't even know if he is a Twistrose." Odar snorted. "We're not presenting anyone with anything until I've heard the verdict of the only one who might know what to do with them."

"Who?" Kepler leaned forward, placing himself between Niklas and Odar. "Who could possibly know better than the Brokeners what's best for Broken?"

Odar's mouth curled up. "The Greenhood. I'm taking them to see the Greenhood."

Chapter Twenty-seven

Purpledusk, Odar had called it, and Niklas could see why. Outside the mismatched windows of the Second Ruby, the day had dimmed to the color of bruises, streaked with pointed shadows. There were no sunsets inside the shrub, or so Kepler had said.

The ferret led the way up the stairs, pointing out where the regulars lived. "Only one bathroom for all of us, and that's in here. Too's room is there, next to Odar's, Castine's is by the stairs, and mine is up in the turret."

"How come you get to stay inside a house?" Niklas asked.

"Remember I told you about Wilders and Petlings? Well, Castine, Too, and me, we're the only Petlings in Broken. It means we were pets before we died, so we were used to life inside a house when we got here. Even Castine, who was rescued from a cat when she was young." He grimaced at his new cut. "But the others are all Wilders, so they're better at slinking around the thorns. If they were free and at peace, they would probably still prefer homes that were mostly open to nature. Not decked out like this." He patted a column carved like a serpent.

"And Odar?"

"Oh, Odar is driven by an entirely different urge." He grinned. "Treasure. Besides, this clearing was his home even before the Breaking."

Back in the common room, the dinner bell rang, and a stream of voices and footsteps followed. Niklas imagined the Brokeners settling around the long table, or into the torn armchairs and singed pillows, eating stew and telling Odar he had lost his mind for letting them stay here. Niklas was glad he didn't have to face the surly fox.

"It's usually my task to ring the bell," Kepler said. "When I'm not being punished for *traipsing*." He stopped in a wedge of warm light that cut across the landing. "Castine is carving," he whispered.

Through the cracked door they could see the squirrel's room. She had stuffed it full of tools and materials, leaving only a den in the middle for herself, where she now worked in the yellow glow of the lantern. Every now and again, she stopped to brush away wood shavings, holding a round object into the light for scrutiny. "Another medallion," Niklas said. "What do they mean?"

Kepler held his out and opened the lid, revealing a carving of a short-haired girl encircled in a ring of twigs. Her eyes had been inlaid with green gems. "This is my Marti," he said. "Roof climber and escape artist, and the fiercest nine-year-old you could ever hope to encounter." He scratched the girl's hair. "At least she was when I came here. She is almost thirteen now, but she is still a perfect rebel."

"How do you know?" asked Niklas.

"I can feel when she is very happy, or very sad, through this. It's like a twinge of electricity, like getting a glimpse of someone you've missed, but far away across a field." He nodded at Castine. "She keeps us sane, that one."

"What are those?" Secret pointed her ear to a pile of strange sculptures pushed against the inner wall. Thorns stuck out of the top, and there were bits of scrap metal and woven panels like the house walls, except smaller.

"Armor," Kepler said. "For when we fight back. Castine made them for us long ago. There's a shirt for each Brokener." He sniffed. "Except Odar. He doesn't want one."

"I thought you said there were only forty-one of you," Niklas said. "It would be a small uprising."

Kepler pulled at his leather cord. "Small, but clever. We could take the Nightmares, if we had a good plan and a true leader."

Castine glanced up at them. "Enough now, Kepler." Maybe it was the carving iron she kept in her mouth, but her voice sounded softer than usual. "You can conspire more in the morning."

* * * * *

They were to sleep in Kepler's turret chamber. It had a patched hammock suspended from the tip of the spire, and a tall window where roses pushed against many-colored panes, and a fireplace, where Kepler set about lighting a fire. "Hope you don't mind the smell too much." He gave a goofy grin. "Ferret thing."

"Not at all," Niklas said. The animal musk was there, but mostly the room smelled like a library. Scorched books lined every wall. A painting sat propped up on a shelf. It showed a dark brown weasel, grim of face, before a backdrop of ships burning in a harbor. It was a little rough, but good enough for Niklas to realize that he had seen the weasel's face before, spouting water in the fountain outside.

"The day of the Breaking," Kepler said, brushing the kindling off his pants. "Odar doesn't like us to dwell on it, but I think we need to remember that, too."

"You painted this?" Secret's brow furrowed. "Yourself?"

"I'll take that as a compliment," Kepler said. "Marcelius here was just a gardener and fresher than me, but when the trolls came, he still stayed behind to fight them. Gave his life so the others could escape. He deserves to be recognized." Kepler picked up a paintbrush and ran his thumb over the soft tip. "I'm going to do a portrait of all the heroes of the Breaking. Odar included, whether he wants it or not."

"Odar is a war hero?" said Niklas. "I thought he didn't appreciate . . . traipsing."

"His method is stay hidden, stay alive," Kepler said. "But you have to understand that Odar wasn't an ordinary citizen of Jewelgard. He only came to the city for, ah, special visits to relieve the Jewelgarders of excess riches. If you take my meaning."

Niklas whistled. "He was a thief!"

"Best raider this side of the mountains. Still is, I guess. Just look at all the stuff he brought back from the ruins. A whole house and everything in it. Without him, no one would have survived. He's the one who taught us how to survive here. Hide inside the Rosa, raid the garden for food." Kepler put the paintbrush back in its cup. "But last spring, Brokeners began disappearing. Four raiders caught, even when they were following the rules. Odar forbade us to leave the Nickwood until we know what's going on."

"But you don't care," Secret said.

"Sure I do. I care that we're almost out of food, except for those blasted mushrooms. I care that if we just hide in here, we won't figure out what's happening. Four dead Brokeners doesn't mean we should cower in the bushes. It means we should fight back." Kepler's eyes shone as he turned to Niklas. "So I'm asking you again: Are you here to help us?"

Niklas never got around to answering, because a

gentle knock sounded at the door. Too hovered on the threshold, clutching a tray with bottles, gauze, and a jug of hot water. "I've come to ask if Secret will let me dress her wound. Even small scratches made by a skullbeak will fester."

"You're a doctor?" Niklas asked.

"No," Too said. "But I'm the closest thing you'll find around here." The little cat stepped into the room. "I promise I'll be careful."

Secret backed toward the window.

Too winced. "I remember my fresher days. It takes some getting used to." She gave the tray to Niklas. "Maybe you should do it."

Niklas raised his eyebrows at Secret, who to his surprise flopped over on the floor so he could get at the gash. He rinsed out the cut with water and clear liquid from a bottle. Secret refused the gauze, but she let him put on an ointment that smelled like Grandma Alma's cough drops. Not even a snarl, and yesterday she wouldn't let him touch her at all.

Kepler leaned on the mantel and watched in silence. When Niklas had finished, the ferret poured the rest of the water into the wash basin and put it next to the hearth, very carefully not looking at the gravy spatters on Secret's chest. "We'll leave you to it, then. Odar said he would take you to the Greenhood first thing in the morning."

"I have a question for you first," Niklas said.

Kepler lit up. "Yes?"

"What happened to that loner in the cottage? Sebastian, was it?"

"Sebastifer." Kepler looked out the window, at the scratching thorns. "No one knows. I hear he insisted on staying in that canyon, so it's likely the Nightmares killed him." His hand went to his medallion. "Well, like Odar said, you should get some rest. You'll need it."

Secret curled up by the fire while Niklas crept into the hammock. The blankets smelled of ferret, but also of nutmeg, just like Rufus, Lin's little vole at home. He wondered what Lin would have made of the Rosa Torquata and this whole strange world. "If Lin were here, I bet she would have come up with a plan to take care of those tunnel roses."

"But she isn't." Secret's good ear tilted back. "What is your plan, other than to follow stray ferrets home?"

Niklas wished he knew how to look so disdainful with just a twist of his ear. "I know you didn't want to come here. I know it's risky with all the hiding and lying. But these Brokeners hate my mother, and I want to find out why." The truth was, he needed to know if she deserved it or not. *What do you want,* he had asked, and the nightmare Erika had pointed up, up. Maybe she wanted him to find the tunnel to this world. "While we keep looking for those garden shears, of course."

"Be careful. You may be good at talking, but that

Kepler isn't half-bad either." Secret licked her paw and began to clean gravy off her chin, ignoring the wash basin with perfect dignity. For some reason, that felt comforting to Niklas.

He picked the Sebastifer and Erika figurines out of his pocket. His mother thought she had gone mad when she heard him call to her, but all the while he had waited for her in that cottage, brought back to life because she missed him so.

"I've been thinking," he said. "About this world and how it works. How the animals awaken when they come here and become either Petlings or Wilders."

Secret stopped grooming.

"I think you awakened, too. Magic from the Realms leaked through the tunnel and made you like the Brokeners. You're my Wilder, and I'm your human boy. Or, we should be, except we didn't know each other."

"I knew you," Secret said. "Hard not to when you stomp around the Summerhill woods like you own them."

"Yes, but this is supposed to be a bond of love. Kepler keeps kissing his medallion of Marti, and they're all so proud of their children. You had seen me, sure, and I had given you the meat. But you couldn't possibly care about me. Right?"

Secret looked away. "When I came out of that cave, I felt . . . hollow. Like your mother's statue. The only thing that seemed to ease it was being around you. So I kept watch."

"I didn't know that," Niklas said.

"Because I know how to sneak," Secret said. "But it wasn't until you let the lambs out that the hollow filled in."

"That's when I became your boy?"

"That's when I knew you needed someone to save your stupid hide. As you've proved many times since then."

"Ha! I would have gotten out of that troll cage eventually." Niklas lay back on his pillow and as the hammock rocked under the spire, he listened to the crackling of the fire and the voices of the guests in the common room that drifted up through the floor. After a while he added, so quietly he wasn't sure she'd hear it, "But thank you."

From deep in Secret's chest came a small, creaky growl that sounded like purring.

Chapter Twenty-eight

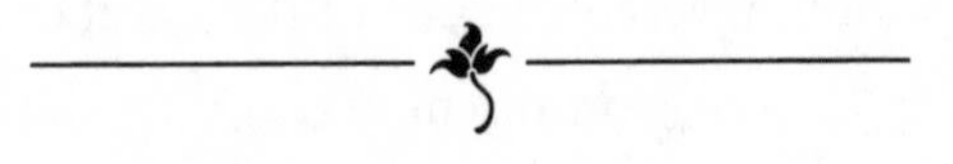

Nightmares wove into Niklas's sleep, an endless coil of crypts, and troll runes making his skin glow, and a nasty voice that whispered, *"Fear in this one, gray as old bones."*

Then he felt a strange tug. Something cold and lonely pushed into his head and pulled him away, into a dream so lucid, it felt real.

He saw kids in the night, three of them, struggling across a moonlit field. A pale-haired girl led the way and two boys brought up the rear. Even before he got close enough to see their faces, he knew who they were: his mother, Uncle Anders, and Peder Molyk. The reason for their slow pace was the heavy object the boys hauled between them.

A cage.

Inside it, a shape darted restlessly back and forth behind the chicken wire walls. The boys put the cage down in the grass, a little too abruptly. The creature in the cage yelped.

"Don't hurt him." Peder Molyk's eyes seemed too big for his face. Niklas had always thought of Molyk as the looming sort, but the only tall thing about twelve-year-old Peder was the cowlick of hair that stuck up from his forehead.

"I'm careful," the lankier Anders said.

Erika grinned. "Hurt him?" She sat down on her haunches and peered into the cage. "We're not hurting him. We're *saving* him. No one will find him where we're going. Not even your father." She gazed up the mountainside, past the tall pine trees and all the way to the snowcapped face of Buttertop. "He'll find shelter there, and plenty of food and water. It's perfect."

A sharp bark sounded from the woods above. Erika got up, beaming with pride. "Good boy." She found a corner of the cage to lift. "Sebastifer says the coast is clear."

They continued up the hill, carrying the cage between them.

None of them saw the dirty water that leaked from the cage, leaving a black trail across Oldmeadow.

Chapter Twenty-Nine

He woke with a paw covering his mouth and found Kepler bent over the hammock. "Shhhh. Don't wake the others."

"What are you doing?" Niklas sat up. Secret still dozed by the fireplace, outlined by the red glow from the embers. The windowpanes showed no signs of dawn.

Kepler patted the backpack he had slung over one shoulder. "I'm taking you on a little expedition," he whispered.

"Against Odar's orders?"

"Oh." Kepler pursed his lips. "My mistake. I didn't take you for the timid sort."

Niklas had grown up with all manner of suspicious grunts, meaningful glances, and unspoken accusations from the people of Willodale. But he wasn't used to having his courage called into question. "I'm not . . ." He received another ferret paw over his lips and lowered his voice. "I'm not timid! I'm just making sure we agree on the facts."

"Excellent!" Kepler said. "Because it really would be a shame to come all this way and not see the garden. Come on. Bring your satchel. And bring twitchy-ear over there, too." He nodded at Secret's now conspicuously still form and crept out the door.

Niklas swung out of the hammock. The floor felt cold, but his boots had warmed up nicely by the fire. As he pulled them on, Secret groaned. "So we're not going to stay put?"

"I thought you were asleep." Niklas tugged her ear-tuft. "Who cares about stupid rules? We'll be back before anyone notices."

Secret swatted his hand away. "Don't push it, cub, or I'll chew your little fingers off." She got up and stretched to properly underline that she, too, knew how to waste someone's time.

No night-lights lit the paths of the sleeping village save for the gold flickers from the Rosa Torquata. In the near-darkness, it was impossible to see all the thorns. But Kepler murmured, "Be grateful for the night. We don't know how long it will hold."

"Don't you have clocks around here?" Niklas stepped carefully through the gnarly web of roots.

"Clocks are of no use in this world. Our time is linked to dreams and games, so it races and slows as it wants to."

Kepler's smile showed blue. "Makes it more interesting to sneak around. By day you get more skullbeaks. By night the trolls are on the prowl."

Makes it harder to break the rules without getting caught, too, Niklas thought, but he didn't say anything.

They all let the Rosa Torquata taste their blood. It let them out into a sparse grove of black-and-white birches scattered across a gentle slope. Niklas had thought that after the creaky, tangled nest of the Nickwood, the air on his face would be a relief. Instead a feeling of unseen danger pressed down on him.

"Snout up!" Kepler said. "Where Nightmares rule, they play tricks on your mind. We'll know if there are trolls about. I hope."

They crawled the last few yards to a rusty fence at the edge of the grove. Kepler picked a collapsible telescope out of his vest pocket and watched for a moment. "Home, sweet home. Not *our* home anymore, but let's not mince words."

At the fence, the hill dropped steeply, and they found themselves at the rim of the valley that cradled the garden of Broken.

Night mist lay lightly on shelves upon shelves of terraced fields set in plunging circles, stitched together by tall hedges, stone fences, and steep embankments. Waterfalls from the mountains fed the water ducts that spread out like a silver spiderweb through the vale. A fjord sliced in between two cliffs in the west, ending in a city of ruins.

The moon hung full between the cliffs, rippling the black water with gold, making the ruins sparkle. "A bit bright for our purposes," Kepler said. "But at least the Nighthouse is mostly blind tonight." He gave each of them a turn with the telescope. "The right cliff at the far end of the fjord."

Thick fog shrouded the bluff, but Niklas could pick out a single black tower that poked up from the blanket of gray. Kepler sniffed. "It used to be a magnificent lighthouse that brought all ships safely into the Kolfjord. But when the Sparrow King conquered it, he put the beacon out to watch in darkness. Secret, do you see any movement in the tower?"

Secret peered awkwardly through the lens, then shook her head. "But I see trolls everywhere in the garden."

She pointed them out to Niklas, patches of green light on the walkways that wound through the fields. "Their eyes."

"Very good," Kepler said. "Stay away from the green light. And stay close."

He led the way into the upper circles, creeping under hedges and sliding on the outside of hewn steps in the rock. From above, the garden had seemed so ordered. But not up close.

Apple trees dropped their blooms into dense shrubs of gold berries. Flame-leafed sugar maples stuck up from a riot of cabbage and weeds. Sparkling insects hummed like violins.

Niklas's heart galloped faster with every field they sidled through. Sure, he had paid countless visits to Molyk and Fale in the cover of night. Sure, he had run pretty fast to avoid being caught. But when the enemy could slice you in half if you didn't think or move fast enough? That was something else entirely.

More than once, they had to dive under the hedges, holding their breath while heavy feet crunched by, leaving sharp claw slices in the gravel.

"Quite a few of them about tonight," Kepler said as they brushed leaves off their thighs. "Hope you don't mind."

"Absolutely not," Niklas said. He didn't mind the trolls, or the dew that soaked his clothes, or the dirt that still clung to the carrots, even after a good rubbing in the grass. They tasted sweeter than any carrot he had ever stolen. They tasted like adventure.

Secret proved an excellent raiding partner. She was the first to hear the trolls on the path, the first to smell them, and the first to catch the green that streaked the mist like headlights. But when Kepler suggested they sneak down to the ruin city, she balked.

"Why? You wanted to show us the garden; we have seen it. You wanted to bring home food; your backpack is full."

"Don't worry, lady fair," said Kepler. "I know a secret way. We won't get caught."

Her tail whipped. "The trolls are stupid, yes, but the two of you are louder than elks on twigs. What is down there that could possibly be worth the risk?"

"Oh, there is something," Kepler said. "Worth the risk and a thousand gold coins, you'll see. If you're up for it."

"We're up for it," Niklas said, ignoring Secret's silence.

As they followed the paths west and down, Secret whispered quickly to Niklas, "You do know he does that on purpose? To make you go with him?"

Niklas shrugged with a smile he hoped was half apologetic and all disarming. Of course he knew. But it didn't matter what sort of games Kepler played.

It wouldn't do to be a coward.

Chapter Thirty

Before the Breaking, Jewelgard had been wealthy, Kepler had said. Niklas had a feeling that was an understatement. The wooden houses had all been taken over by ivy and roses, but the roof tiles and trimmings still showed through. They all glittered faintly, as if they had been treated with powdered gems.

Kepler guided them through alleys and dark lanes, flitting from shadow to shadow. Every few minutes, they heard trolls in the distance, squabbling over some unknown prize. It seemed whatever order had kept them quiet up in the garden no longer applied. "Probably they're not expecting us," Kepler said. But even he stiffened whenever the howls went up, and once he made them back silently out of an alley and go in a different direction.

"Those Brokeners that went missing," Secret said. "How did they get caught?"

"We don't know," Kepler admitted. "All four disappeared during the day, so it can't have been the trolls. But there wasn't any blood, either, and the skullbeaks usually leave plenty of that." He stopped by a tear in a tall fence, through which a house could be glimpsed. "We're here."

The house held up better than most buildings in Broken. Other than the red roof tiles, there was nothing spectacular about it, nothing worth risking their hides for, anyway.

"A house," Secret said, not so impressed.

"An *inn,*" Kepler said, leading them through a smashed window.

The common room was besieged by shrubs. Except for a big old iron stove in the kitchen, the furniture was gone. "Odar took everything that could be salvaged," Kepler said. "He would have lugged off the stove as well if it didn't make too much noise."

"Why this particular inn?" Niklas nudged a mold-licked shard of glass with his boot. "Was it his favorite?"

"Yes, but that's not why. The Ruby was the site of Jewelgard's last stand. On the final day of the Breaking, the few remaining citizens hid out here, keeping the enemy at bay with sticks and stones. They were failing." Kepler pointed out the front window, to a cobbled square. "That was the moment when the heroes stepped up. Julia, the leader of the Hoof clan, led the horses in a charge against the trolls. Marcelius volunteered to stay behind and make it look like everyone was still trapped. And Odar surprised everyone by offering to lead the rest out the back and to his smuggler's hideout in the Nickwood." He turned to Niklas. "The Ruby isn't just an inn, or even just a place where history unfolded. It's proof that the Nightmares can be beaten." Kepler made a solemn pause. "Plus, it keeps a secret."

In the back of the common room there was a mosaic puzzled into the plaster. It showed a garden with fruit-laden trees and once-colorful falcons. But the wings were chipped and the glass dulled by dust.

Kepler ran his fingers along the mosaic until they struck an unassuming bird with no glitter, just a pattern of swirls and dots on the tail feather. Secret and Niklas flinched when the feather flashed under Kepler's hand. The stone shifted until a crack formed in the wall, just big enough to step inside. "It's cloak magic," Kepler said. "Done by one of Odar's associates a long time ago."

Inside the tunnel they found a narrow staircase that cut down into the ground, lit by a line of glass that glowed in the dark. Kepler's tail bristled with excitement. "We're moving under the city now, but smell how fresh the air is? No trolls this way, that's for certain. You know Odar: Stay hidden, stay alive."

"How come you know about this tunnel?" Secret's voice sounded stiff.

"Odar showed it to me." Kepler laughed. "When I was a

fresher, he was the one who taught me the garden. Said I had stripes, which is Raccoon for guts, or possibly insanity."

"So he taught you everything you know and lets you live in his house. Still you sneak around behind his back."

"That's not . . ." Kepler went quiet for a moment. "I don't mean to betray Odar, and neither does Castine. We just want him to come around. If we bring him enough facts, he'll understand that we need to do something, or we won't survive. And if Odar believes we should fight, all of Broken will."

Kepler brushed aside a curtain of ivy and turned to Secret. His sly grin was gone. "That's all I wish for."

They stepped out into a walled orchard.

The trees were dressed for all seasons. Fat, white flowers and tiny buds shared boughs with leaves and ripe apples, pears and plums. Each fruit caught the moonlight and sent it dancing on the wall and grass so the entire garden shimmered. They looked like gems.

"The jewel orchard," Kepler said, smugness restored in his voice.

"It's beautiful," Niklas said, but the words seemed poor. The garden was magnificent and resplendent and luminous, and all sorts of words that he liked to tease Lin about using in her maps and log books. He felt a twinge of sadness that she couldn't see this. "Why haven't the trolls broken it?"

"Oh, I'm sure the trolls could smash in the front gate if they wanted, but they don't. I think they're afraid of this place. There's something powerful in the soil here, an old kind of magic that has no use for Nightmares. After Odar's new orders, I'm the only one who comes here."

Niklas glanced around at the lush, even grass and pebbled pathways that curled under the trees. Not a dropped twig, not a rotting fruit. Unless the old sort of magic also trimmed lawns and cut weeds, *someone* tended this garden. "Kepler," he said. "How long has it been since your last visit?"

But Kepler had already climbed into a morello tree. Soon after, he whistled softly up in the canopy. "Catch!"

Secret snatched the pair of berries that fell out of the tree. They looked like morellos, dark red and ripe, except they were glazed in sparkling facets that clinked against Secret's claws.

Kepler skipped into an apple tree, then thumped to the ground beside them. "I know you haven't warmed to non-meat just yet, lady fair, but I promise you, ruby morellos will change your mind." When Secret just glared at the morellos, he plucked one of them off its stem and popped it in his mouth.

The morello cracked, like the most delicate glass breaking. Pink juice dribbled down Kepler's chin as he shifted the berry carefully around in his mouth. "See, most bake the fruit into pies or some such, and use the shards for art and ornaments. That's missing half the fun and most of the taste, if you ask me. You just have to watch your tongue."

He had kept his hand behind his back, but now he held it out to Niklas. "For you." He placed a perfect red-and-green fruit in Niklas's upturned palm. "A diamond apple."

Niklas let it sit in his hand. It felt heavier than a normal apple, and cool and dewy, like a glass of lemonade on a hot day. How it could have a scent, being encased in diamonds and all, he had no idea. But it smelled like cinnamon and sour-apple candy. Reflected light danced across Secret's and Kepler's faces as Niklas lifted the diamond apple to his lips.

An eerie, plaintive hooting cut the air.

Kepler spat out the morello stone, shoulders suddenly locked.

"What?" The diamond apple fell out of Niklas's hand, hitting the grass with a tinkle. "Is it the skullbeaks?

Kepler's whiskers bristled. "It sounds a little like them, but they shouldn't be out now."

"I hear trolls," Secret said.

"I'll look." Kepler darted up a pear tree that leaned against the orchard walls. Niklas grasped the trunk, put the sole of his boot against the bark, and shimmied after him.

The secret tunnel had brought them to the very center of the town, where a round, tiled plaza called the Falcon Circle separated the jewel orchard from the tip of the fjord. Beyond a grand marble fountain, two ugly, square barracks barred the water's edge from view. There were trolls outside the barracks, lots of them.

Secret wasn't looking at the trolls. She was staring up through the pear tree at another building that loomed beyond the city on its tall bluff, wreathed in mists.

The Nighthouse.

"If that's the enemy you want to beat," she said, "you'll never even get close enough to fire your bow." In her eyes Niklas thought he saw the same hopeless pity that had convinced him she felt sorry for Rag the first time he met her.

She was right, though. The only access to the Nighthouse was a road that climbed up the cliff. Guard posts and huge wicker nests poked up everywhere. There must be at least fifty of them between the ruin city and the castle.

"Maybe not." Kepler shook Secret's verdict off like water. "But there are other ways."

The hooting filled the air again, deep and nasal. It came from the Nighthouse.

"It's a . . ." Secret tilted her head to find the right word. "Foghorn."

They all saw it now: A thick woolen wall had come in from the ocean, filling the mouth of the fjord.

"A foghorn means there's a ship," Kepler said. "I've never been this close to the docks with a ship coming in. Odar insists that we all leave the garden at the first sight of a mast, since it brings out every Nightmare in Broken. But . . ." He licked his lips. "I've heard the trolls talk. The

Sparrow King is involved in some sort of trade. He makes something very secret. Something that involves *cages.*"

Niklas felt a cold tug in his chest, almost like the one that had pulled him into the Oldmeadow dream. "What kind of cages?"

"Don't know. But I sure would like to find out."

Niklas frowned at the barracks. "Maybe we should, then. Do you know any other ways to get to the dock? One where we wouldn't be seen?"

Kepler turned to him. "You think we should go spy on the ship?"

"I think any information you can bring home to Odar is interesting." So was the link between his mother and this world, and the mysterious cages that she kept dragging around in his dreams, but Niklas didn't mention those. He also didn't look at Secret, even if he could feel her eyes on him.

Kepler pointed to the east of the Falcon Square. "Lostbook Hill. It curves out along the harbor, so we can see the docks from there."

"And be seen," Secret said. "This is stupid, cub."

"There is a fine line between brave and stupid," Kepler said. "But this won't be for the faint of heart."

"My heart is fine," Niklas said.

"Then mine is, too." Kepler looked so pleased that it almost dulled the sting of Secret's silence.

Chapter Thirty-One

By the time they reached Lostbook, dawn was bleaching the sky, picking out their shapes against the ruins. All the houses here were rubble, as if the Nightmares had taken special care to destroy them. Instead, ivy had grown in, clinging to stalks of tall weed like green ghost walls, excellent for spying.

"This used to be Bookhill," Kepler said. "It was the richest part of town, studded with libraries, book shops, and antiquaries. But trolls don't have much use for that kind of wealth. One of the first things they did was torch the entire neighborhood."

They found a gap in the ivy from which they had a view of the docks. The visiting ship lay at anchor already. Next to the plaster drabness of the barracks, it looked like treasure. The dark hull and masts had been reinforced with what appeared to be glass, which Kepler reckoned was magical coating to protect them from the monsters of the Frothsea. The lowered and tucked sails rested upon the beams like black snow.

"They're unloading," Secret said. With the telescope, Niklas could also see the trolls that swarmed all over the dock. The cargo was boxes that required two crews just to get them down the ladder.

Could be crates, could be cages.

"Secret, can you tell what they've got there?" Niklas asked in his most humble voice. On the way here, she had showed him in at least nine different cat-ways she wasn't pleased with him, including tail-swishes and cold stares. But she took the telescope.

"Cages." She bared her teeth. "With living creatures inside."

"Can you see what kind of creature?"

"No."

Niklas rubbed his forehead. His little plan had seemed so clever in the jewel orchard. Finding out what was in the cages would get him two things at once: both a clue about his nightmares and a way to give Kepler a little bit of what he wanted. Niklas wasn't stupid. He noticed all the hints about being the Twistrose that Broken needed. He had wanted to play the hero part, just for a little bit. "If only we could get closer."

Kepler fetched his medallion out from his vest and twirled it fast. "We could go down to the docks. If we were really crazy."

The wide slope between the ivy ruins and the docks was covered with brambles. They might be thick enough to hide them. Or not.

"Have you done it before?" Niklas asked.

Kepler shook his head. "I don't see why it shouldn't work as long as the skullbeaks aren't about."

"It's nearly dawn," Secret said.

"Yes," said Kepler. "But it's very slow today. I think we have enough time." He put his medallion back under his vest. "I've got my Marti for luck, so I'm set."

Niklas pushed his chin up. He felt more comfortable in this hero role by the minute. "Kepler knows what he's doing, Secret. You know what they say. Better to be crazy than a coward."

They moved very, very carefully down the hill, keeping hands and paws light. But when they got to the edge of the brambles, it turned out to be all for nothing. Even if they crept along the skirts of the shrubs until the very end, the barracks blocked the view of the ship. They couldn't see the cages.

"Happy now?" Secret backed deeper into the leaf shade with the weary face of someone who had once again been proven right, but remained too dignified to gloat.

"Not very," Niklas admitted. The last piece of land between the brambles and the docks was a strip of yellow, limp grass, a few rotten planks, and the occasional rock. Only a single, brave juniper bush stuck up in the middle.

Kepler nodded to himself. "Lady fair. Twistrose. You wait here."

"What?" Niklas wrenched around to face Kepler. "You can't go out there alone!"

"I thought you said it was better to be crazy than a coward. I should be able to see the cages from that juniper."

Secret's tail thumped. "The docks are thick with trolls."

"Well, they're busy unloading, aren't they? Besides, they won't be around for much longer." Kepler glanced up at the sky. Gold licked the mountaintops at the valley's rim. "When the sun comes up, they'll have to crawl back into their holes."

"Then there will be skullbeaks." Secret's voice had turned flat, a sure sign that she was seething inside. "They'll see you. You know they will."

"But they're not out yet." Kepler eased off his backpack and handed it to Niklas. "The timing is perfect. Look, you're the Twistrose. We shouldn't risk you. And the odds are better if it's just me."

"So stupid."

Secret was probably right about that. Niklas had no idea what the odds were, but they couldn't be very good. *Don't do it,* he should say. *It's not worth the risk.* But it had never before been Niklas's job to talk someone out of a dare. The words stuck to his tongue. Instead he cleared his throat. "You're sure?"

"These are my woods, not yours. Meanwhile, why don't the two of you think up a great explanation for why we're here in the first place? We're going to want to share this with Odar when we get back." Kepler pulled up the hood of his vest. "Make it sound like this was all your idea."

"But be careful." Niklas slapped Kepler on the shoulder, because it seemed like something you should do when you let people go into danger. He slumped back into the dirt and tried to look calm and collected.

Kepler winked at them, and slipped off.

From the shadows they saw him worm across the field until he scurried under the lonely juniper, unseen for now.

"Terrible sneaking," Secret muttered.

Niklas didn't reply. He hadn't felt so awful about watching someone disappear since the Rosenquists drove their battered red car down the road from Summerhill. He promised himself: The next time he and Lin raided Mr. Molyk's orchard, he wasn't going to ask her to wait by the fence and keep lookout. If there ever was a next time.

Somehow Secret sensed the sinking pit in his belly. "You're not used to being left behind."

"I'm *very* used to being left behind," Niklas said. "Just not for this kind of thing."

They waited.

Niklas had no idea how much time had passed. It felt like hours, but the sun had yet to clear the mountains completely. It couldn't be long, though. Above the barracks, the tip of the ship's glass-covered mast now blazed with the first rays, but still Kepler made no sign of coming back. Niklas's eyes hurt from trying to spot him inside the juniper. "What is he doing?"

Secret cocked her good ear. "Not spying on the cages, because they're done with those. They're rolling something up the planks now. Barrels, I think."

Niklas's sinking pit hit the bottom of his belly.

"Maybe he got stuck or something. We have to go get him."

Secret tensed beside him. "Too late. The nests."

Niklas peered out through the branches to the cliff on the far side of the valley. Along the Nighthouse road skullbeaks had emerged. They sat perched atop their wicker nests, hundreds of them, turning their heads like searchlights.

They had begun their watch early.

Niklas used the foulest words he knew, ones he had heard Uncle Anders say when something went wrong in the barn.

"Swear all you like," Secret hissed. "But stay still. If their eyesight is as good as Kepler claims, we're not safe here."

Niklas ducked his head. "When Kepler comes back, I'm going to tell him a thing or two about perfect timing. It's no good if you're too slow."

"*If* he comes back," Secret said.

"Maybe if he just sits tight," Niklas whispered.

In answer, a high-pitched keening grew in the distance. It started as one voice and became a wailing choir as the skullbeaks all took flight and came gliding across the valley on their ghostly wings. They headed straight for the yellow grass, sounding like an air-raid alarm.

Hoooowoooooo.

"How did they see him? The sun isn't up yet. *I* can't even see him."

The dark green leaves of the lonely bush began jerking hard, and Niklas bit his knuckles. "Come on," he whispered. "Get out of there!"

But Kepler didn't get out of there. The flock of skullbeaks was already upon him. They circled above the bush, churning the air with their bones and beaks. One of the birds dipped into the shrub and came out again with a spitting ferret clutched in its claws.

For a moment Kepler hung suspended in the air, stretched and struggling. Something tethered him to the bush; a length of dark rope coiled around his ankle. Another skullbeak dove in and cut the rope with its beak. The first bone bird rose quickly with its prey.

It didn't go far. Instead of flying toward the Nighthouse, it dumped Kepler outside the barracks. The skullbeak flock went back to circling, howling in triumph.

Kepler hit the ground hard and tumbled to a stop in

front of the barrack door. He got up slowly, coughing from the dust, trying and failing to put his weight on his leg.

"Run," Niklas whispered, but even without the leg injury, Kepler would not have been able to run. The door opened and trolls poured out, surrounding their prisoner in seconds.

Kepler lifted his chin to face his captors.

Under the brambles, Niklas felt like he had been punched.

Even Secret gave a tiny whimper.

In the barrack doorway stood a great, bald troll. She was covered in tattoos and scars.

She sneered as she beckoned for the troll guards to bring the prisoner inside. The doors thundered shut after them.

Kepler had been taken by Rafsa.

Chapter Thirty-two

Rafsa was here.

Somehow the troll witch had escaped the poisoned stew and wriggled through to this world.

Niklas got up on his knees.

"Get down." Secret hissed into his ear, but Niklas wasn't listening. He only heard the skullbeaks hooting and hooting, like a storm in his head. What was it Rafsa had told him when she marked his arm? *You know I like my little games.* And now she had Kepler for a plaything behind those barrack doors.

He clenched his fists.

Secret rose up on her hind legs to pin him back to the ground. "Niklas!"

He knew what she was going to say, so he pressed his lips together and turned away to show he wasn't listening. She said it anyway. "We can't go after him."

"You said Rafsa ate the stew!" Even he heard how unfair that was. Secret had done everything she could to stop Kepler. It wasn't her fault.

They stared at each other. The skullbeaks left in a cloud of screeches, returning to their guard posts. Secret's voice was very quiet as she eased off him. "She did. I saw her."

Niklas leaned against a bramble stem. "Then how can she be here?"

"I don't know. But troll witch or no troll witch, Kepler would still be a prisoner. We can't go get him."

"We have to." Niklas crossed his arms. "Rafsa will kill him."

"If they catch us, they will kill *us.* And Summerhill and everyone there will be lost because there's no one left to stop the taint."

"Then we won't let them catch us! Don't you see? This is why the Brokeners hate my mother. Rafsa is her creature, her invention. She uses her runes to do evil things. I can't just leave Kepler to be whatever it is Rafsa does to her victims. And I should have . . ." He swallowed.

Secret watched him a long moment. It felt like she was looking straight into his head. *I should have stopped him,* Niklas thought. "I know it's crazy, but let's do it anyway. Just this once."

Secret closed her eyes. Her stance softened. "All right. Just this once."

"We fooled them in the troll caves. We can do it again."

Niklas rolled over and stared hard across the field. "But we'll need a good plan."

The barracks looked like a prison to him now. The slits in the walls were all fortified with thick bars and fine-masked net. That left only the door, but Rafsa had posted two guards outside. They stood at either side of the entrance, leaning on spiky clubs.

Niklas grabbed a handful of loose stones and shoved them in his pocket. "Come on. Let's get closer to the barracks."

They were making their way along the edge of the brambles, when Niklas tripped over a stone and shoved it out of position. Beneath it there was a nest of black vines.

"I think this is the stuff that was wrapped around Kepler's leg," Niklas said. "He must have gotten himself tangled. But Kepler doesn't exactly strike me as the clumsy kind."

"He's not." Secret lifted her lip to taste the air around the nest. "Don't you recognize it? There are no thorns on this one, but it's the same smell from the tunnel. Sweet, but foul. Treacherous."

Niklas pushed another stone gently to the side. Under it more dark vine covered the ground. A tendril lifted for a moment, searching for something to ensnare. Thorns slid out like claws. When it didn't find a victim, it pulled its thorns in and settled back into the weave.

"What if the whole hill is crawling with the stuff?" Niklas shuddered as he put the stone back. If they hadn't moved so carefully down the slope, the vines might have caught them, too. "Wait. Do you think this is what happened to those other Brokeners? The ones that disappeared?"

"Maybe," Secret said. "Because I don't think the skullbeaks saw him. I think the dark vine called them."

Niklas winced. "We should have gone after him sooner. We could have gotten him out."

Secret didn't argue. Instead she said, "What's the plan?"

They were as close to the barrack doors as they could get without leaving the brambles. The shrubs curved outward here like a widow's peak, and a glance upward confirmed Niklas's suspicion: As long as the skullbeaks didn't leave their nests, the barracks were tall enough to shield them from their eyes. The troll guards still waited outside the door, however. There was no getting around that. "We're going to make a muck boot," Niklas said. "Or rather, get rid of Mr. Molyk so I can get at his boots."

"Muck boots." Secret wrinkled her nose.

Niklas scooped the rocks out of his pocket. "See, what I've learned is that if you don't want people to see what you're doing, make them look somewhere else." He weighed the stones in his hand. "Let's just hope it works on trolls as well."

He stood up, trying not to think of how visible he must

be against the dark green leaves, and tossed the stones as hard as he could before he crouched back down.

They sailed in a perfect arc across the blasted grass, over the juniper bush, and clattered to the ground beyond the barracks. The troll guards sniffed the air, raised their clubs, and left the door.

Niklas and Secret waited until the trolls were nearly by the corner, then sidled across the grass. Secret led the way, melting from planks to shadows to stones, until they reached the door.

They opened it and stole through the crack.

Inside, the barn reeked of muck and sour milk, laced with an unsettling, rank smell that Niklas thought might be scared animal. When his eyes adjusted, he saw that they were in a crude hallway with doors leading in every direction. Through bars in the dockside doors, they could see a train of wagons draped with heavy, black cloth. The cages and the mysterious creatures inside were probably stacked beneath the covers.

Behind the right door, they heard rumbling and grunting as someone rolled heavy objects along the floor. The barrels Secret had mentioned. Behind the left door, they heard hard, deep voices. They were coming closer.

Seconds later the door burst open and Rafsa appeared, followed by a brood of trolls dressed in bulky cloaks.

The troll witch looked much worse for wear. She had fresh burn marks on her skull and arms, her lips oozed with cracks, and her bone armor had horrible, meaty splotches on the front. But she still smiled as if she had just been served a juicy little morsel on a silver platter. "Oh no," she said to one of her broodlings. "The plan is not off. It had to wait a little, is all. The Sparrow King has a new way now. A better way. You should all sharpen your claws."

"We get to fight?" said one of the trolls.

Rafsa answered with a grin.

"What about the prisoner?"

Rafsa wrapped the cloak around her body. "Just get into the wagons," she said. "The sun is almost here, and the king will be very interested to hear what came out of the bushes." She pushed open the dockside doors. "Oh yes, he will."

If any of the brood had thought to look up at that moment, they would have seen a boy and a lynx, dangling from pulleys above their heads, in a manner that Mrs. Ottem of Ottem farm would not appreciate.

But none did, and the whole band of trolls pulled up their hoods and disappeared into the pale dawn.

Niklas and Secret waited until the squeak of wheels had died down before they dropped to the floor again. They heard no rolling of barrels, no voices or footsteps. The barn was silent but for the buzzing of lazy flies.

"Did you see if they had Kepler?" Niklas said. "Those cloaks could have hidden anything."

Secret didn't answer. She had pushed open the door from which Rafsa had emerged and stood on the threshold, tail tucked in and hind legs low.

The bars hadn't lied. This was a prison.

The wan light that leaked in through the slits near the ceiling did little to lift the darkness in the barn, and it didn't at all reach into the pens that lined the walls, some fortified with iron, others covered with nets of troll rope. Niklas hurried down the middle, peering into the boxes, finding only empty ones. They must have taken him, then.

But Secret didn't seem convinced. Niklas watched her lope along the pens, nostrils flaring, until she reached the far corner of the barn. There she turned and looked back at him, golden eyes wide and scared. Her good ear twitched along with a small noise.

Drip. Drip. Drip.

From the last pen came a slow trickle of black water. It was not one of the troll rope boxes, and the barred metal gate was not properly locked. But still the creature that lay curled up against the wall made no effort to escape. His light gray stripes had turned brown from something sticky that smelled both sweet and rotten, like spoiling fruit.

"Kepler," Niklas said, trying to keep the horror out of his voice. "Can you hear me?"

"Idiots," Kepler whispered. His eyes glinted purple. "Why have you come? They'll be back. They'll get you."

"Shhh." Niklas crept into the pen with him. "The trolls have left, at least for now. We have to . . . Oh." So that's why Kepler hadn't gotten up. The ferret had a wound on his chest, right near the opening of his vest.

"They took my Marti." Kepler waved to the corner of the pen, where his medallion lay, cracked in the muck. "They broke her."

Secret snarled, scruff raised. Niklas didn't think he had ever seen her angrier.

"That's . . . not good," he said. "But Castine can make you a new one, right? She carves fast, you said so yourself. As for this little scratch, I'm sure Too can stitch it up for you. We just have to get you home and you'll be good as new."

For want of bandages, he buttoned Kepler's vest over the cut. Kepler blinked hard, as if he tried to remember something, but all that came out was a small mewl. Niklas helped him to his feet. "Come on."

Secret didn't meet his eyes as they supported Kepler along the pens.

Exactly how they were going to make it back without the skullbeaks noticing, he had no idea. But suddenly they heard creaks and splashes out on the fjord, and clipped voices barking orders. Niklas climbed up to peer out from a seaward-facing slit. He couldn't believe their luck.

The entire host of skullbeaks had left their nests to follow the glass ship out the fjord.

As it glided off with its mysterious cargo, and the black wagons rolled up the Nighthouse road, three thieves crept home, hiding under bushes and hedges, two of them carrying the third.

No trolls attacked and no skullbeaks struck while they made their way through the ruin city, and the dark vine that peeked out through greenery in the morning sun did not snare them. But as they climbed the tiers of the garden, Kepler moaned and whimpered. His vest ran dark with blood, and halfway up the valley side he passed out.

The Nightmare work was already done.

Chapter Thirty-three

Odar stared down his snout at Kepler's still form. They had put the ferret on the long table while Castine scrambled off to wake Too, and Odar stood beside him, brewing up a storm.

"Don't be, uh . . ." Niklas cleared his throat as Odar shifted his smolder-coal gaze to him. "I meant to say it was my idea to go into the garden."

Odar kept him squirming for a little while, then sighed. "I know you're trying to be brave. No wonder he likes you so well. He loves nothing more than to admire himself in a mirror."

"It was never to show off." The voice came from the fireplace, where Secret sat as close to the flames as she could get without singeing her fur. "Not once he saw the ship. He wanted to bring back information he thought you should have."

"Well, then." Odar kept his voice gruff, but Niklas thought he saw surprise on the raccoon's face. "Tell me what you learned."

They did, Niklas speaking for the most part, Secret adding her observations where she thought Niklas was too hasty. Especially she described the vine that had entangled Kepler in detail: inky, withered skin, hooked thorns that could be retracted. Odar pulled his whiskers. "You don't think that vine belonged in the brambles."

"No," Secret said.

"Neither do I." Odar sat down on the bench, watching Kepler's chest rise and fall. "This morning, just before you came home, there were strange tremors in the ground. No injuries, just a tumbled shelf and some shed roof tiles. But I think the shaking came from the Rosa Torquata itself."

The stairway rattled, and Too came blustering into the common room with thunderous steps for one so small. She carried her doctor's basket, and her eyes were black circles. "What happened?"

"Trolls," said Niklas. "They cut him. He's full of some sort of sticky liquid, too. I think they made him drink it."

"All right." Too walked around the table, lifting Kepler's lids and feeling his nose. She winced at his black chin and swollen ankle, but looked pleased when she prodded his belly. At last she undid the buttons of Kepler's vest. "Oh," she said. "Stitches won't do for this. Not by a far cry." She turned to Odar. "I'll need the book."

Odar blew air out his nostrils, but he went into the kitchen and fetched a book with bloated covers.

"Don't worry, Kepler." Too riffled through the pages. "I have something that will help." She cracked the book open on a page and put it on the table, facedown. "I need to rinse the cut first. Try and stay still." She glanced up at Niklas as she shook a blue flask. "If you want to help, you could try talking about something else."

Niklas understood. When his mother died, it helped when strangers came to the farm and talked about random things that had nothing to do with her death. It didn't much matter what, as long as some of their normal life rubbed off on him.

"So, Too. How did you get your name?"

Too poured the liquid over Kepler's chest. "My boy, Magnus, named me. He was only six when they picked me up at the shelter. His mother pointed out another kitten, but Magnus said, 'That one is cute, too.' And it stuck."

Niklas laughed and Too nodded. "It's very funny, my name. But you don't know what it can do."

She turned the book over. The open page had a mark on it that Niklas thought must be a kind of rune. Not the harsh cuts of a troll rune, but softer, swirlier lines with dots and flourishes. Beneath it a word was printed: *heal.*

"You know healing magic?"

"Not exactly." Too picked a quill and a bottle of ink out from her bag. "My boy was very sick when he got me. We were a good match, because it turned out I was sick, too." She lifted her medallion briefly to her cheek. "We spent most days tucked up in bed. He read to me and I listened. Odar says he's never met another Petling who knew books *before* they came here." She smiled. "I learned lots of things from reading. How to bake pies, stitch wounds."

"So that's how you picked up your doctor skills," Niklas said.

"One day Odar asked if I wanted to try it with a magic book." Too grimaced. "I think you need special tools, though, because the runes never work when I draw them myself. But I figured out how to do this." She dipped the quill in the ink and drew an & sign right beside the pretty rune, hooking the double loop so it bound them together. "See? Now the rune is mine."

Niklas was impressed. "You take other people's magic and make it your own?"

Too shrugged. "All Brokeners are thieves. I just happen to steal runes." She tore the page out of the old book. "Only problem is, it uses up the rune. After this, we'll have no more healing magic."

She tried to put the page on Kepler's chest, but he curled up into a ball.

"Please," Too said. "I need you to stay still for this."

Somewhere in the pain, Kepler heard and understood. But he couldn't keep from flinching, not until Secret came over to the table. He smiled at her. "I knew you'd come, lady fair. You wouldn't give up on our team."

"What team?"

"You know, our raiding team. You'll be the eyes and ears, I'll be the . . ." He whimpered as Too tried to put the book page on his cut.

"Idiot," Secret finished for him. She put her big paws on Kepler's shoulders and held him down. "I'll finish you myself if you don't stop squirming."

That helped. Too placed the paper perfectly on top of Kepler's wound, closed her eyes, and said, "I, Too, call this rune."

The sign blazed bright. Smoke stung Niklas's nose, and when it cleared, a scorched blotch had replaced the *heal* rune.

Kepler breathed a long sigh. "Thank you."

Too stroked his cheek. "Just don't tell a real rune master, if you ever meet one. I don't think I'm supposed to be able to do that." But Kepler had already fallen asleep. The rune had healed his chest completely, and his ankle looked much better.

"He's all right now?" Secret pulled her paws back.

"As well as I can make him," Too said. "He needs to rest."

"Good." Secret left the room and slipped up the stairs. She must be exhausted. They hadn't exactly gotten a lot of sleep last night. Niklas was about to excuse himself, but Odar put a hand on his arm. "Not so fast, boy. I'd like to hear that story one more time. You carried a prisoner out of the troll barracks without being noticed?"

The front door banged open, and Castine came running into the room. "Odar! Too! You have to come quick."

The raccoon frowned. "Can't it wait?"

"No." Castine's eyes bulged. "Gidea's hurt. Too, bring your bag!"

And just like that, Niklas's interrogation was over. Odar and Too followed Castine out into the morning, leaving Niklas alone with the sleeping patient.

Kepler's wound may be healed, but he still cried softly in his sleep. Niklas tucked a pillow under the ferret's head and sat down beside the table. There he waited until Kepler's breath grew steady.

When Niklas entered the turret chamber, Secret wasn't sleeping at all. She waited bolt upright by the fire, ear turned back, beating her tail on the floor.

"It *was* your fault, you know." She met his eyes.

Niklas froze. Here he thought things had taken a turn for the better. Kepler was healed and they had made it out of the garden alive and with crucial information. But Secret looked every bit as mad as she had been when they found Kepler in the pens.

"With the lamb, it was bad luck mostly," she said. "You were too blind to see that the woods had changed. But this, tonight?" She bared her teeth. "You knew it was stupid. You knew Kepler would do anything to make you believe what he believes. You could have stopped him in the garden, in the jewel orchard, in Lostbook, under the brambles. All those times, you could have called it off."

She was right. Even about Rag. Niklas had been so busy blaming the trolls and even Mr. Molyk, but they hadn't let the lambs into the woods. He had. Guilt sluiced through every part of his body, cold and deadening. "I didn't mean for anyone to get hurt. We were just playing dare."

Secret turned away, but this time Niklas was pretty sure it was a gesture of disgust. "Why do you do that? Put on that false mask and pretend you're not afraid?"

"I don't—" Niklas began, but Secret cut him off.

"You forget I can hear your heartbeat."

In the silence that followed, Niklas's heart betrayed him terribly, kicking so hard, he thought all of Broken must hear it. But he never got around to figuring out an answer, because someone clicked their tongue behind them.

"Save your quarrel for later." Odar stood in the doorway. "We have bigger problems. I didn't want to say this in front of the others, not while they're heartbroken over Kepler. But while you went on your little expedition, I went back to the canyon. Your gate should have closed behind you, but it's wide open."

Niklas already suspected that, since Rafsa had come through there. But what he said was, "Oh."

"Oh yes." Odar narrowed his eyes at him. "And Gidea? She swears a thorn cut her while she was sitting outside her den, minding her own business. Almost took her eye out." Odar turned his back and started down the stairs. "We're going to see the Greenhood."

Chapter Thirty-Four

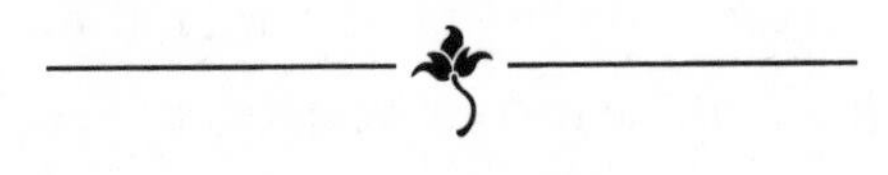

Odar wasn't all bad, Niklas decided.

The raccoon may have dragged them out into the Nick-wood again, but at least he had brought breakfast. The bread was made with spices and walnuts and still hot from the oven. Every tenth step Niklas stopped to take a bite. It wasn't safe to walk and eat at the same time.

Secret hadn't said anything to him since the Second Ruby, but Niklas noticed that she had eaten the bread with relish, even repeating to herself the flavors Odar said he'd added to the dough, aniseed and maple syrup, as if they were a magic spell.

The ground fell away beneath them in overgrown cracks and gulleys. White roses still bloomed here and there, but there were also roots that poked through shelves in the rock. Odar drew to a stop before a dense net of thorns. "I will take you inside to see the Greenhood, but you must swear never to tell anyone where this place is."

"All right," Niklas said.

"Not even the other Brokeners."

Secret gathered her whiskers. "Why not?"

"The task of the Greenhoods is to tend the Rosa Torquata, on behalf of all the Realms. Our Greenhood can't be burdened with the Brokeners' problems. She doesn't belong to them."

"But she belongs to an old smuggler?" Secret swished her tail.

Odar lifted an eyebrow. "Many years ago, when I was a *young* smuggler, I made a deal with her. I promised I would bring her food and news, help messengers from her order find their way, guard her back. In return I was allowed stay in the Nickwood. And that's the only reason there is a Broken. She lets a ragtag band of thieves hide under her skirts because if she didn't, they would be lost. You included."

The raccoon let the thorns prick his palm. They drew aside like a stage curtain, revealing a cavern carved into living wood, lit by the twinkling lights of the Rosa.

"Idun?" Odar's voice frayed into echoes, even if the room was lined with branches. Niklas had the feeling that the Rosa Torquata whispered back to them. "Idun Greenhood, are you there?"

A squeak sounded, and a figure in a deep green cowl emerged from behind a table. "Odar? Is that you?"

"Of course it is." Odar stepped into the room, belly first and grin fixed. But Niklas noticed how he wrung his hands behind his back. "Why are you hiding?"

"Oh, no reason." The Greenhood stood up, holding on to the table with knuckled fingers. "I heard the thorns rattle, and . . ." At the sight of Niklas, she startled. "A Twistrose!"

Idun pushed her cowl back. She was a brown rodent, a gerbil, Niklas thought. Her creaky voice told him she must be ancient. "Where did you come from, child? And how?" She took a step forward, but sank back against the table to steady herself. She favored her arm, which was wrapped in bandages.

"Easy now." Odar opened his backpack and took out a small flask. "You shouldn't be down here alone, Idun. You need someone to help you shoulder the burden. An apprentice."

"Perhaps." Idun accepted the flask with a nod. "Yet it is no small responsibility to bring an apprentice down here. It can get a bit . . ." She made a small gesture.

Niklas peered around at the giant roots and snaking vines. They made him feel like an insect, tiny and squashable. "Dangerous," he suggested.

"I was going to say overwhelming, but you are right. This is not a place for the weak of mind." The Greenhood took a swig. "Real starmead! I've not tasted that in years."

She wiped her mouth. "Now tell me. How and why did you find your way here, young man?"

"Through a crack in the mountain," Niklas said. "It was a coincidence more than anything. I didn't know it led here."

"We discovered him in Sebastifer's canyon two nights ago," Odar said. "Alone with his Wilder here. They say they came together."

Idun's eyes never left Niklas. "Where is your key?"

"That's one of the reasons I brought him here. He says he doesn't have one." Odar stepped close to Idun and murmured into her ear. Her eyes grew wide, then narrow.

Niklas glanced at Secret, who kept her face carefully blank.

Idun hobbled over, put her bony hands under Niklas's chin, and lifted his face. "What is your name?"

"Niklas," Niklas said, and when the Greenhood waited for more, he added, "Rosenquist. Niklas Rosenquist."

Idun nodded to herself. "Odar, my friend," she said, handing him the flask. "It may be my ears playing tricks on me, but I think I hear someone outside. Would you please make sure you were not followed here?"

Looking none too pleased, Odar disappeared back through the curtain.

"Come." The old gerbil led Niklas and Secret into a smaller alcove of arched branches around a massive stem. A square of the stem had been cleared of bark, like a window. Along the frame there were intricate runes carved, the swirly kind Too had used to heal Kepler. The bare wood within looked soft and alive, pulsing with golden light. Niklas wanted very much to put his hand against it.

"Do not touch it," Idun said sharply. "This is a speakwood. A place to commune with the Rosa Torquata. It can only be used by a Greenhood."

"All right," Niklas said, putting his hand in his pocket.

Idun's fingertips danced across the speakwood, and the air shimmered between her black claws and the white wood. "When a Twistrose plea comes, this is where I feed it the key," she said. "I press it against the speakwood and ask for help on behalf of the Realm who made the request. The Rosa Torquata absorbs the key and sends it through to your world."

She opened a small casket that sat next to the speakwood. It was full of crumpled gold. "These are keys I tried to send through this spring. The Rosa Torquata crushed and spat out each and every one."

"It wouldn't help?" Secret's good ear had turned out, and her mangled one hung low.

"Wouldn't or couldn't, I don't know which."

"Maybe the Rosa didn't like whoever asked," Niklas said.

"I hope that is not the case," Idun said. "Because I did the asking. For the first time in Greenhood history, I saw no other solution."

She turned her black eyes to Niklas. "Only those with a key in their possession can pass through a gate from Earth to the Realms. Whoever tries it without a key, will burn. So tell me the truth this time. Where is yours?"

Niklas suddenly remembered something the old voice inside the mountain tunnel had said right before it let him pass. *He is just a boy with a dead key . . .* He opened his satchel and brought out Uncle Anders's handkerchief. "The only thing I can think of that I carry is this."

He unfolded the fabric. A whiff of aging wood tickled his nose as he opened it, revealing the thorny twig he had found inside his mother's statue.

Idun let out a faint hiss. "May I?"

Suddenly Niklas didn't want to give it up, this briar his mother had hidden in her heart for all those years. But Idun didn't wait for his reply. She snatched it and held it up against the light. "Decades old." She gave him an appraising look. "Where did you get this? Was it delivered to you?"

"I found it," Niklas said.

"This is a Twistrose Key. Or it was, before it withered." She smelled the shriveled twig, then put the key back into the handkerchief. "But apparently it still works for you. You had better hold on to it, Niklas *Summerhill.*"

Niklas held his breath, thoughts racing. How did she know?

"No need to be scared," Idun said. "Your secret is still yours. Why do you think I sent Odar away? But I know who owned this key."

The gerbil limped over to a bookcase and picked out a heavy ledger. "This is the Book of Twistrose. We keep records of all who have been called." She let the pages flow past her fingers, and Niklas saw hundreds of entries sift by, names and years and places.

"Here." Idun let the pages come to rest, laying her knuckled hand next to an entry. "Erika Summerhill. She was called October third twenty-five years ago, by the realm of Jewelgard. But she never came."

Niklas stared at the page.

Twenty-five years ago, his mother would have been his age. Like the statue. Like the Erika of his latest dreams. He felt woozy as the pieces clicked into place. His mother's twig was a key. The key was a call for help, a call to become a Twistrose. But . . .

"But the Breaking happened twenty-five years ago," he said.

"It did," Idun replied. "That is why she was called. To stop the troll invasion." She moved her hand and revealed the last part of Erika's entry.

Secret went rigid beside him. "Your heart! Cub, say something. *What is wrong?*"

But Niklas couldn't speak for the thunder in his ears.

A word was written behind his mother's name.

Thornghost.

Chapter Thirty-five

He could almost hear her voice, bound to the memory by white tubes and taped needles. *Keep him away from me. I'm dangerous. I'm a Thornghost.*

"But if she didn't come, then . . . the Breaking was my mother's fault?"

"The Rosa Torquata presents you with a key," Idun said. "It can't make you use it. You must choose to come. Some don't."

"That's why they hate her." Niklas had been convinced it was because his mother had created Rafsa. But it was because she failed to save them.

She didn't come.

"We call them Thornghosts because they remain shadows of what could have been. It is a kindness that they never know the destruction they cause. For them it is merely a road not taken. An invitation passed up. But for us it means disaster."

Erika knew, of that Niklas was certain. He remembered Anne Rosenquist's scratchy tape and the awkward conversation before the lullaby.

Every legend starts somewhere. Why not with you?

Because it didn't.

What he didn't know was *why* she hadn't come.

The pages had begun to shift, slipping into a more familiar place in the book. Niklas lifted his hand to stop them, but Idun gave a little gasp as if she remembered something. She locked her fingers around his wrist with surprising strength for one so frail-looking.

Secret growled at her.

Niklas felt a pang of relief that she still wanted to protect him.

"I apologize," Idun said quickly. She let go of Niklas's hand, but closed the book. "Odar?" Her brittle voice suddenly carried, amplified by echoes and whispers. "Come back inside. We must go to the map room. There is something you all should know."

No daylight could ever reach so deep into the ground, but glossy, serrated leaves grew in the map room anyway, covering the walls in dense layers. At first Niklas didn't understand how the chamber had earned its name, because the only feature that reminded him of maps was a silver star in the stone floor that showed north, south, east, and west. But when Idun brushed her hand over the leaves, she woke up a pattern of twinkles that spread around the chamber, some linked with flashing lines.

It looked like a star chart.

"Are they constellations?"

"Not quite," Idun said, "though the light is related, all taken from the sun. This is a map of the Rosa Torquata. Each node of light represents a place where the Rosa's power is active. Palisades and guard posts. Speakwoods and maps. Every possible gate that links our world to yours."

"Like the one in Sebastifer's canyon?"

"Yes. We call them scargates." Idun walked over to the northern reach of the map and traced a line to a node that glowed steady. "You are right. This gate is open. Do you see how the light is too bright? Feverish, almost?" She cupped the glowing leaf in her hand and lifted it.

A chill trickled down Niklas's spine.

The wood beneath was riddled with withered vine. Idun was right. It did look infected.

Or tainted.

"Dark vine," he whispered.

At the sound of Niklas's voice, a small tendril of the dark vine broke free from the wall. Its thorns creaked softly as they slid out.

Niklas backed into Secret.

The vine hovered in the air, swaying like a snake.

For a moment, they all held their breath. Then the branches of the map room shuddered, and the tendril slithered back behind the leaf. Niklas felt as if he had just escaped a hunter.

"You have seen it before." Idun did not sound surprised.

"It catches raiders in the garden," Secret said. "Tangles them until the skullbeaks come."

"Skullbeaks?" Idun said. "It helps the *skullbeaks?*"

"It sure looked that way. It also grows in the tunnel where we came through the mountain," Niklas added.

Idun's whiskers trembled. "And what happened in the tunnel?"

"It got a little heated," Niklas said. "There were two voices, two creatures arguing with each other. Old voice and nasty voice, I called them. One wanted to help us, but the other wanted us dead."

"Two voices? That might perhaps be the dark vine and the Rosa Torquata, but only rarely does the Rosa speak to someone other than a Greenhood. But of course it could not watch someone try to kill a human boy." Idun stroked the leaf gently. "No more than it could watch the dark vine attack its guardian in her sleep."

Odar startled. "That's what happened to your arm?"

"The vine did it," Idun said. She lifted leaf after leaf.

The dark vine lurked under all of them. "It is vile, and it is spreading everywhere in the world."

"Even in the Nickwood?" Odar said.

"Even in the Nickwood, even as we speak."

"But I've never seen such a plant," the raccoon said. "Where does it come from?"

"I've been pondering that question for a long time. It began as one blackened creeper coiled around a root where the Rosa comes near the garden's edge. I cut it off and closed the wound from the thorns. But the dark vine returned, smothering the sunbursts of the Rosa Torquata. One creeper became many, and more, until I couldn't keep up." She tugged at her cowl. "A few months ago, it gained the upper hand. So I tried to call a Twistrose."

Niklas stared up at the flickering nodes. The infected canyon gate was a single star in a sky of leaves. "These lights are places all over your world. If the Rosa is taken over, would they be in trouble, too? Not just everyone in Broken?"

Idun shook her head. "If the Rosa Torquata loses to this enemy, *everyone* is in danger. Not just everyone in this world. Do not forget, it was in the tunnel. It is probably the reason the gate is open and infected."

Niklas and Secret shared a glance. At last they knew the source of the taint that threatened Summerhill. No garden shears in this world, or any world, were big enough to cut it. "Do you know how to get rid of it?"

"I'm afraid not," Idun said. "But I am convinced it is not natural. Someone is behind this."

"Someone is growing the dark vine on purpose?" Odar's voice was small.

"Yes. And with your news of the canyon and the skullbeaks, I have an idea who it is. The Rosa is very powerful, very capable of defending itself. To get close enough to hurt it in any way, I think you would need to use a speakwood."

She found two bright nodes, neither very far from Sebastifer's canyon. "This easternmost node is the speakwood I guard, and this . . ."

She tried touching the other, but snatched her hand away as if stung. "Is its twin. Jewelgard was special among the Realms. It had not only one, but two speakwoods within its borders. One a secret, nestled deep among the Rosa's roots. The other placed on a magnificent rose tree that sent its rays of sunlight into the night. A beacon, to show the way for travelers."

Odar gawked at her. "Surely you're not serious? There is a speakwood in the Nighthouse?"

"I'm afraid so. An old one inside the tower itself."

"And you've left it to the Sparrow King all these years?" Niklas rubbed his forehead. "Isn't that a bit stupid?"

"The beacon was extinguished a while after the Breaking, so I assumed he had destroyed it. Only the Rosa's chosen guardians could use a speakwood. If the Sparrow King tried, the Rosa would kill him. It does not tolerate Nightmares. Or so I believed." Idun bowed her head. "It seems we must all pay the price for my carelessness."

"The Sparrow King is no ordinary Nightmare," Odar said. "He may look the part, but his actions are far more deliberate. He conducts experiments. He rules, and he is clever."

And he has a new and better plan, thought Niklas.

Idun nodded. "The Sparrow King is behind this, though I do not know how he does it, or why. I wonder if he knows the magnitude of ruin he is about to cause."

Chapter Thirty-six

They had begun the slow and meticulous trip back to the Second Ruby when Secret said, "You want to go to the Nighthouse, don't you."

She kept her voice hushed, the words calm. If Niklas hadn't known her, he might have believed she asked so quietly to keep Odar from hearing. But he did know her. She might as well have snarled at him.

"I think that my mother . . ." He hesitated, not sure what to call the creature that had appeared on the Oldmeadow trail. "I don't think the Erika we saw before we left Summerhill was an ordinary Nightmare, either. I don't know why my mother failed these people. She's a Thornghost, so maybe she deserves their hate. But she pointed up toward the gate. I think she wanted me to come here. To fix her mess."

Secret didn't reply. Niklas pressed on.

"You heard what Idun said. The Nighthouse is the

source of the dark vine, which means it's the source of the taint. We have to—"

Secret cut him off. "I also heard what Odar said. The Nighthouse was considered impossible to take, even before the trolls and the skullbeak nests. Sheer drops and slick rock and runes that guard the skies."

"The Sparrow King took it."

"He had an army." Secret sighed. "When we went after Kepler, you said we would do the impossible, crazy thing just this once. I agreed. Once. Niklas, you can't sneak, you can't fight, and you can't defeat an army of Nightmares."

"Then you won't come with me?" Niklas fought hard to keep his voice level.

"That depends," Secret said. "I'll come if you stop lying. If you stop trying to trick me into doing things, or pretending you don't hear me when I say things you don't like. If you trust me as much as I trust you."

Niklas swallowed. "That sounds fair. I've thought about your question. Why I prefer crazy over coward."

As they climbed through the thickets and thorns, Niklas told Secret what happened the day his mother died. He told her why the word *Thornghost* made his heart pound, and what he had promised himself in Oldmeadow that evening. "I decided that I'd rather be the rascal prince than the pitiful orphan."

"Oh my stupid, stupid cub," Secret said. "Whoever said you had only two choices?"

Niklas had to think on that one, too. And when the lights of the inn appeared behind the branches, winking them home through the softness of purpledusk, he thought he might have an answer.

He just hoped it wouldn't cost him his head.

Chapter Thirty-seven

They sat gathered in the common room, foxes, badgers, rabbits and mice, and the Second Ruby regulars. All forty-one souls in Broken plus their two guests, crammed in between looted art and memories. Their faces glowed with firelight as Odar told them of the dark vine, and the Sparrow King, and the speakwood that was hidden in the very heart of his nest.

"That's how it is, my friends," Odar finished. "We have to find a way to go to the Nighthouse and stop the Sparrow King from doing whatever it is he's doing to the Rosa Torquata. And we have to do it now."

A map of Broken lay spread out on the long table, held down by splintered magnifying stones rescued from the city hall. The seven rings of the garden twinkled with gilded legends drawn in a time when pavilions and gazebos were more than burnt-out husks, and the Nighthouse's beacon still cast its ray onto the Kolfjord. The Brokeners stared at all of it, as if a spark of hope would somehow present itself if they looked hard enough.

But the silence stretched, and from his stool by the bar, Niklas watched as tails lowered, ears drooped, heads sank.

"We'll never make it past the docks," the fox Gidea said. Her injured eye was covered with a bandage, but the other held cold resignation. "We have no troll's bane. That evil witch Rafsa torched every oak tree within a hundred miles."

"The skullbeaks will get us if we go by day," Castine said, never looking up from her whittling. "They'll peck our hearts out in moments."

Too had tucked in her tail. "And if the dark vine is everywhere . . ."

"Even if we got through all that," a badger said, "at the top of the Frothcliff road, the drawbridge would still be up. The Nighthouse can't be taken."

Odar nodded grimly. "I know. But we still have to find a way."

Niklas noticed how the raccoon didn't use the word *impossible*.

"I know a way."

Everyone turned toward the voice. It came from the corner where Kepler sat huddled under his cloak. "Actually, it's more of a staircase up the cliffs above the Frothsea, across the fjord. It leads directly into the castle." He coughed. "I found it last spring."

Odar showed his teeth, but it wasn't exactly a smile. "You want us to believe you crossed the Kolfjord? On your own?"

Kepler came up to the long table. "The fjord has changed since last winter. When the tide is out, a narrow bridge of sand rises from the water." He drew a line at the mouth of the fjord.

Castine put down her carving iron. "But Kepler, why would you go there? Of all ridiculous risks to take, you—"

Kepler lifted his hand to silence her. "Because when I was out breaking Odar's no raiding rule, I overheard the trolls talking. The Sparrow King has a secret prisoner. One he won't lose for anything in the world. One that would destroy 'the great plan' if he escaped."

Niklas glanced at Secret. Rafsa had mentioned both a prisoner and a plan in the barracks. They had assumed she meant Kepler, but could there be another?

Kepler reached behind the counter and brought out the painting he had been hiding there since the beginning of the meeting. It was the portrait of Marcelius the gardener. Kepler's hero. The dark brown weasel now carried a pair of garden shears, which Kepler must have added while they were visiting the Greenhood. "That's why."

"You can't believe it's him?" Castine twisted her fingers. "Marcelius died in the Breaking."

"I don't know for certain it's him," Kepler said. "But I don't care either, so long as rescuing the prisoner will ruin the Sparrow King's plan." He looked around at all the Brokeners. "Low tide is at the half-morning mark. The skullbeaks will be watching, but a few of us could make it. Two raiders, three at the most."

Odar's nostrils flared. "The stairs lead into the castle, and no one is guarding it? That doesn't sound like the Sparrow King to me."

"He might not know about it. It's very hard to find." Kepler's eyes burned bright. "I didn't go inside, because the tide was coming in. But I meant to go back as soon as I found someone dedicated enough to come with me."

"You mean crazy enough." Odar's voice was calm, but he loomed over Kepler like a storm cloud. Castine looked utterly betrayed. She wore a brim-eyed face that could cut your heart in half.

Kepler didn't notice. "I mean someone who cares more about Broken than someone else's rules. Someone who is not too scared to risk their own skin." His eyes flicked to Niklas. "Someone brave enough."

No one spoke; the air in the common room felt static. Niklas felt the weight of everyone's stare, especially Secret's. He cleared his throat. "I have something to say."

Muttering and whispers gathered under the beams like smoke.

Niklas couldn't hear all of it, but he picked out the words *not a Twistrose.*

"That's true," he said above the din. "I'm not a Twistrose. No one called me. I just stumbled through the mountain, and ever since I got here, I've been trying to fix my own problems. The thing is, my problems and your problems come from the same root. Because my mother was Erika Summerhill." The whispers died out, and Niklas's voice sounded awfully loud and alone. "I'm the son of the Thornghost."

There. It was out. No way back, and no escape, either, if the Brokeners decided to turn against him.

In the corner of his eye, Niklas saw Secret edge closer, ready to protect him.

But no one lifted a paw. No one even snarled or said an angry word. Instead Odar laughed, of all things. "You humans with your old wars and grudges," he said, stroking his whiskers. "You thought we would care about that? It wasn't you who failed Jewelgard, Niklas. So Erika Summerhill happens to be your mother. That doesn't mean she guides your hand or makes your choices."

"You don't hate me for being her son?"

Heads shook around the room. Too even smiled at him, and Kepler's eyes were liquid and dark. But it was Secret's face he looked for. Was this honest enough for her?

She squinted and looked away.

Niklas let out his breath. "Then I think that Secret and I should go with Kepler to the Nighthouse."

* * * * *

Morning would come swiftly, and there was no telling when. So the three secret raiders waited in the common room for the right time to enter the garden.

Secret climbed up under the rafters, and soon she snored softly above their heads. Kepler lay curled up in a chair by the fire. He couldn't seem to get warm enough, and he shivered in his sleep.

Niklas and Odar stayed up a while longer, poring over the map.

"Jewelgard had no wall or defensive works," Odar explained. "We had always been protected by the land itself: the peaks, the fjord, and the magic of the earth. There were trolls in the mountains, sure, but they were made for darkness and deep caves, not a sundrenched valley. They could never take Jewelgard to hold. Not unless they had an ally. Someone to rule by day."

"The Sparrow King," Niklas said.

Odar nodded. "And his skullbeaks. They showed up a few weeks after the Breaking. Three at first, then more and more until the sky went dark with bones."

The embers in the fireplace crackled, and Kepler buried his snout in his arms with a little cry. Niklas felt sick at the thought of dragging him back into the Nightmares' reach. He could only hope he was doing the right thing.

"All those names in the Book of Twistrose," he said. "They were chosen."

"That is true." Odar nudged at the magnifying stone. "The Rosa Torquata chose them because they were somehow suited for their task. When your mother was picked, the news spread like dandelion seeds all over Jewelgard. The creator of Rafsa would return to bring the troll witch down. Sebastifer became a hero then. Never mind that he was a fresher who did nothing but sit and carve images of his girl. Everyone wanted to shake his paw. An honor guard went with him to the canyon to wait. He couldn't stop talking about this wonderful girl who had saved him from the shotgun. He was convinced she would save us all."

"But she never came."

"No. The gate withered day by day. The honor guard left to help defend the city. Only Sebastifer remained in that canyon. He refused to give up."

Niklas thought about Erika's entry in the Book of Twistrose, marked by the shameful Thornghost name. Sebastifer must have been so heartbroken. "Even if she had answered the call, what could she have done against an army of trolls?"

Odar scraped at the red jewel that marked off the Ruby Inn. "Your mother knew Rafsa better than anyone, and she knew how to fight trolls. But I believe most of the magic lies in the legend itself. People expect the Twistrose to be able to save them. If she had come, many more Jewelgarders would have chosen to stay and fight instead of fleeing the city. We might have stood a chance."

"That's what Kepler believes," Niklas said. "You need a hero to lead, and the rest will find their courage."

"Instead of putting all our faith in some legend, we should have found a way to fight them off. We had teeth and claws and heart. That's not nothing." Odar sighed. "But Kepler is wrong. Hero or no, forty-one souls against a troll army isn't courage. It's crazy."

Niklas nodded at the chair where Kepler slept. "Do you think he's strong enough for the raid?"

Odar grunted. "In all my years here, I've never met a more stubborn lad. He knows you need him to find the right cove. He won't fail you if you don't fail him."

Niklas winced. "Maybe I'm the one who is crazy for volunteering. You heard the other Brokeners. I'm not a Twistrose. The Rosa didn't pick me. I came here uninvited."

"But you came. Sometimes you have to choose yourself."

Over by the fire, the whimpers had stopped. Though the ferret kept his eyes shut, Niklas thought that he was listening, too. "How?"

"Can you think of any reasons that you may be suited for this task?"

"Because my mother was a Thornghost and I should make up for what she did."

"No. Why *you* are suited for *this* task."

Niklas shrugged. "Unless you count by Secret's impossible standards, I am good at sneaking."

"And?"

"I know Rafsa, and I know how to fight trolls."

"Even better," said Odar. "You're willing to risk your life for the sake of others. You proved as much when you went into those barracks to save Kepler."

"And that makes me a Twistrose?"

"No." Odar placed the magnifying stone over the Nighthouse. "It makes you perfect for a task with no hope."

Chapter Thirty-eight

In the small, stretched hours, somewhere between waking and sleep, Niklas curled up in a dark cage. The sound from Kepler's pen in the barracks whispered by his ear.

Drip, drip, drip.

He knew he had to stay asleep and stay quiet. If the sound of his heartbeat got too loud, they would hear. His arm burned where Rafsa had marked him, and when he peered out through his lashes to look, his skin glowed with magic. But it wasn't the *break* rune anymore. It was an eye inside a square.

Awake.

Niklas opened his eyes.

He was in Sorrowdeep.

In the middle of Sorrowdeep and so cold.

He saw his mother. Twelve years old and the captain of a small rowing boat. Anders was there, too, and Peder

Molyk. Sebastifer at the bow, barking hard. Wedged between them was the cage. They were sinking.

The little boat foundered fast. The children scooped water over the gunwale, all of them crying, until there was no gunwale anymore, just a pale frame in the dark water. They were all in the lake, and Sebastifer's barks turned to yips as he treaded the water fast, fast. The boys splashed around in panic first, then made for land. But Erika wasn't with them. She was below, deep under. Her pale hair billowed as she clawed at something on the bottom of the lake. Something heavy, something impossible to shift.

The cage.

Bubbles rose in frantic streams from Erika's mouth and from between the bars, but they grew smaller in size now, and farther between. She had no breath left, but Erika wouldn't let go. She kept tugging, kept wriggling.

Pearls of air clung to her lashes as her hands slowed.

A shadow came from above and stuck his snout under her arms, jolting her into action, pushing her up toward the splintered moonlight.

Erika kicked and kicked.

When she broke the surface of Sorrowdeep, she was alone.

Chapter Thirty-nine

He rubbed the sleep from his eyes and packed his things into his satchel. Might as well bring everything. Chances were they wouldn't come back here.

"Make sure you get some bread, too." Secret melted down from her beam. The smell of fresh baking wafted out from the kitchen.

Niklas smiled. "Wouldn't go without." He would have to learn how to make that bread if they made it back home. *When,* he told himself. No point in inviting the bad luck.

"What was it about?" Secret said. "The nightmare?"

Niklas closed the lid of his satchel. He must have been thrashing in his sleep, then. "Oh, the usual. Sorrowdeep. Drowning. Mixed with some nice troll runes this time."

Secret tilted her head. "You're scared, and with good reason. I don't need dreams to tell me this won't end well."

Niklas shrugged, but the image of the pearly air slipping up through the dark water jostled its way into his head and left his fingers clammy. At the threshold Secret stopped and flicked her ear back. "You can only be brave if you're scared in the first place, cub. Come on. Kepler is waiting for us."

Dawn trickled through the leaves of the Rosa Torquata, promising a gray day. Lucky: It might make it easier to escape the hollow eyes of the skullbeaks. Kepler had made a big fuss out of Secret's fur, and she had grudgingly agreed to wear a drab cloak to hide it.

She pulled it on now, one whisker short of pouting, when Castine called behind them, "Wait."

The squirrel stood on the steps to the Second Ruby clutching something in her paws. "I can't let you go to the Nighthouse without these." She held out two small discs, each fastened at the end of a leather cord. They were carved from wood and painted in mist blue, dark rust, and gold. She opened the lid. Even in the wan light, Niklas could see what they represented: a boy and a lynx.

Medallions.

She approached Niklas first. The medallion settled against his chest, heavier than he had expected, but also oddly comforting. The lynx's ears were the tips of diamond apple spikes, and flecks of jet patterned her fur. Castine was the one who seemed to hate his mother the most, but from her tired eyes, Niklas guessed she had stayed up all night to finish these. He smiled at her. "I didn't think the human got one. Thank you."

She smiled back. "It was Sebastifer who gave me the idea, once upon a time. He couldn't carve for the life of him with his dog paws, but he showed me how to pour the love into the wood. I never got to give him a medallion. He would want you to have one instead."

Then it was Secret's turn. She lifted her paw to study her medallion. The boy's face within the lid was mostly blank, but the sapphire eyes and mop of dark hair definitely belonged to Niklas.

"I didn't have time to do the features," Castine said. "I'll finish it when you return. So see that you do."

For the first time, Niklas felt the sting of the medallion. It was like an extra heartbeat that planted a feeling in his chest. Gratitude. "You're very kind." Secret shut the lid and looked away. "Maybe you can make a new one for Kepler first."

Castine frowned at the ferret, who stood by the fountain. Petals drifted down around him, some landing in the water, and he watched them drench and dissolve. "They broke his Marti," Secret said.

"Okay." Castine sucked in a deep breath. "Just keep him safe if you can."

Kepler was supposed to keep them safe, Niklas thought, or as safe as they could be, headed for the Sparrow King's nest. But as he watched their guide ease his weight over to his injured leg, he knew that Castine was right. "All he needs to do is show us the stairs, and we'll do the rest," he promised.

Castine nodded and skipped back to the steps, where Odar and Too had come out through the door with the scent of aniseed. Kepler stirred, nose twitching. "That's enough for good-byes," he said. "Let's go before the other Brokeners show up, too. And before . . ." He pointed vaguely at the thousands of thorns around them, each sharp enough to slice through bone. There was no need to add the rest.

They chose a different path through the garden this time, staying on the seventh circle among the pear and plum trees until they reached the far end of the valley, near the left bluff. There they carved their way down to the fjord, struggling along the tall stone fence that marked the border. The banks were so thick with dark vine that they often had to double back to find another way.

But Kepler brought them down to the shore without once coming near the enemy or exposing them to the pale sky.

"What is that smell?" Niklas crinkled his nose as they crawled to the edge of the fjord. The wind reeked of salty sulfur. "Not trolls, I hope?"

Secret snorted. "No, that's the smell of low tide. Morning breath of the ocean."

Obviously lynxes got to travel more than farm boys. He felt a sting of jealousy. "How do you know?"

"I've been there, in the cold months. The water is poison. Not good if you want to live."

Right in front of them, the causeway formed a crescent across the bay. It measured maybe ten yards across and was littered with seaweed that stretched out on the sand, limp and oozing.

Mysterious prisoner or no, Niklas couldn't believe Kepler had gone out there alone. How did he know that there was something to find on the other side?

"Have you done this many times?"

"Just the once." Kepler's voice came out clipped, as if he had trouble squeezing air out of his lungs. He glanced up at the sky. "Morning has flowed faster than I had hoped. We have to go, or we'll be caught out there."

The ocean licked at the bank from both sides, lifting the seaweed as it foamed past. The sand was so drenched, it felt wobbly. Their feet made shallow marks that filled with water as they darted along the causeway. Suddenly Secret tugged them to a stop. "Don't move," she said in the very calm way that Niklas had learned meant deadly danger. They pulled down the hoods of their sand-colored cloaks.

"What?" Niklas whispered. Secret glanced upward. The

Nighthouse loomed atop the cliff, wreathed in wisps of fog. A skullbeak was circling the dome. Now it banked out over the fjord, hollow scream rising as it came closer.

Kepler squeezed his lids shut. His left hand grasped for his Marti medallion, but found nothing. His breath grew so wheezy, Niklas was sure the skullbeak would hear. But it didn't. It turned back and headed for the docks.

"That was lucky," Niklas muttered as they clambered up on the far cliff.

"Very," Secret said. But the look she gave Kepler was full of worry.

Chapter Forty

The ledge wound along the base of the cliff at the high tide mark, no more than a foot wide and near impossible to find if you didn't know it was there. Somehow Kepler had discovered it anyway on his previous expedition, and he led them now, inching along the ledge with his back turned to the Frothsea.

Below them, sharp rocks jutted out of the roaring water, and they felt the spray of each wave. Every four feet or so there was a hollow in the rock near their shoulders. They could easily be mistaken for natural cracks, but when you stuck your hand inside, the hollows curled inward to make a concealed handle, perfect for holding on to when the wind gusted or a big wave came in.

Someone had crafted these handles, as well as the path they secured.

Niklas tilted his head back. Far above, the mountain

gave way to smoother stone. The castle leaned out over the edge, and he could see the Nighthouse as a black half-moon. A flock of skullbeaks wheeled over the tower, but whether it was luck or the smuggler's cloaks that kept them hidden, they still went unnoticed.

Kepler sidled along with his eyes shut, as if his fingers knew more than he did. Suddenly he stopped by a narrow opening in the rock. It looked like just another weather-worn crack, and the ledge continued on. Kepler slipped into the opening, spidering along by way of crude foot-holds. Niklas had to shout to be heard above the din of the ocean. "Are you sure this is the right place?"

Kepler pointed at a blotch in the cliff wall. Niklas had thought it was a patch of lichen, but when he bent down to inspect it, he saw that Kepler was right. The gold leaf of Jewelgard.

The crack turned out to be a cove that curled in on itself like a spiral, and at the deepest crook nestled a staircase. The steps rose beyond the funnel of the cove and climbed wildly along the face of the cliff lined with old seagull nests and tufts of bleached grass. There was no railing and after a while, Niklas decided to stop looking down at the foaming waves. When they took a rare moment to rest, he asked, "How come the skullbeaks haven't found this?"

Kepler put a finger over his lips and pointed up. "Better be silent." The castle walls loomed taller now, cut from dull, black glass. The ever-present Nighthouse fog trailed down like hanging moss. It smelled sweet and rotten. Niklas couldn't see any sign of life, and the skullbeaks had not been out for a while. Yet the nightmare feeling had never weighed as heavily on him as on these stairs. The shifting, brooding quality of the air sent prickles down his back.

At last the steps ended with a door in the mountain wall. It was made of weathered wood and reinforced by metal scrollwork of entangled thorns. There was no handle or keyhole, but a single thorn poked out in the middle. Kepler nodded at Niklas, and whispered, "Let it taste you."

"You're sure?" Secret frowned at Kepler. "That's what you did last time?"

"Yes." Kepler clutched at his chest where Marti's medallion belonged, his fingers searching until the other paw came up to stop it. "It's just like the gate thorns of the Nickwood. I'm worried it will taste that disgusting troll poison in my blood. But it will let you in. You're a Twistrose."

"Not a real one," Niklas said. He pressed the pad of his thumb against the tip until a drop of blood came out. The door swung open with a creak. A passageway continued upward into the mountain, dark but for glimmering tiles of glass on the steps.

A sound whispered down to meet them: a swooshing swelling and dying down, as if the sea had a brother deep in the castle.

Kepler swayed slightly. Niklas was none too certain that their guide could manage more stairs without falling backward, so he put his arm around Kepler's shoulders. "Let's go together."

Kepler didn't protest. "Careful," he said. "The door is heavy."

It slammed shut as soon as Secret had passed the threshold as the last of the three, leaving them in the ghostly sheen. The inside of the door had no handle, no thorn.

Secret's tail thumped against Niklas's legs. "I hope no one heard that boom."

Kepler turned back. The light picked out only the stripes of his face. "The trolls don't know about this passage, or we would have smelled them."

"Let's keep going," Niklas said.

They emerged through a slim, concealed door behind a pillar in the corner of a courtyard. A wooden gallery enclosed the yard, but the rest was all smoky, dark stone. The massive walls had turrets at each corner, and in the middle of the west wall, the hulking round tower of the Nighthouse disappeared into thicker mist. All of it was covered with creeping dark vines.

Niklas had the strangest feeling he had seen this before.

He turned in a circle, taking in the flagstones, the crenellated curtain walls, the gatehouse in the east with the drawbridge raised against the lowered grate. But the pieces didn't click into place until a gust of wind lifted the fog around the Nighthouse. The dome had a wraparound balcony and a wide band of windows under ridged half-moon tiles that looked like fingernails.

"It's my mother's bird castle!" He rubbed his forehead. How could she have known exactly what it looked like? Somehow the Nighthouse had made it into her dreams with photographic precision.

"What are you doing?" Secret's voice was not her normal calm or even flat. It sounded slurry with uncertainty. She wasn't talking to Niklas. Her eyes were trained on Kepler. The ferret had slipped away from them and made his way to the gate. Next to the gate hung a large bell with a clapper for gripping. An alarm bell.

"Nothing."

"Then why do you reek like a coward?"

Kepler grasped and grasped at his chest, leaning against the wall. "I . . . I. Ngh." His other hand flew up to stop the clawing.

"Kepler," Niklas began, but then he stopped, staring at Kepler's hand in horror as it moved slowly toward the bell. "What are you doing?"

Kepler glared at his fingers on the clapper. His eyes bulged. "It . . . It's my task to ring the bell now."

"But they'll know we're here," Niklas said.

"The Sparrow King already knows. He knows everything."

"I actually trusted you," Secret said. *"So stupid."* She

turned to Niklas, eyes watering. "What should we do? Attack him before he rings the bell?"

"No!" Niklas touched her scruff. They'd never reach him in time to stop him. And this was Kepler, brave, hopeful Kepler, who dreamed of freeing Broken.

"Have to . . ." Kepler almost gagged to get the words out. "Ring the bell!"

His hand swung the clapper hard against the metal of the bell. The noise rolled around the courtyard, rose up along the tower of the Nighthouse, and fled into the sky.

The skullbeaks answered, letting their *hoooowooooo* break loose over the ruin city. Inside the castle sounded a long, shrill troll cry. And up in the Nighthouse, a tall shape stepped in front of the window, beak curved like a plague-doctor.

The Sparrow King was watching.

Chapter Forty-one

Kepler kept the bell ringing, ringing. The peals thundered in Niklas's head, making it impossible to think. They had to hide, but where? The door where they had emerged from the sea stairs had closed. The only other exits from the courtyard were the drawbridge and the castle door, behind which thundering footsteps approached. The trolls were awake in there. Outside the walls, the skullbeaks howled.

Hoooowoooo.

Secret turned her mangled ear to him, as if to say, *You decide our next move.*

Niklas couldn't think of any moves. There was nothing to do but wait to be captured.

Dark vine was creeping up where the concealed door had been, smothering the wall with its thorny web, exactly like the roses his mother had carved on the Summerhill birdhouse.

Wait.

If this was his mother's Nightmare castle down to every detail—if she had really dreamt about this place back in her bed in Summerhill—then maybe she knew more about it than what the surface showed. In the birdhouse, she had hidden two secret compartments. One at the top of the tower, and one beneath the round flagstone! Niklas searched the courtyard, and there it was: right at the foot of the Nighthouse, a round stone etched with a thorn.

He sprinted over to it. The flagstone measured two feet across. It lay completely flush with the rest of the courtyard. He needed to spring it open, but how?

He pressed the stone. Nothing.

He knocked on it, stepped on it, scratched the thorn, used his fingernails to dig into the surrounding mortar. Nothing.

Hooooowooooo.

For a short, desperate moment Niklas wished Lin were there. She solved riddles all the time, like it was nothing, but he had never been able to figure out the answer to anything.

Except he *had.* This past week he had. He had found out his mother's secrets.

Exactly how the worlds were connected, Niklas had no idea. But maybe there was some of Erika in this place, too? With her, things always moved in circles: The spire must be screwed off, the statue spun around, the medallion twisted to open the secret chamber of her heart.

He put the heels of his hands on the stone and used his whole weight to turn it around. It moved with surprising ease. When it had turned full circle, it lifted two inches out of the ground, revealing a handle along the edge.

"Quick," he said to Secret. "Help me get it out!"

Secret lifted the hatch, but at the last moment, she glanced across the courtyard at Kepler.

Tears leaked down the ferret's face as he rang the bell harder and faster, filling the castle with a mad clangor. His eyes were shut. He couldn't see where they were going.

Niklas and Secret jumped through the hatch.

The cellar echoed with sounds: hooting and screeching from the courtyard above, footsteps pounding through hallways. Doors slammed and voices shouted, but no one came running down the same tunnel as Secret and Niklas. He almost dared hope they moved in a separate, concealed grid, until they found a lone, lit lantern on the wall, sputtering with rancid oil.

The trolls had been here not too long ago.

Niklas patted Secret on the back. "At least we'll see where we're going. Maybe we'll luck out again and find another exit."

"We're moving deeper into the mountain." Secret turned away from the flickering light. "And it was never luck. Not Kepler's rescue, not the sneaking. Odar was right. It was too easy." She hissed. "I shouldn't have trusted him."

"We shouldn't have brought him in the first place. He changed after the barracks, Secret. They broke him." *And it was my fault he ended up there,* Niklas thought. They couldn't hear the bell anymore. Either they had come too far belowground, or Kepler had stopped. But the desperate ringing still played in Niklas's head.

"Not so soft-hearted, cub," Secret said, but the angle of her neck was anything but hard.

Dirt and half-gnawed animal bones lined the hallways, and the sour-milk stink wafted out of the stairwells. Secret sniffed the empty frame of a door that had been torn clean off its hinges, revealing a nest of dirty beds within. "Used to be oak."

Niklas grimaced. "Rafsa is nothing if not thorough." He could very well imagine the troll witch striding down these tunnels, bone armor clattering, claws scritching against the stone, ordering doors to be removed.

Secret stopped, nostrils flaring.

"What is it?" Niklas couldn't smell anything other than troll stink.

"Fur and old piss," Secret said. "But something else, too. Something sweet and burnt, like in Kepler's pen in the barracks."

They turned the corner.

"Oh no," Niklas whispered. "No, that can't be right!"

Kepler hadn't lied about everything, not about the troll conversation he had overheard. But he had guessed wrong about the prisoner. It wasn't Marcelius.

They stood on the doorway of a dank cell, full of filthy rushes. Behind the bars, the sole prisoner slept in the middle of the floor. He was hooked up by needles and long, snaking tubes to a flask mounted on a hospital rack. The flask contained a black liquid that dripped, dripped, dripped into the veins of a bone-thin dog.

Niklas knew this dog: the floppy ears, the black patches, and the gentle curve of his snout. And not just from the figurine in his pocket. From his dreams as well.

"Sebastifer?" Niklas took a step forward. "Can you hear me?"

Sebastifer whimpered in his sleep. Just like Kepler had done.

"Don't be scared," Niklas said. "I'm Erika's son. Your girl Erika? I'm going to help you." He tugged at the heavy padlock on the cell door. "Just please wake up?"

But Sebastifer didn't stir. The liquid dripped and dripped. Troll poison, Kepler had called it.

"We have to get in there," Niklas said. "We have to get that stuff away from him." He began kicking around in the rotten straw.

"What are you doing?" Secret murmured into his ear. "We won't be able to break that lock."

"We won't have to." Niklas found what he was looking for. Trolls were messy. Of course they had tossed discarded needles on the floor. They were gooey and horrible, but they would work. He wiped them off on the rushes and stuck them into the padlock.

"You know how to pick a lock." Secret couldn't hide the pleased smirk on her face.

"I borrowed one of Lin's dad's research books. How else would I get into the Fale cellars for plum jam?" Niklas wiggled the final needle into the hole. "Don't tell Mrs. Fale. Or my grandmother."

The lock sprang open, and the cage door creaked on its hinges.

Sebastifer still didn't move. When Niklas unhooked him from the needles and untangled him from the tubes, he kicked and yelped in his sleep. He was dreaming. Niklas tried shaking him and even pinched his wet black nose, but no matter what he did, Sebastifer would not wake.

"I don't think he can." Niklas felt his chest clench. "Look at his fur."

Sebastifer had been marked, top to bottom, with troll runes. Niklas recognized the one from the sleeping stone trolls in the cave, the eye that meant *awake.* He had to use his mother's rune book to decipher the others: *Sleep.*

Dream. A long fang meant *obey.* And one he had only seen twice before, on the lid of his mother's troll-hunting casket. And on Rafsa herself, cut deep on her entire lower arm. A four-pointed star that meant *power.*

"They've bound him with magic." Niklas closed the book. "We're going to have to lift him up and take him with us."

"And go where?" Secret's bad ear drooped. "We don't know where we are, and we may have to bolt at any moment. You know we can't outrun the trolls if we're carrying him between us."

She lifted her paw and put it gently on Sebastifer's shoulder. At the touch, Sebastifer turned over in his sleep and whined. "The night grows dark, Erika. But I can't find you!"

That's because she's gone, Niklas thought. *She can't help you, or us, or anyone.* His eyes stung.

As his vision blurred, Sebastifer's whimpers filled his head. There was something about them. They were just snippets, but there was a pattern. A melody. One Niklas had heard before.

"Wake now, little rose," he sang, trying to fit the song over the sounds. "The night grows dark and old . . ." He faltered. It was all he could remember of his mother's lullaby. But for a brief moment, Sebastifer's tail and ears had twitched. *Had he heard?*

At the bottom of his satchel Niklas found a wrinkled

sheet of paper and smoothed it out on his knees. He had jotted down the words from the tape in Morello House, only a few days ago, although it seemed like a thousand.

He couldn't bear to look at Sebastifer as he sang, so instead he watched Secret, and her golden eyes rimmed in black and white, and her lone ear tuft and spotted fur, so out of place in this cell.

Wake now, little rose,
The night grows dark and old.
Your feet must find the trail tonight,
To Sorrowdeep the cold.

Wait now, little dog,
Your voice will carry through.
The key lies in her hand tonight,
Sebastifer the true.

Sleep then, ghost of thorns,
If you can't play the part.
Your love will lead you nowhere when
It's locked inside your heart.

Somewhere during the second verse, Sebastifer fell silent, and when Niklas finished the last line of the song, he turned back, expecting to see the dog resting peacefully. Instead Sebastifer sat upright, staring right at him.

Clouds of black drifted across his eyes, but his nostrils flared.

"Erika, is that you?"

"No," Niklas said. "She couldn't come. I'm sorry."

The dog scratched his ear, and when he looked at Niklas again, his eyes were weary, but clear. "You smell like her. Like woods and night mist and fun."

The black liquid leaked down his face like ink tears.

"Here." Niklas held out his water bottle.

Sebastifer drank in big gulps. He looked terribly weak. Secret gave him her loaf of aniseed bread, and it was gone in two bites.

"Thank you." Sebastifer sighed. "It's been a long time since I had fresh bread."

Very long, Niklas thought, since before Erika carved the bird castle, at the very least. How else would she know where to place his prison? Suddenly he remembered what Kepler had said: The prisoner would destroy the Sparrow King's plans if he escaped. "Do you know why they kept you down here?"

"To keep the canyon gate open." Sebastifer's eyes clouded over, as if the words were pulling him back into the dream. "I have to keep it open for my girl, Erika. She is a Twistrose. I'm waiting for her."

"I know. I'm sorry." Niklas took a painful breath. "Erika isn't coming. She's dead. She died seven years ago, when I was little. I'm her son. Niklas."

Sebastifer shook off the drowsiness again. "I . . . know. Yes, I remember. I felt her slip away, but I get so confused. You're Niklas?"

"Yes."

The dog wagged his tail. "I've been dreaming about you. Something about boots with muck in them? And a girl named Lin who left? And Alma is old now?"

Niklas nodded. "Lin left, but I have Secret now. And Grandma Alma is old, but she's okay. Except . . ." He wondered how lucid the dog was. He looked so weak. But he had to try to explain. "I came here to close the gate in the canyon. The one you've been keeping open? Magic from the Realms is leaking through it into our world, poisoning the Summerchild. There are trolls in the woods."

Sebastifer's eyebrows shot up in the middle. "Trolls? They went to Summerhill?"

"That's not even half of it. The Sparrow King is doing something terrible here, in this world. I don't know what it is, but it involves the Rosa Torquata and the dark vine that is spreading everywhere. I think it's breaking the canyon gate open."

"Yes." Sebastifer blinked. "You're right. That's what they want. They want to make a big hole to Summerhill." His ears wilted. "They told me I could see Erika if I only kept waiting. Instead I've been helping them with their plan. I'm so sorry . . ."

"It is him, then," Secret said. "Sebastifer is the prisoner

Kepler talked about. The one whose rescue would ruin the whole plan." She wrinkled her nose at the medical equipment that lay in an ugly pile on the floor. "So is it ruined now?"

Niklas had no idea. "Only one way to be sure. Sebastifer, we have to get you out of here."

A door slammed. Troll voices bellowed, still a ways off, but closer than before. Niklas put his hand carefully on the old dog's shoulder. "Do you know a way out? We can't go back where we came from. The skullbeaks will probably be waiting by that trapdoor like Tobis by his favorite mouse hole."

Sebastifer brightened at the mention of the Summerhill cat. "That sneaky old scoundrel. He's still around, then?" He stood up tall and looked Niklas in the eyes. "I wish I could help, but there is no way out of this castle for us. The trolls watch all the doors. Like cats, yes."

Niklas bit his lip. He heard footsteps now. "Then do you know where we could hide until we think of something?"

Sebastifer's ears perked up. "Yes, I do! There is a place not far from here where the trolls never go."

"Why not?" Secret said, ever suspicious.

Sebastifer's smile looked almost happy. "Because they're too scared."

Chapter Forty-two

They had walked into another trap.

That was Niklas's first and almost overwhelming thought as they stepped into the vault. The entire room was filled with skullbeaks, perched on banisters, soaring under the ceiling or laid out on a worktable in the middle of the room, cloth wings spread out.

Niklas felt Secret coil up, ready to spring.

"Wait!" Sebastifer slunk across the floor, tail tucked in. "They're not dangerous. Not yet. This is where the Sparrow King makes them. This is his workshop."

There were tongs, bone cutters, scissors, and needles. Rolls of cloth and kegs of fluids. And piles and piles of bones, on the table and in big wicker baskets along the walls.

Some skullbeaks hung suspended from hooks, looking

complete to Niklas's eye, but Sebastifer shook his head. "They don't have Thorndrip in them yet."

"You mean the black liquid they put in you?"

"The Sparrow King injects it into their beaks and then Rafsa wakes them with her runes. They're not alive, not truly. They're bound to him with a talisman, one he wears around his neck. He sees what they see, they do what he wants."

Niklas walked over to the table, where the wings of an enormous skullbeak trailed over the edges. It was the biggest one they had seen yet. He dared himself to go closer, closer, until he stared straight into its empty eyes. "They remind me of my mother's mobiles in the bird room."

"That's because they *are* your mother's mobiles. The Sparrow King got the idea from Erika." Sebastifer wagged his tail briefly. "She had such a talent for making things, my girl."

"But how could he know about her designs?" Niklas rubbed his forehead. "Unless . . . you told him?"

"I never meant to." Sebastifer pushed back some of the matted fur on his arm. "He found out through this."

His forearm was marked with a triangle with an *R* inside. Niklas didn't recognize it from his mother's notebook. "Rafsa makes her own runes? What does it do?"

"It lets you read my mind. Whether I want you to or not." Sebastifer coughed, and Niklas gave him another swig of his water bottle. He swallowed gratefully. "We were linked, Erika and I. At first it was sheer stubbornness. Mine mostly. I refused to leave that canyon, even after the gate had closed. You know us dogs. We don't give up."

Niklas had never known any dogs, but he nodded anyway. Over by the door, as far away from the skullbeaks as the room would allow, Secret rolled her eyes. She had picked that one up from Castine.

Sebastifer didn't see it. "But later, it was magic." A cloud of oily brown scudded over his blue irises. "The Sparrow King had Rafsa carve her runes on me so the bond never snapped. It just lasted and lasted, way too much love and sadness, driving us slowly mad with regret."

He squinted up at the half-finished skullbeaks circling, and when he continued, his voice sounded so tired. "Night after night the bad dreams streamed from my head into hers. Fever dreams, Thorndrip dreams. Of the Breaking and the ruin. Of Rafsa and the Sparrow King. Of Sorrowdeep and the death she had caused." He hung his head. "I couldn't keep my last moments from tormenting me at night, so they tormented her as well."

"*You* sent her the nightmares?"

"I didn't want to, but the runes and Thorndrip were so strong. In return, I got glimpses of Summerhill as the dreamer saw it. First Erika, and when she died . . ."

"Me." Niklas stood very still. So that was where the nightmares came from. All those evenings he had hid under his covers, trying his best not to invite the dreams, and they didn't come from his head at all.

Sebastifer nodded. "Sometimes your uncle, sometimes your grandmother. But you were closer."

All the guilt in the world showed in the slant of his brows. "I am so sorry. For everything."

Niklas couldn't meet his eyes. His mother spent the rest of her life dreaming of the most horrible thing that had happened to her, over and over. No wonder her mind broke. Suddenly he felt a warm pulse against his chest. The medallion. He grabbed it and turned around.

Secret's fur bristled, and her stare was molten gold. She was holding her medallion, too. "It's not your fault," she said. "They did that to you. To *all* of you. They should pay for it."

"Is that the reason the nightmare Erika pointed up the trail?" Niklas had thought it was a message from his mother, but it maybe was Sebastifer's dream, Sebastifer pleading for someone to rescue him from his prison cell.

Sebastifer held his arm out to Niklas. "I know you must wonder why she didn't come. It's here if you want to look."

The *read* rune.

Niklas hesitated. The rune looked sorer than the others, as if it had been activated often. "Won't it hurt?"

"Go on," Sebastifer said. "I think you should see for yourself."

Niklas put his hand on Sebastifer's arm. It felt hot, and hotter still when the rune lit up red under his fingers. He looked up, about to snatch his fingers away. Sebastifer was gone, his eyes hidden by Thorndrip. Then the cold tug took Niklas, too. He heard Secret snarl, but she was so far away, which was no wonder, because Niklas no longer found himself in the skullbeak shop.

He was at Sorrowdeep, where the twelve-year-old Erika stood on the beach by the finger rock. In the palm of her hand, she held a golden key. It had rose petals for a head, and thorns for teeth, and the word *Twistrose* engraved on the stem.

On the far side of Sorrowdeep, light glowed in the avalanche crack. A distant voice swept over the lake. Could be barks, could be echoes. It was hard to tell.

Erika stepped into the water. The bottom sloped hard. Shivering all over, she tried to see her feet, but they were lost in the mud. A current came out of the deep to brush against her skin. Somehow it seemed angry. Intent, as if it wanted to pull her down.

She closed her eyes. This strange and wonderful key had appeared on her windowsill, waiting for her to use it. Now she thought she heard Sebastifer, calling for her. All she had to do was get in the water and swim. If she could just see his face . . .

Instead she saw the cage on the bottom, door rusted shut, filled with white bones.

She opened her eyes. Her tears made rings in the lake, and she thought she might burst from shame. But she couldn't do it. She couldn't swim across Sorrowdeep.

She stepped out of the water and went home.

Erika's tears had showed up unbidden on Niklas's face. He wiped them with the back of his hand. "What was that inside the cage?"

"A mink cub from the Molyk farm," Sebastifer said, so calm now, and so sad. "It got sick when it was a newborn, but Peder had nursed it back to health, despite his father's rule of never getting attached. Now he couldn't bear for it to get the buzzer."

"They were saving him," Niklas said. His mother's words in the dream made sense. It all made sense now.

"They were going to release him in the Summerchild cave. It might not have worked anyway, but Erika didn't know that. She just wanted to help. But the boat sank, and so did the cage."

"The mink drowned."

"He did." Sebastifer sighed. "That cage carried all her guilt and sadness, for me, for that cub. You should have seen her that summer, Niklas. All those nightmares. Her head became a cage, too."

Niklas breathed out. "I guess I understand why it's in the dreams now. It had nothing to do with those cages from the ship after all." Which meant the whole trip to Lostbook was based on a wrong guess. Kepler's capture was for nothing.

Sebastifer's ears shot up. "There are cages that come from ships?"

"For the Sparrow King's trade," Niklas said. "We snuck down to the docks to see a shipment come in, but we never found out what the cages contained."

Sebastifer's eyes glazed over for a moment, as if he was struggling to recall something. He wagged his tail slowly, then faster and faster. "I remember now! The trade!" He hobbled toward the door, tail still whipping. "We have to get there before the trolls sniff us out!"

"Get where?" Niklas hurried after him.

"The ballroom!" The old dog looked over his shoulder. "Our chance to escape!"

Chapter Forty-three

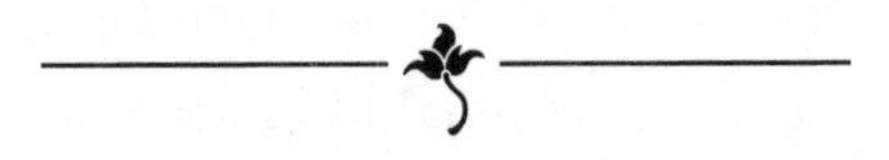

Niklas and Secret had woven their way deep into the cellars of the castle, but Sebastifer led them always up, on stairs and secret ladders. Every now and then, he stopped to listen. Sometimes Niklas heard the eerie whooshing drifting down the tunnel. Other times the floor trembled, and the sound of fire and steam rolled down to meet them, along with the cloying smell that Secret hated so much. "Not that way." Sebastifer doubled back to herd them along. "There's no way out from the Thorndrip factory."

They snuck past storage rooms full of grains, empty glass containers, and a strange kind of medical equipment made of metal circles, hollow spikes, and linked pots and tubes. "Thorndrippers," Sebastifer said. "For the factory." Niklas allowed himself a shudder. He had a feeling he didn't want to know what went on there.

Several times Sebastifer led them to a clever hiding place right before a group of trolls barged past.

"He certainly knows his way around," Niklas whispered as he and Secret pressed against the wall behind a rotten tapestry while Sebastifer checked to see if the coast was clear.

"Especially for someone who has been locked up in a cell," Secret murmured. "And have you noticed his eyes are cloudy again?"

When they came out from behind the tapestry, they found Sebastifer watching them. "I'm not lying," he said. "I have been locked up. But when Rafsa reads me, I get a glimpse of her mind, too. Never the Sparrow King, but her thoughts roll through in a thick haze of hate. I'm leading you by her memories."

The whooshing grew louder now, and at the end of a wide corridor, Sebastifer stopped and lifted his paw. "The cages."

They stepped into a big hall. Niklas could see how this might once have been a ballroom. The ceiling that soared high above them was painted with animals and delicate roses, and light filtered in through a huge stained-glass window in sparkling blues and reds. But it was no longer a room for dancing. Instead it held the crates from the glass ship.

They lined every wall, all the way from the floor to the ceiling. At last they learned what the Sparrow King needed for his secret trade. The cages teemed with tens of thousands of fluttering brown wings, beady black eyes, and little yellow beaks straining for food and freedom.

Sparrows.

Niklas had wondered why the Sparrow King had chosen his name. Here the reason towered above them, cage after cage, row after row. "What does he want with them?"

"They don't come out of this castle alive." Sebastifer whined softly. "They go into the factory and then they go into the barrels. The Sparrow King turns them into Thorndrip."

"Thorndrip is made from sparrows?" Niklas pushed away the thought of Sebastifer's tubes.

The old dog nodded. "I've read Rafsa's thoughts on this. More and more ships come, more and more sparrows die." He pointed toward the next room, visible through a tall, vaulted archway. It held hundreds of black barrels, stacked almost as high as the cages. Most were sealed and ready to be transported down to the docks but there was also a pile of discarded barrels and chipped lids. "We won't be able to close them properly," Sebastifer said. "But trolls are sloppy. I think they won't notice."

"You mean for us to hide in them!" Niklas smiled.

"There will be guards at the docks, too, but we stand a much better chance than inside the castle walls."

They loaded their escape barrels onto the waiting wagons. Secret poured into hers, somehow fitting comfortably even though she was the biggest of them. Niklas helped Sebastifer clamber into his, then scurried into the last one, clutching his lid. "Ready?"

Sebastifer nodded. "See you on the other side."

Niklas hunched down, pulling the lid into place.

In the sweet-smelling darkness he listened. Somewhere in the hallways, he heard shrill shouts. The trolls must have their scent.

But he also heard the sparrows, calling, chirping, flapping in their cages.

Waiting to go to the factory.

He stood back up. The lid slid off. He tried to catch it, but it clattered to the floor. Secret peeked out at him. "What's wrong?"

"I can't do it." He climbed back out of the barrel as if it held scalding water. "I can't leave them to be squeezed into juice or whatever happens to them down there. It's not right." After a deep breath, he added, "I'm going to let the sparrows out."

Secret opened her mouth, but he cut her off. "I have to. I know it's not our mission, but I can't leave them."

"I know you can't," said Secret calmly. "But this is a closed room. The sparrows will have nowhere to go."

"We'll figure it out! Maybe if we're quick, we'll make it before the trolls find us. Will you help?"

"Stupid cub." Secret jumped down from the wagon. "You always ask such silly questions."

Sebastifer stood up from his barrel, too. The inky tears

showed on his face again, but his dog-grin was wide and happy. "You really are her son."

Together they returned to the pens.

They dragged two of the heavy cages in front of the door, and then they began their work. Sebastifer listened for the trolls. Secret took care of the cages she could reach from the floor, while Niklas climbed the stacks. He pushed open the latches, working as fast as he ever had.

If he had any hope that the trolls wouldn't hear what they were doing, they were quickly dashed.

One by one the doors burst open, releasing a cloud of sparrows, squeaking the loudest they knew how at the joy of stretching their wings. Soon they formed a vast, billowing flock that filled the great hall with feathers and trills.

Secret turned her ears down and out, to shield herself from the cacophony. "Now what," she called to Niklas.

Niklas churned on the inside, too. With the lambs, he had been trying to make trouble. But setting the sparrows free felt different. Like it truly mattered that these birds should have blue skies under their wings. It felt like something a hero might do. It felt right. His breath rushed too fast as he pointed to the giant leaded glass window. "We break them out."

They began a frantic search for something that would be light enough for Niklas to carry up the wall, but heavy enough to smash through the thick panes. Secret had just found a hooked metal rod, probably for lifting crates, when the noise died.

They turned around to find that the birds had all settled down, on cage doors, on ledges and sills, watching in utter silence.

Lost feathers drifted to the floor, and Niklas's heart fell with them.

And then the pounding began, like rolling thunder. The trolls were at the door.

Secret whimpered, tucking her tail in.

Sebastifer leaned against the wall, black spots drifting across his eyeballs, tail hanging limp. His brows were lifted in the middle. "She is here."

He closed his eyes as the double door scraped open, pushing the cages out of the way like they weighed nothing. A rasping voice cut the air.

"The boy-enemy! Come once again to Rafsa's den."

Rafsa crossed the stone floor with her long claws extended, clicking and rattling in her heavy bone armor. A good twenty troll guards piled in after her, green eyes lit and hungry, brandishing sabers and spears.

At the sight of Sebastifer, the troll witch tilted her head, and Niklas thought the hatred on her scarred face grew even hotter for a moment. "I see you've found our prisoner. You think that matters? You think freeing him will help you?" She spat on the floor. "We don't need him and his dreams anymore. The plan is too big for him now. It's too big for you."

She walked past Sebastifer, until she hulked over Niklas in all her smelly, scarred glory. "I would love to play a game with you, for what you did with the stew. Ruined our big night. Killed all my broodlings. Almost killed me, too. Clever boy."

She let out her purple tongue and licked her four-pointed star tattoo. "But Rafsa can't be killed, oh no. She can't burn, she can't die from bane. No matter what you do, Rafsa comes back to catch you."

She snatched at his arm. Her long fingers grazed the troll rune, which began to sear and itch beneath his shirt sleeve.

Niklas wrenched his arm away, backing up against the cages. Secret was right beside him. "No chance of escaping this," he whispered as the trolls circled around to cover both exits.

"None," Secret agreed.

They tried anyway, ducking to the side and racing for the nearest stack to try and pull themselves up. But Rafsa lashed at Niklas with her claw, and a sheet of red fell in front of his eyes.

"Sleep now, boy," she said as he crumpled to the floor. "The king wants you in his tower."

Darkness followed.

Chapter Forty-four

When Niklas came to, the air no longer smelled like sour milk. It smelled like roses.

"Are you all right, cub?" Secret's face hovered above him. Her worry poured into him from everywhere, from her eyes, from the softness of her paw on his shoulder, from the medallion around his neck.

"I'm fine. Just . . ." He touched his fingers to his forehead. Someone had bandaged his wound. "Just help me up. Where are we?"

"We're in the Nighthouse. Rafsa shoved us in here and shut the door. There are guards, but they stay outside." Secret glanced around at the curved walls and the stairs that wound around a wide column in the middle of the tower.

"I don't think the trolls are allowed in here," Sebastifer said. "The room is too unbroken."

He was right. It might as well belong to a separate castle altogether. Instead of dirt and rubble, there were china figurines. Instead of bone splinters along the walls, there were books on polished shelves, and a warming fireplace.

Suddenly Nightmares broke the illusion of comfort. Two skullbeaks dropped out of the darkness under the ceiling, wind rushing through their skulls. They gathered their cloth-wings and landed on the floor beside them. Moving their beaks in unison, they pointed toward the stairs.

Niklas looked at Secret. "Won't do to be a coward," she said softly.

No, it wouldn't. They walked up the stairs together, their heartbeats echoing through the medallions.

The stairs emerged into a round room. Apart from the circle of windows where the beacon's light had once escaped, and the door out to the wraparound balcony, the Rosa Torquata covered every inch of the chamber. A thick stem grew up from a hole in the floor and reached all the way up to the dome, where it spread into hundreds of rose-laden boughs that traced the ceiling and trailed down the mirror-clad sides.

It was very sick. The dark vine crawled everywhere, infesting every branch and twig, turning the roses black, and the scent unctuous. The starlight pulse had been strangled, leaving the Rosa Torquata of the Nighthouse completely dark.

Next to the stem a figure stood waiting, tall and deadly with his long-beaked skull. The ruler of Nightmares, the creator of skullbeaks. The killer of birds.

The Sparrow King.

He gave Niklas the same pinch in the guts as the skeleton birds that stood lined up around the room, following their every movement. Except the skullbeaks watched with hollow eyes. But the Sparrow King saw. The Sparrow King knew. And as his coal-fire gaze settled on Niklas, he had the feeling the Sparrow King hated him.

He didn't quite know how to reply when the king said, "I've been waiting for you, Niklas. Would you care for some fruit? It's from my own orchard."

He extended an arm toward the sole piece of furniture in the room: a big and nasty cage made from the living rosebush, with long, hungry thorns. Just like the one in Erika's bird castle, though it didn't contain a child. Instead it doubled as a desk, holding books and quills, crystal glasses, flasks and silver boxes, another bottle of the Emerald River starmead, and a bowl of magnificent diamond apples.

Secret gave a long, pained growl. Niklas turned and found her staring at a cowed shape that faced the wall behind the cage, positioned among lanterns and other discarded lighthouse paraphernalia.

Niklas went cold.

Kepler.

The Sparrow King ignored Niklas's silence. "Perhaps later, then. Or have you come to my castle to sample my real riches?" He ran his gloved fingers along a rack of three glass flasks, all filled with dark brown liquid. "A flask of Thorndrip is worth twenty baskets of sapphire plums."

He picked one from the rack and swirled it so weepy marks formed on the glass. "You know, I had no thought for trade when I invented this. I read about a new device using thorns to drain blood. The professor who designed it could not quite make it work, so I thought I would improve it. But if Rafsa had not suggested we bind the blood with troll runes, I would have failed." He raised the flask as in a toast to Niklas. "Don't you find it extraordinary that magical power can be distilled from sparrows? The very least important of creatures? It's something to do with the pain, Rafsa tells me. I'm sure a *human* understands the irony."

"No." Niklas made his voice as frosty as he could for someone whose heart thundered way too fast. "I think it's evil."

The Sparrow King said, "Truly? Then I'm sure you'll become more enlightened as you change from child to grown-up." The black roses followed his path as he walked to his desk, like eyes with a hundred dark lids. "I expect you've come to look at this?" In the middle of the trunk the bark had been peeled back in a ring and secured with runes.

The speakwood.

The wood within pulsed sickly and gray. "Perhaps you've figured out by now that it is the source of my sway over the Rosa."

The Sparrow King opened a silver box and pulled out a long syringe. With precise, steady movements, he pierced the wax lid of the Thorndrip flask and sucked the contents into the syringe. "Do you know this rune?" He drew a sharp V with the tip of the needle. Niklas knew it.

Obey.

"It is most useful." A small flick of the Sparrow King's wrist acknowledged Kepler. "Some, like your young ferret friend here, require a simple version carved somewhere on their body, and their will belongs to me."

Niklas's thoughts raced. Kepler was carved with a troll rune? That was the reason he had betrayed them? Secret went still beside him.

The Sparrow King crossed the floor until he stood right behind Kepler. "Turn around."

Kepler turned around. He did not look at his friends. Niklas looked at him, but he didn't see any troll runes on the ferret's body.

The Sparrow King snapped his fingers on Kepler's snout. "I don't need to keep him in the cage, because he is already caged." Kepler's eyes welled up, but he didn't move.

"I could hardly believe it when I saw a human child in the canyon," the Sparrow King said. "Especially when I recognized you as the son of a Thornghost. Oh yes, I've seen your dreams. Sebastifer has been most obliging."

Sebastifer's tail and ears hung heavy. "It's okay," Niklas said. "You couldn't help it."

The Sparrow King nodded. His beak drew a sharp V, too. "Neither could young Kepler here. Rafsa didn't want to risk you slipping through her claws again. She left Kepler in the barracks so he could bring you here." He patted Kepler's chest. Kepler's right hand moved to defend himself, but the left one brought it down as before. Secret snarled, but the Sparrow King's eyes glittered inside their hollows. "I told him to stay. So he stays, like a good boy."

The Sparrow King's cloak billowed as he returned to the trunk of the Rosa Torquata. "Other and more powerful creatures require a constant reminder to perform their tasks. A refill." He buried his syringe into the speakwood. As he pushed down the piston, black streaks appeared in the wood to form the *obey* rune.

The dark vine stirred all around the room as the Sparrow King pressed his palm against the rune. "Rosa Torquata. I would like you to listen."

There was something wrong with that hand, something that nagged Niklas like a buzzing gnat. But he couldn't think straight. His knees felt too watery, his chest too tight. *You must find a way,* Odar had said, and here they were, in the same room as the speakwood, while the poisoning took place. Skullbeaks loomed behind him, ready to put their beaks through his shoulder if he tried a move. But he couldn't have come all this way just to goggle like a stupid cub. He cleared his throat.

"Whatever your plan is, you have to stop. The dark vine is making the Rosa sick. You're putting everyone, including yourself, in danger."

"Yes." The Sparrow King raised his skull eyes toward the windows. The mist had cleared away to reveal a sky of darkness and stars, diamonds crushed and scattered. "Night has come to Broken. What do you think your thieving friends inside the shrub are doing at this moment? Toasting their toes by the fire? Drinking the last of their mead? I noticed you have left the apples hanging this year. Odar must be running out." His breath sounded wheezy inside the beak. "My guess is that most of them are asleep in their pathetic little shelters, surrounded by deadly thorns."

"How do you know all this," Kepler croaked. "You're not one of us. You're a Nightmare."

The Sparrow King lowered his voice. "Oh, but I am both."

Niklas knew enough about roles to tell when someone had stopped playing one. This was no longer the king of Nightmares speaking. This was someone else. He stared at the hand, the crystal glass, and the hand again.

Of course.

A beak that large could never drink from a crystal glass.

And there were four fingers on that glove, all of which pointed forward.

"You're no sparrow," Niklas said. "You're no bird at all!"

The Sparrow King watched Niklas for a moment. Then he hooked his fingers under the beak and began to ease his skull off its joint. The bird mask came off to reveal a pointed weasel face of dark brown and snowy white, with quick eyes and small, sharp teeth.

"Rafsa was right. You are a clever boy."

By the wall, Kepler gave a strangled cry. They had all seen that face before, in a portrait in the Second Ruby.

It belonged to Kepler's great hero Marcelius.

Chapter Forty-five

Kepler stood doubled over, as if his hero had cut him far worse than a troll claw ever could. His mouth worked and worked, but no words came out, so Niklas said them for him. "But you're their hero. They adore you!"

Marcelius cocked his head. Without the ponderous mask, his movements were fast and nimble. "Is that what they say now? They didn't much care for me before the Breaking. Turned their snouts up at my thoughts and theories, like they turned their snouts up at me. Made me a gardener when I wanted to be a runemaster. Kicked me out as a Greenhood apprentice." He tossed his sleek neck. "All because I didn't fit into any of their categories. I'm not a Petling like Kepler. I never lived in a warm house full of treats and love. And I'm not a Wilder like your cat there. I never knew a moment of freedom." He bared his teeth at the bars of thorns under his desk. "I'm best forgotten, because the truth is too ugly to remember. But I remember every closed door, every click of the tongue, every grunt of pity."

With unsettling speed, he prepared another shot, sank the needle into the speakwood, and set his hand against the rune. "Rosa Torquata. I would like you to wake the thorns of the Nickwood and kill the Brokeners in their beds."

"No!" The word burst out of Kepler's mouth. He tore away from the wall. With his right hand he pawed at his chest so hard, it undid some of Too's healing. Red light pulsed in his fresh wounds, coming from under his fur. *Oh, you nasty witch,* Niklas thought. So that's why they hadn't seen the *obey* rune. Rafsa had put it on the inside of Kepler's torn skin, knowing they would do their best to close the gash.

Kepler's fingers came away bloody as his other hand tore them away from his chest. The red light kept pulsing, but Kepler still found the strength to lunge at Marcelius, face screwed up with anger and grief.

The skullbeaks plucked him out of the air like a frisky kitten. Niklas found himself hurtling toward the speakwood, but the skullbeaks got him, too, pinning him to the floor. One of them curled its claw around his arm. The troll rune began to sear and thud under his shirtsleeve. Beside him Secret bucked and snarled, batting her paws at the skeleton birds to get to him. She tore off a bone and sent it clattering across the floor, but it didn't matter. There were too many.

"Enough of that," Marcelius said, touching his amulet briefly. "I want them reasonably whole."

The skullbeaks stepped back immediately, and Secret hissed at them as she placed herself between Niklas and the enemy.

"It's okay, Secret," Niklas called, easing his sleeve away from his burning skin. *Don't give them a reason to kill you,* he thought, willing the feeling to go through the medallion, but he said, "Don't worry."

Marcelius frowned at Kepler, who lay panting on the tiles. "Not as weak as I assumed, then." He shrugged. "It doesn't matter. My will is already surging through the Rosa like venom through a snake's tooth."

The fight had gone out of Kepler. Sebastifer stood quiet and still, arms hanging limp from his frail form. Secret had retreated to the one thing she needed to do: guard Niklas's back.

Niklas thought of the small houses built entirely from the Rosa's gifts, and of the sprawling collection of memories that was the Second Ruby, and the candlelit long table where no one would eat aniseed bread anymore.

The *obey* rune in the speakwood throbbed and throbbed.

"Call it off! The Brokeners are kind people," he said, trying to sound steady and convincing. "You might think of them as thieves, but all they have done is make a living out of scraps."

Marcelius stroked his white chin, appearing to consider

Niklas's plea. "The Brokeners ought to blame themselves. I tried telling them about the potential of troll runes. Magic in this world is usually tempered. Balanced. But Erika Summerhill made the troll runes with no safety pin. They could do almost anything as long as the pain was sufficient. But the librarians and scholars laughed at me."

"That was twenty-five years ago." Niklas's smile felt stiff and wrong, but he pressed on. "They keep a sculpture of you in the village. Kepler painted a portrait. It's true that they love you." Niklas nodded at the box of syringes on the desk. "You can save them. Just call it off."

Marcelius walked over to his desk, ran his fingers over the box. "You're right. I don't much care that the Brokeners laughed at me back then."

He picked out another syringe, weighing it in his hand. "In fact, I don't care about them at all. When Rafsa broke down the door to the Ruby that night, I found her more reasonable than anyone I had met so far on this side. We figured out we had a common purpose, she and I." He snapped the box shut with a grin, and there it was again, that hot hatred burning against Niklas's skin. "The canyon gate."

Niklas felt his smile slip. "I know that's your plan, but I don't understand why. You have a whole kingdom here. Jewels and a castle. Why do you want to open the canyon gate?"

"Don't you know yet?" Marcelius smiled. "Rafsa's reason should be easy to figure out. She was the first troll with magic, and it was powerful enough to allow her to cross the border. When the gate opened for Erika twenty-five years ago, Rafsa snuck through to Willodale and stayed there until the gate narrowed and the magic grew thin. Ever since, she has wanted nothing more than to claim her homeland for her brood."

"And your reason?"

"I want her to succeed."

Marcelius approached them slowly, each step thudding on the tiles. "That is why I decided to become the Sparrow King. I want Rafsa and her brood to destroy every farm and field of Willodale, to torch and kill and ruin as they yearn for, as you *created* them to yearn for. But most of all I want the cages burned."

Cages? The sparrow cages flashed through Niklas's head, but that made no sense at all.

Marcelius licked his teeth. "Did you know that the grass that grows around an apple tree tastes like fruit? No? It doesn't, actually, but that was how I imagined it from my pen. I longed to sniff at the sweet roots and hunt for field mice in the night. To swim in the cool, green river and feel the water slip off my fur when I returned with fish." He shrugged. "Or perhaps I just thought that I did. The line between the animal I once was and the creature I became is blurred. But one thing I know was real. The cage."

He pulled up before them, stretching his long neck until he loomed tall. Right now he seemed more terrifying to Niklas than the skull mask ever had. "The pens where they kept us must burn. Old Molyk can go on top of the pyre, and if your murderer of a mother were not already dead, I would gladly add her to the flames."

Niklas's ribs felt too tight. Old Molyk. The pens. His mother saying, *We're not hurting him. We're saving him.*

Marcelius wasn't a weasel at all. He was a mink.

As if he could follow the thoughts in Niklas's head, he lifted his skullbeak amulet. Within the spiky jewel glass encasing, there was a small, worn center of wood. One of Castine's medallions. Marcelius opened it. There was a boy inside, a boy with dark hair that stuck up in the front. Peder Molyk.

Marcelius was the mink cub who drowned.

With a yelp, Sebastifer sagged to his knees. Secret caught him.

Marcelius shook his head. "Poor, stupid dog. All those years and you never guessed who was behind the mask. I did have Rafsa carve a *hide* rune on me so you wouldn't catch it when I read your dreams, but still you should have known. Have you told the others what happened that night, Sebastifer? How the children all crawled out of the black waters, but not you and I?"

Sebastifer swallowed hard. "They loved us, Marcelius. We wouldn't be here otherwise."

Marcelius clicked the medallion shut in the casing. "If Peder had truly missed me, he would have sat by Sorrowdeep and mourned me as much as Erika mourned you. The Rosa Torquata could have picked him to be Jewelgard's Twistrose. He knew about the troll runes, he knew about the hunt. But of course it chose her. My murderer. The Thornghost."

He pushed the needle into the last flask of Thorndrip.

"I've waited twenty-five years to have my revenge. And now the Rosa no longer has the strength to resist my commands. You see, I worked on it for the longest time. Injected it with Thorndrip. Helped the dark vine grow. The Rosa resisted and resisted." He tapped the syringe. "Then, last spring, the solution occurred to me. Instead of just the injections, I could feed the blood directly to the Rosa. No boiling, no nonsense. No sparrows. I caught some bigger fowl to use for my purpose. Strictly speaking, they were two rodents, a fox, and an otter."

Kepler moaned.

"The missing Brokeners." Secret growled. "You killed them."

"Indeed I did. And that is when the magic happened. That is when the crack in the mountain truly began to widen. A few days ago, it was wide enough for Rafsa to awaken her brood, a plan you managed to bumble your way into ruining. But I'm glad you did. This is better."

He gave the speakwood a third and final shot, and said, "Rosa Torquata. I would like you to open the cage."

A shudder went through the rose tree. Black veins shot

out from the speakwood, spreading along the branches, and the flowers opened wide. The thorns creaked open, too, and now Niklas saw that the cage had no bottom. It was just a black hole in the floor. Like a gullet. "A dog who should be long dead, a ferret who gave everything for his beliefs, a lynx who awakened before her time, and a boy who fancied himself a Twistrose. If that diet doesn't finally break her, I don't know what will." He touched his amulet, making it glint red under his fingers. The skull-beaks crowded in behind them, herding them toward the opening. Secret tried to fend them off, but got a beak in her shoulder in response.

"Tonight the canyon gate will not just open. It will shatter like a dam, and the Nightmares will flood all of Wildodale and wash away the filth."

Niklas wanted to shout, but his throat wouldn't let him. "You've had your revenge on my mother, many times over," he whispered. "And Peder Molyk already burnt down the pens. He keeps sheep now."

Marcelius waited a while before he spoke. "Then they can burn down his house instead and the entire farm with it." His skull mask gleamed blue as he pulled it back on. It slipped into place with a sucking sound. The Sparrow King's voice sounded hollow once more as he touched his amulet and said, "Throw them in the cage."

Chapter Forty-six

They tumbled into the dark well, crashing along the branches until they reached the bottom. The ground was cushioned with shed petals that broke their fall enough to leave them bruised but not injured. The trunk of the Rosa Torquata grew along one side, sending reedy branches out along the walls. Its roses were black, and it was nearly smothered by the dark vine that riddled the entire well. Red light seeped out between the dark vine's serrated leaves, illuminating white objects that hung hooked onto the thorns. Bones and skulls.

"The missing Brokeners," Kepler said through his teeth.

"We have to climb back out." Niklas gripped the trunk and tried to place his foot somewhere, but all the thorns of the dark vine turned toward him like knives. He backed to the center of the well, struggling to find his balance in the slippery rose heap. Far above, branches wove tight across the opening, closing them in completely.

"Maybe we can find another way out," he said.

"I don't think there is one." Sebastifer's eyes glazed over as he searched through the memories Rafsa had leaked into his head.

"There isn't," said Kepler. "I read the rose tree was here before they constructed the lighthouse. They built a central column around the stem to protect it. We're inside it. There is nowhere we can go, nothing we can do to . . ." His voice petered out.

Niklas glanced at Kepler. "Do you think it's too late? That the Brokeners are already dead?"

The ferret shook his head firmly. "They'll fight back. Odar has stripes, and you've seen how wary Castine is. No enemy can sneak up on her."

Not even if the enemy is all around her? If it's someone she trusts with her life? If she's asleep in her bed? But Niklas didn't say those things out loud. What good would it do?

"Did *you* know?" Secret suddenly asked, studying Kepler's face. "That you were leading us here to betray us?"

"Sometimes." Kepler stared at his clenched hands. "But when I tried to tell you, my tongue went numb and I couldn't speak. Then I forgot again."

"Why the causeway?" asked Niklas. "Why not parade us up the road? The skullbeaks wouldn't have touched us."

"Rafsa didn't think you would believe me. She told me

to take you across the sand." Kepler swallowed pitifully.

"You had never even seen the sea stairs before." Secret's voice was quiet.

"No. Rafsa put the route in my head. I told the truth about the prisoner, though." He bowed his head. "I really thought it was Marcelius. I thought he was a hero."

His right hand trembled as it came up to touch his chest, but as always, it was brought down again by the other hand. "I've been trying to get rid of it. But I can't. The rune won't let me." He finally looked up at Secret.

Secret met his gaze for a long moment. Then she lunged at him in one fluid motion, nose crinkled in a terrible sneer.

"Secret! Stop!" Niklas cried out, but Secret paid him no mind. She sank her teeth into Kepler's chest and tore out a patch of fur with one ferocious bite. Blood seeped down her chin when she spat it out.

Kepler hadn't even lifted his arms to defend himself. He looked a little shaken, but he buttoned his vest over the wound as a makeshift bandage once more. "Thank you, lady fair." He got a small lantern out of his pocket, lit it, and pointed it at Secret. "I knew I could count on you."

Secret squinted and looked away. "It had to be done."

The lantern light caught something stirring on the floor between them. A long creeper of dark vine had crawled across the petal heap. It hooked its thorns into the patch of fur and dragged it back under the leaves.

Niklas barely had time to yell "Look out!" before a hundred vines broke through the leaves, scuttling across the floor like spider legs.

The first curled around Secret's ankle. She wrenched around with a thin mewl.

Niklas wanted to help her, but vines caught his leg, too. They all tried to pull free, but the creepers only tightened. The ugly brown thorns came out. Secret growled again as one of them licked across her chin where Kepler's blood was still wet.

Niklas yelled, "Stop!"

All around the well the leaves rustled, and the faintest echo whispered back.

Stop, stop, stop.

The vines pulled back, hung in the air like sniffing snakes. All the thorns twisted so they pointed at Niklas, trembling as if they strained against something.

The dark vine was listening.

But what would he say? Niklas tried and failed to bring out his winning smile. Begging for mock-mercy from his grandmother was a game. This was not. "Please," he said. "Don't . . ."

One of the vines lashed out. It hit Niklas in the arm and stuck a thorn through his skin, tasting him. The leaves began flapping.

"It's the little liar! The little thief!"

It was the nasty voice from the mountain tunnel. It

rasped like claws against a windowpane, loud enough to shake Niklas's spine. "Still frightened, still scared."

The vines woke from their strange suspension, whipping around every foot, paw, and arm.

All four of them hung in the web, caught.

A big thorn stabbed Secret's paw. She screamed in panic. Her thrashing made the thorns tear her skin. The terror that flowed through the medallion made Niklas dizzy. Or was that his own fear?

"Secret!" Kepler was trying to catch her attention. Even though the vines held his wrist cruelly, he managed to turn his light in her direction. It bounced off her golden fur as she bucked and fought.

Some of the light fell on the wall behind her.

Niklas gasped. One of the Rosa Torquata's black flowers had turned bright red, just like it did when it tasted someone's blood. But the Rosa hadn't tasted them. The dark vine had. Niklas thought the dark vine was a separate plant, an infestation that squeezed all reason and will out of the Rosa Torquata, turned it into something it was not. A parasite. But maybe it wasn't?

"Kepler," Niklas cried, still fighting the panic from the medallion. "Point your light at the leaves by the trunk!"

Kepler looked confused, but he did as Niklas said. Under the leaves, the dark vine grew right out of the Rosa Torquata's trunk. It was no parasite, but part of the giant rosebush.

Their enemy was the Rosa Torquata itself.

The most powerful creature in this world.

Niklas's heart pounded. *You can only be brave if you're scared in the first place,* Secret had told him. Well, he was scared now, scared for his life. But he had to try. There had been two voices in the tunnel, and one of them wanted to help. Something had stopped the dark vine from attacking him in the Greenhood's map room, and something had made the dark vine hesitate here in the well.

The old voice, the part of the Rosa Torquata that could not watch someone kill a human boy. He had to get through to it.

Niklas drew a deep breath. If there ever was a time to find the right words, this was it.

"You know what the people of Willodale say about me? 'That Niklas Summerhill. He's such a rascal and trouble-maker, but he sure was brave when his mother died.' Well, they're wrong. I was so terrified, I didn't dare talk to anyone."

"Silence," the nasty voice hissed. The vine slithered around his neck. It only had to tighten and he would be all out of both words and breath. But Niklas continued. "Just because someone makes you out to be brave or scared or evil, it doesn't mean it's the whole truth."

"You are no one," said the nasty voice. "You are just a boy with a dead key."

"Maybe," Niklas said. "What I'm saying is still true. The

dark vine is you, but it's only part of you. You can . . ."
The vine constricted, and his last words came out a croak. "You can fight it."

The vine around his neck dropped away. All the black roses opened wide, watching him through their many lids. In the circle of Kepler's flashlight, the red rose turned pale. Pale like the roses of the Nickwood. Like the true Rosa Torquata.

Niklas stared at the single white bloom, willing the change to spread. *Come on,* he thought. *Fight!* But the Rosa Torquata didn't change and didn't heal and didn't move.

Not until a dark vine snared around the healed rose and pinched it off. It dropped into the fallen petals.

No. His words weren't enough. The dark part of the Rosa was too strong.

Thorns buried deeper into his legs and arms. Fear flashed through the medallions, racing back and forth between him and Secret like electric heartbeats. *Are we going to die here? Are we going to be skulls and bones tangled in the thorns?*

No!

"Don't give up!" He wasn't sure if he was pleading with the Rosa, or Secret, or himself. "Please don't . . ."

The dark vine pulled taut and yanked him off balance. The world turned upside down as it lifted him by the ankle, higher and higher into the air.

Far below he heard Secret roar.

With a dizzying twist, the dark vine whirled him about and sent him flying into the trunk of the Rosa Torquata.

The air left his lungs. Rough bark scratched him as he slid down along the stem. The petals at the bottom broke his fall, but he landed in a crumpled heap, head ringing. His chest throbbed and the bandage leaked blood down the side of his face. He had no idea if he could get up.

The dark vine didn't seem to find it very likely, because for now it ignored him, concentrating its attack on the others. They were still fighting, Secret snarling and writhing, Kepler and Sebastifer using their teeth. Vines coiled around them like tentacles. Thorns buried deep into their fur and stayed there, sucking their blood.

They *were* going to die. Niklas wanted to get up, but his limbs wouldn't listen. He closed his eyes and rested his cheek against the trunk of the Rosa Torquata, just for a moment. It felt soft and smooth, almost like a cheek against his own.

Smooth?

Niklas opened his eyes.

His fall had pushed aside a pile of rotting petals, exposing more of the trunk. He was leaning on pale wood where a patch of the bark had been cleared away in a rune-rimmed square.

Another speakwood!

It had to be very old. The wood inside the square was cracked and the runes barely visible. But it was there.

Maybe it was a speakwood they had used before the lighthouse was built? Niklas sat up. Blood from his cheek had left a dark smudge in the middle. It disappeared, absorbing into the Rosa.

Niklas scrambled onto his knees. He had an idea. Somewhere in the wild terror, he felt Secret reflect the feeling back at him. *Hope?*

Yes, if he could get it right. He was no Greenhood or chosen guardian, but this was no time to worry about rules. Sometimes you had to choose yourself.

Niklas fumbled his satchel open and brought out his mother's book, riffled through it until he found the runes he needed. Erika's bold ink strokes were easy to read in the red light from the dark vine. Niklas dipped his fingertip in the trickle of blood from his forehead and copied her runes as precisely as he could. A square with an eye inside. A four-pointed star.

Awake. Power.

For a moment the runes rested on the surface of the speakwood, black like oil. *Come on,* Niklas thought again. *Please wake up!*

The blood sank into the grain of the wood, but the runes remained visible as soft lines. A flicker of white light appeared along the streaks, faint at first, then stronger and stronger, until both runes pulsed with starlight like a beating heart.

Then a blinding flash of force sent Niklas tumbling

backward into the petal heap. Tremors shook the trunk of the Rosa Torquata, and a deep voice thundered, "Enough!"

The old voice. It sounded angry. No. *Furious.*

The walls of rosewood flexed. The branches writhed, the thorns grew longer. The Rosa Torquata struck like a thousand snakes, but not at the four prisoners. It turned its thorns on itself, slicing the withered, black tendrils clean off at the roots. The dark vine fell to the floor around them in a nasty, crackling rattle.

All the roses had turned pale now, and among them twinkling lights ignited, one by one, spreading out until a sky of tiny stars filled the whole shaft.

Sebastifer, Kepler, and Secret watched Niklas with shining eyes. "You did it," Sebastifer whispered. "You're her son, and you did it!"

"The Rosa did it," Niklas said. "I helped it wake up, but it healed itself." He put his palm on the speakwood and said, "Thank you!"

The Rosa didn't answer, not with the nasty voice and not with the old one. Instead it creaked and shifted, braiding branch with branch, making a ladder for them along the trunk.

Another burst of brilliant yellow light flashed through the well, this time from the chamber far above.

The cage had opened.

Chapter Forty-seven

It was a long climb up the ladder. The rungs gave slightly, and even though the Rosa had averted its thorns, they had to be careful. Sometimes a burst of light filled the shaft, but they saw no movement at the top, no skull-headed silhouette peering down.

When they emerged from the hole, the Sparrow King's desk was empty and the door to the balcony was open to the moonlit night. But Marcelius himself and his guards were gone.

The light bursts that illuminated the whole chamber came from the upper speakwood. Rid of its dark veins and Rafsa's obey rune, the ring of wood gleamed clear, framed above and below by glowing signs.

Secret's good ear turned toward the open door. "I hear yelling and screaming."

They all stepped out onto the balcony.

The castle courtyard lay abandoned, the Nighthouse road empty. But far away at the bottom of the hill there were Nightmares in the Falcon Circle. The entire plaza between the jewel orchard and the docks milled with trolls.

Trolls by the hundreds, claws out, shrieking and howling for battle. Above the jewel orchard, skullbeaks flew in a churning cloud, directed by the Sparrow King himself. He sat atop the giant skullbeak they had seen in the workshop, awakened now, big as a skeleton dragon. They circled above the docks, amulet glowing red in the Sparrow King's hand.

And inside the jewel orchard, barely visible along the top of the walls: strange creatures with spikes.

"What are those?" Niklas squinted. "Another kind of Nightmare?"

"No." Secret lashed her tail. "It's the Brokeners!"

"You mean they're not dead?" Kepler rummaged in his vest pocket and produced his telescope. He leaned so far over the railing, it seemed he might fly down to join the battle. "They're in armor! They're *fighting!*"

Sebastifer wagged his scraggly tail. "They must have gotten away somehow!"

But when Niklas looked through the telescope, he felt a cold claw in his gut. The Brokeners hadn't gotten away. They had gotten themselves trapped.

The trolls hadn't breached the gates to the orchard yet, but it was only a matter of time, and not a lot of it. They were crawling up the outside of the walls like ants.

The Brokeners did their best to push them back. They didn't have swords or axes, but they had teeth and claws and hearts. As Odar said, it wasn't nothing. The raccoon himself stood on top of the wall, brandishing the sign of the Second Ruby for a weapon. "That sign is oak," Kepler said. "That crazy, brave old hero!"

But neither was it enough.

The gates shattered. The stubs swung open, revealing the Brokeners inside. They stood in tight ranks, three deep across the opening. Niklas thought he saw the tiny form of Too, nearly drowning in her spiky armor. Odar jumped down from the wall and landed in front of the line, batting off troll claws with his sign like he had led rebel armies his entire life. But they still resembled a ragtag band of petty thieves that had stumbled into an army of executioners.

This wasn't going to be a fight. It would be a slaughter.

"I need my bow!" Kepler gripped the railing. "I need to get down there!"

"You can't reach them," Secret said. "Castine is already doing her best. Look."

They couldn't see her behind the orchard walls, but it must be her firing into the skullbeak flock. Her arrows rose up like reverted shooting stars. But even if the odd wing of cloth burst into flames, it didn't make much of a difference. There were too many skullbeaks.

"We have to do something!" Niklas clenched his fists. But what could they do against an army of Nightmares?

Nothing. Unless they knew their weaknesses. Something that would take out all of them, at once.

"If only we had acorns," he groaned.

"Or dawn would come," Secret said. But there was no sign of it, not even a graying in the east. Niklas wished he could pull the sun over the horizon and into the valley.

The sun.

Something the Greenhood had said stirred at the back of his mind. *A rose tree that sent its rays of sunlight into the night.* "A beacon, to show the way . . ." He said it out loud, trying out the idea on his tongue.

"What?" Secret turned her good ear toward him.

"Petrify," he whispered, because he knew a girl who was good with words like that. Niklas bolted for the balcony door. "The lighthouse!" he called. "We have to get it working!"

The Rosa had pulled its living branches back from the walls and ceiling, curling them into a lovely tree. The speakwood formed a bright ribbon around the stem. But Niklas quickly realized he had no idea how to turn the light bursts into a lighthouse ray.

"We need the beacon lens to focus the light," Kepler said. "It's over by the wall. I glared at it for hours."

"You know how to work the lighthouse." Secret didn't sound surprised.

"Lady fair, I've been waiting to take back this place since I got here. Of course I know how to work it. In theory." Kepler pulled the sheet off a three-foot-tall round object with a hole in the middle. The lens shimmered in angles and layers of jewel glass. It was crafted like a ring that opened up on hinges. "Huh. It doesn't look like the ones in the book." He cleared his throat. "But I think it goes around the speakwood."

Niklas and Secret helped him carry it over to the Rosa Torquata. It clasped perfectly around the stem. "It should probably sit on a base that swivels," Kepler said. "But we'll need to hold it in place and turn it to control the ray." He glanced up at Secret. "Together?"

"I suppose." She helped him lift the lens so it enclosed the speakwood.

"Better shut your eyes," Niklas said. "It's going to get pretty bright."

"Better hurry," Kepler said. "It's going to get pretty heavy, too."

Niklas ran back outside, where Sebastifer was watching the battle. "How are they doing down there?"

Sebastifer's tail drooped as he handed Niklas the telescope. "Let's hope your plan works."

There were crumpled forms outside the orchard gates. Niklas didn't see how many.

Yes, he thought. *Better hurry.*

The first ray of light shot out of the beacon and out across the Frothsea, blasting the moon out of the water with its wedge of gold.

"To the left," Niklas yelled, and Kepler and Secret

turned the lens. The beam swept across the mouth of the Kolfjord before it went out.

"More left," Niklas yelled.

The second ray hit the ivy ruins of Lostbook and almost made it to the docks before it went out.

The third ray struck the Falcon Circle, licking over the tiles like a tongue of light. Shooting in from above, it grazed everything, spared nothing. Everywhere it hit, the trolls turned to stone.

No ugly screams rent the night. There were no gargles or howls to blend with the skullbeaks' cry. Just a sudden silence as their limbs froze. Once the beam had done its work, a host of standing stones filled the circle. Alive no more. Dangerous no more.

Odar swung his sign an extra time, stopped. He looked around at the stone trolls. Looked up at the flashing beacon. And as he pointed up to the Nighthouse, the other Brokeners howled, waving madly, a giant roar that could be heard all the way up on the bluff.

But there was one living creature who did not join in the cheer. The Sparrow King wrenched around on his bird of bones. He, too, saw the beacon. His skull mask glinted as the ray passed over him again. Then came a red flash from his amulet as his great skullbeak banked, head hooting as it set course for the Nighthouse.

"Put the lens down," Niklas yelled. "The trolls are out, but the Sparrow King is coming!"

"What now," said Sebastifer. "Hide inside the tower?"

Probably a good idea, Niklas thought. The only reasonable thing to do, really. Except the skullbeaks over the jewel orchard hadn't moved. The wind brought the sound of their skulls: *Hoooooowoooo*. Now the cloud formed into a whirling, rattling funnel of death that touched down in the garden. They must be striking blind, and jewel trees provided some cover, but the Brokeners were still like fish in a barrel in there.

Secret and Kepler came rushing out on the balcony, drawn by the distant screams. "We have to stop him," Niklas said. "He controls the skullbeaks with his amulet. We have to take it from him!"

The Sparrow King held the spiky disc in his hand. They could knock it out of his hand. They *had to* knock it out of his hand. But Kepler had no bow, Secret couldn't reach, Sebastifer was no fighter, and Niklas for once in his life found himself without a single stone to throw.

"I need a rock," he said. "Something to throw!" He pawed through his satchel, but there was nothing there that could help, not unless the Sparrow King came close enough to be hit by a book. "Secret, look inside," he called, but Kepler stopped her before she could go.

"No time." Kepler fished his broken Marti medallion out of his vest pocket. "But I have this."

"You're sure?" Niklas's hand drifted to his own medallion, felt a soft sting. "Maybe I should use my own . . ."

"This is broken already." Kepler placed the locket in Niklas's hand. "Just make it count."

The medallion was cracked, but heavy. It felt like it could count if he hit well.

The Sparrow King was getting near. Niklas waited until the great skullbeak flapped its wings over the courtyard, so close that he could see Marcelius's eyes burning inside the mask.

Don't miss now.

He hurled the medallion at the Sparrow King.

It may have been sheer luck, or it may have been all those stones Niklas had thrown at Mr. Molyk's rusty barn roof. But whether it was one or the other, the medallion hit the Sparrow King's hand, knocking the amulet out of his fingers.

The amulet fell through the air, flashing red all the way down to the courtyard. The spiky glass shattered on the flagstones, leaving Peder's medallion bare.

Above the jewel orchard, all the skullbeaks came apart and tumbled to the ground. Not as Nightmares, but as cloth and empty skulls, raining bones into the garden.

They did not fall alone. The giant skullbeak's wings stopped. It careened down and to the side until it crashed into the grand hall, smashing the leaded glass window of the ballroom.

The Sparrow King was thrown off. He caught the ledge

below the window and dangled by his fingertips. His mask pulled to the side, so heavy now. But Marcelius couldn't let go of the ledge to take it off, or he would fall.

Something fluttered above his head. A sparrow. Another appeared in the frame of the broken window. It perched for a moment between the shards of sparkling glass before it took flight. Suddenly a great cloud of birds streamed out through the opening and gathered in the sky. The caged sparrows had been flying loose inside the ballroom, and now at last, they were free.

Chirping and screeching, the flock grew and grew, hovering over the courtyard as if it waited for something.

But the last sparrow didn't join them. It flew down to the Sparrow King's mask and began pecking at the holes. It was only little, but the Sparrow King still couldn't help himself. He had to cover his eyes.

So he fell.

The sparrow flock dove after him and caught him before he hit the courtyard. It rose up into the sky with Marcelius trapped inside, hanging by his cloak like a black tangle in the center. And while the lighthouse sent its flashes into the night, the birds struck out over the sea, carrying the Sparrow King into the horizon, to meet whatever fate they thought fair.

Chapter Forty-eight

It was Odar's idea to hold the feast in the Falcon Circle. "We always celebrated here back in the Jewelgard days, so why not? Standing stones or not, the city is ours now."

They cleared away the troll filth and withered dark vine, the shattered bones and broken skulls, and the tiles emerged for all to see, gems glittering between the flagstones in a sweeping pattern of soaring wings. Odar had three Brokeners carry the old stove out of the Ruby's kitchen, and he fetched his last bottles of starmead all the way from the Second Ruby himself. Now the smells of baking drifted across the plaza, crisping crust and aniseed, sweet apple and cardamom.

"Let's have a toast while we wait," Odar bellowed out to the Brokeners gathered by the fountain, starmead cups in hand. A bonfire burned at the tile falcon's heart, and torches and floating candles in the fountain's water painted the Falcon Circle gold. "To Niklas, the not-quite Twistrose, and Secret, his not-quite Wilder! Though only one of them has fur, I say they both earned their stripes this night!"

The Brokeners cheered until Secret licked her paw, thoroughly embarrassed. But Niklas knew she enjoyed every second of praise, just like he did. He raised his cup in thanks.

The air in the valley felt so different now that the trolls had left. The salty ocean breeze had swept away the evil smells, and blended now with the scents of the garden. The Brokeners had changed, too. They stretched taller and moved more easily, and their fur picked up the gleam from the lights and the jewels of the orchard.

"And to Kepler!" Everyone fell quiet as Odar held his cup high. "There is much to be said for keeping the treasures of an entire people safe. But I'll be scratched if hope isn't the greatest treasure of all."

Kepler stared at him in confusion for a moment, but then he grinned. "There is much to be said for showing up for the fight, too, even dressed in an apron. Don't worry, Odar. Next time we'll make sure you have a proper coat of armor."

"Ha!" Secret was the first to laugh, and it spread all over the plaza. Odar laughed louder than anyone, tipping his cup to Kepler.

It turned out Too did know the healing rune after all.

She held a doctor's court inside the jewel orchard, sharing her magic with everyone who needed it. Niklas came to her last, when no one was looking. She healed his head wound, but Niklas had one more request. "Don't tell anyone," he said, unbuttoning his sleeve. "But you've given me an idea. I just need your help."

The smashed orchard gates had been removed entirely. Once the toasting was done, Petlings and Wilders walked along the silver gravel paths, some for memories and some to see the garden for the first time. To tide them over until the apple cakes were ready, Gidea the fox had brought baskets and filled them up with diamond apples, emerald pears, sapphire plums, and ruby morellos. At last Niklas had a bite of fresh jewel fruit. "Huh," he said to the diamond apple. The shards crackled with just the right twist of sour candy, while the flesh melted tart and sweet on his tongue, filled with all the tastes of a warm summer.

"Good?" Secret sat beside him on the marble steps of the fountain, brushing away crumpled leaves with her tail.

"Very." Niklas licked the diamond shard, careful not to slice his tongue. "But Willodale apples taste better to me."

"You mean Molyk apples," Secret said.

"I have no idea what you're talking about." Niklas took another bite to hide his smile. "Speaking of which, why didn't you try to stop me in the sparrow pens tonight? It was sort of doomed to go wrong, that trick."

"Because you didn't free those birds to cover yourself or

to prove a point or annoy the grown-ups. You did it because it was right and it had to be done."

Niklas made a mock frown. "That sounds strangely like praise."

Secret yawned, but the medallion tingled as she leaned against him. "Don't think it makes you any less of a cub. Just slightly less stupid."

Niklas tossed the core into a pile of roots. "You're right. I do like them better when I've worked for them." He smiled at her. "Don't tell my grandmother."

Time slowed toward morning like dark, sweet marmalade. Someone brought in fiddles and a drum so everyone could dance while they waited for the stew that cooked over the bonfire. Niklas had talked to each and every Brokener now, and between all the slaps on the back, the well-dones, and the better-late-than-nevers, he had pieced together the events of the night.

The Greenhood had come to the Second Ruby, telling Odar they must flee or fight. The Brokeners didn't hesitate at all: Out came the armor, and Odar had led everyone into the gardens and through the tunnel of the jewel orchard to either hide in the only place the dark vine had not yet reached, or if that didn't work: to make a final stand.

Sebastifer sat in a folding chair at the rim of the music and the light. He looked tired, but he wagged his tail when

Niklas brought over a cup of starmead. "Thank you, boy."

Together they watched the revelers. Right now, Castine skipped about in the middle of the circle, tail bound with tinkling bells and legs so quick they were almost a blur. She grinned wide at the shouts and whoops she got from the others.

"I've been wondering about something," Niklas said. "Rafsa marked you with a *sleep* rune to keep you under, and a *dream* rune to make you reach for my mother, and the one for power to make you strong enough to keep the gate open. But why the rune for *awake*? Doesn't that go against the others?"

Sebastifer looked away. "They put that on me because I'm not supposed to be here. When our humans die, we don't linger. We leave. Become travelers. I've been aching to go for seven years."

"Oh." Niklas wanted to say something comforting, but he couldn't think of anything that would help. Instead he asked, "But where do you go?"

"No one knows. Travelers leave in the middle of the night, and there are no bodies or anything. Many think that we get to be with our children again." He shrugged. "Like Odar said, there's no greater treasure than hope."

Niklas nodded at Castine, who kept glancing over at them. She had spent half the evening by Sebastifer's side. "I bet she's itching to make an Erika medallion for you."

Sebastifer smiled. "I've got my own, back at the cabin.

They're not as pretty, but I sure worked my fingers off to make them."

"She did the same." Niklas found the little figurine from the bird castle and held it out for him to take.

Sebastifer ran his claw gently along the back of the carved dog. "Well, she was slightly more talented than me. Thank you for showing it to me." He closed Niklas's fingers around the figurine. "But you keep it. Put it where it belongs. I have a gift for you, though."

He smoothed back the fur on his arm, bringing out the *read* rune. "I know how you remember the day your mother died. No one can take that memory away. But I could show you how it looked for her."

Niklas stared at the rune. "You want me to see her dying thoughts?"

"Yes. But it's not what you think."

And it wasn't. Niklas put his hand on the rune, expecting the cold tug to take him to the memory of a pale and scared boy standing in the doorway and then backing into the dark hallway. He expected fear and pain and the word *Thornghost*. Instead it showed him a blur of sunny images, fraying at the edges. Niklas tucked into his bed in the yellow room. Niklas throwing rocks in the Summerchild. Niklas wide-eyed over a page in the science books. Niklas chasing Tobis across the yard, laughing and light, fading slowly, until he and everything was gone.

He opened his eyes and found Sebastifer's brows pulled

up in that odd combination of heartbreaking and warm particular to dogs. "It's not good to carry guilt for things you can't help."

Niklas couldn't speak. His throat hurt too much. He just nodded and put the dog figurine into his pocket. Over by the Ruby's great stove, Odar shouted with a tray in his arms. "Apple cakes are ready! Get them while they're hot!"

Sebastifer nudged his shoulder. "Go dance with your cat. I've never heard of a lynx Wilder before, but if you ask me, she's quite something."

"Yes, she is," Niklas said, searching for her golden fur in the crowd. "But please don't tell her that, or she'll be impossible to talk to."

"I won't," Sebastifer said, squinting up at the stars. "But you should."

He found Secret at the entrance of the jewel orchard, in deep conversation with Idun Greenhood, who to everyone's surprise had come down from the woods to join the party. His cat, as Sebastifer called her, leaned gracefully against the gate post, no longer self-conscious on two legs. Niklas felt a small sting of worry. How long had they been away from home? He had lost track of the nights, but it couldn't be much more than a week since they met in the oak tree. She had changed so much since then. How would it feel for her to change back to a normal lynx?

"There you are," she said when he came close. Niklas knew that voice, the calm one that meant danger. "You need to listen. Idun has something to tell you."

"About my mother?" Niklas saw that Idun was carrying the Book of Twistrose. He had been wondering if the fall of the Sparrow King would blot out the Thornghost stain on his mother's name. Maybe the two of them together would make a whole Twistrose. "It wasn't fair, you know. Couldn't she have gone through a different gate, one that didn't mean crossing Sorrowdeep? She almost drowned there!"

Idun shook her head. "I don't know why the Rosa did that. But it's not infallible, as the Sparrow King proved. Runes or no runes, it should never have tolerated him." Idun hugged her book. "I fear I bear some of the blame. Marcelius of Molyk was once my apprentice. But I found him feeding blood into the speakwood, so I threw him out. I thought I removed him from the danger, and later I believed him dead. But it was I who gave him the tools he needed to feed his hate." She lifted her chin. "However, that is not why I must speak with you."

"It's not?"

Secret's eyes brimmed with reflections from the jewel trees. "It's about Summerhill. Niklas, we came here to stop the thing that caused the taint."

"And we have," Niklas said, staring from one to the other. "Haven't we? The Rosa Torquata destroyed all the dark vine?"

Idun inclined her head. "It did." She brushed the Book of Twistrose with her fingertips. "But say you have a bowl of clear water. And say you have a pen that dribbles ink into the bowl. Even if you remove the pen after a while, the water will still be blue."

Niklas rubbed his forehead. "What do you mean?"

"She means," Secret said quietly, "that whatever magic has already passed through the gate will still be there."

"And whatever monster." Idun put her hand lightly on Niklas's sleeve, and he understood. Rafsa. That's why her standing stone was not to be found. She had left for safer ground. She had gone home.

On the mosaic of the Falcon Circle, the Brokeners still clapped and laughed. Odar and Gidea twirled around in the center now, and Too capered about with an apple cake in each hand. Only Kepler glanced their way over the rim of his cup. He sat on the fountain perched on the hind leg of a marble horse, looking content. The horror of the *obey* rune seemed to be slipping off him like a bad dream.

"We can't tell them," Niklas said. "They're celebrating."

"You can go quietly if you like," Idun said. "It's what we do when the time comes. We leave them dancing."

Dancing? Niklas turned to look at Sebastifer's place. It was empty, save for his cup of starmead placed neatly on the seat of the folding chair. *Go dance with your cat,* he had said, and meanwhile he had gone, and all his memories of Erika with him. To travel only he knew where. Niklas whispered, "You leave them dancing."

Idun pulled her cowl up. "I'll let the Rosa know you are ready. Farewell, Niklas." She bowed. "Secret."

As they edged closer to the darker parts of the feast, where there were more shadows than torches, Niklas snuck two apple cakes, like a thief in the night. Which was his favorite part to play, but right now, he would have liked to give everyone a hug instead.

"You've hugged them all already tonight," Secret said. "Once more doesn't matter."

"Yes, it does," Niklas said. "You should at least say good-bye to Kepler."

Secret frowned at the fountain, where the marble horse now pranced alone with no ferret to keep it company. She shook her head. "No need."

Chapter Forty-nine

This time they left Jewelgard by the main road. Even covered with weeds and crumbled leaves, it was smoother than the paths, and before they knew it, they had reached the end of the garden. Niklas turned to look one last time at the silver-dipped terraces, at the black mirror of the fjord and the moon that hung between the two cliffs at the opposite end of the valley. The lighthouse that was no longer the Nighthouse flashed with the pulse of the Rosa Torquata.

"I wonder if they'll be able to repair the castle after the trolls," Niklas said.

"The mending has begun already," Secret said. "Notice the air?"

Suddenly Niklas knew what had felt so different in the Falcon Circle and all the way up here. It wasn't just the smell. The creeping Nightmare horror was gone, pushed outside of the border, where it belonged.

"I guess that this realm is no longer Broken, then." Niklas said.

"Not so cheesy," Secret muttered. But Niklas still caught her smiling when she thought he wasn't looking.

Nightmare territory though it was, the canyon lay peaceful and still. Niklas didn't have much hope of finding Sebastifer there, but he still poked his head inside the cottage. Filled with dust-specked moonlight, it felt even more abandoned than before. Someone had taken all the Erika figurines from the windowsills. "Safe travels, wherever you're going," Niklas said into the cottage. "You were the best dog anyone could wish for." The quilt and the empty sills did not reply.

The last time they saw the gate, dark vine had filled the crack in the canyon wall. But now the dark vine was gone, as were the vicious thorns, and the tunnel had opened. Flickers of the Rosa Torquata seemed to beckon them inside.

"Come on. Let's go home." Niklas glanced up at the starry sky one final time, then climbed into the tunnel.

"Hello?" he called. "Rosa Torquata? Can you hear me?" He brought out the old, withered rose twig from his satchel. "I have the key."

Neither the old nor the nasty voice answered. Instead Niklas heard a quiet voice behind him.

"Cub."

Secret stood outside the archway. Niklas turned back and stopped on the threshold. A few spindly vines, gentle and thorn-less, shot across the opening, as if to warn him: Don't step outside. "What's going on?"

"I can't go." Secret took a step back.

"What do you mean?" The words came out louder than Niklas meant. "We have to go home! We have to save Summerhill!"

Secret leaned forward and put her paw through the gate. Immediately her fur started smoldering. Fine tendrils of smoke curled out between her claws. She jerked back and licked the sparks. "This is the reason for Rafsa's scars. She burns when she comes this way, even if she is covered in runes to make it through."

The smell of scorched hair stung Niklas's nose, but still he didn't understand. "But we came here together. The Rosa let us through!"

"It let you through because you had a Twistrose key. It let me through for a different reason." Secret sat down in the black sand, just as she had when they first arrived. "Idun explained it to me. I can't go back, because I don't belong in the other world anymore."

"Because you're . . ." Niklas swallowed and swallowed. *I feel strange,* Secret had said when they entered the tunnel the first time. Because she was dying, because of him. "I didn't know," he whispered.

"If you had known, do you think it would have stopped me from coming with you? It won't do to be a coward." Her yellow eyes were liquid. "Which is why you have to go now. Hurry."

"I can't . . ." Niklas's palms felt clammy. He gripped his medallion. "I can't face Rafsa by myself."

"Yes, you can. That troll witch has nothing on your courage. Not now when you know how to use it." The feeling that streamed through the medallion was sad, but also proud. "You will do what has to be done. You will save Summerhill. I will stay here."

"Well, I'm not going to leave you. You're . . ." Niklas faltered. He didn't know how to tell her that she was his only friend now, and that if he had to go back without her, he would be alone again. And every wonderful thing that had somehow found its way into his life would be gone, just gone. Instead he said, "You'll be alone in Nightmare territory."

Secret snorted. "Not exactly. Kepler has been following us since we left the feast. He's hiding in the vegetable patch." She glanced over her shoulder. "Poor guy doesn't know how to sneak. I think I'll have to teach him."

Niklas bit his lip. Of course there was no need for Secret to say good-bye to Kepler, because Kepler wouldn't be the one to lose her.

Secret lifted her huge, white paw, holding it up to the invisible border that would separate them forever. Niklas reached outside and held it tight. He had no idea how to let go.

"Don't be sad, cub." Secret pushed her forehead against his hand. It was the most cat-like sign of love she had ever given him. "There is something else I have to tell you. The Greenhood let slip a little secret from the Book of Twistrose." She tried a smile. "A name. I don't think you're supposed to know, but as you say, who cares about stupid rules?"

She whispered it to him, and it was the only reason Niklas found the courage to turn his back and go through the tunnel.

Chapter Fifty

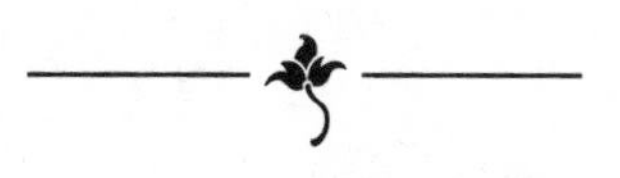

The Rosa Torquata had pulled back from Secret's winter cave, leaving her ledge and the small pool to darkness. Niklas used his hands to find his way through the old avalanche. His nose, too, because the troll stench wafted out from the entrance to the troll caves. But he couldn't hear anything, neither footsteps nor howls. Breathing as shallowly as possible, he chose the smelly tunnel. Fresh torches burned in all the sconces. Rafsa had been here not long ago.

For this fight, Niklas would be alone and without weapons. Except there was one place where he might be able to find some bane, even if it happened to be in gravy form. But when he reached the kitchen, he found it scoured clean. Every last spoonful of bane-poisoned stew had been scraped out of the kettle. Rafsa was nothing if not thorough.

Still no sound broke the silence in the troll nest. Niklas pushed farther in, past the tunnel where he had been caged and kept, and into the great hall.

The six trolls that died from the stew stood gathered near the door. They had turned back to stone, with crumbling holes in the middle where the bane had done its work. One had an ear-like lump where his neck would be. Niklas stepped around him.

"Oh no," he said, forgetting for a moment that Secret wasn't there to hear it.

The hall flickered with torchlight. Jagged shadows danced on the walls. The giant stalactites that Rafsa had so carefully bound and carved with *awake* runes had all cracked open, leaving piles of rubble beneath each. The sleeping trolls within were nowhere to be seen.

Wherever Rafsa had gone, she had brought her army.

As soon as he emerged into the moonlit night, he knew he would not be crossing Sorrowdeep by boat. The little vessel lay in pieces on the pebbly beach, crushed by a boulder that had broken loose from the mountain wall. He had no choice but to swim. Niklas squinted across the pond. The water lilies had withered. He could almost sense the taint brimming beneath the mirror calm of the surface.

In the distance a sound went up: a sharp, unbroken

keening that rose and fell like a siren. Niklas knew it, because he had heard it a thousand times. Deep in the valley, at the Summerhill border, the screaming stone wailed, even if there was not a breath of wind. He had no doubt that Rafsa made it so.

He had to go home.

He cleared his throat and took a step forward. Some pebbles rolled off the beach into the water. The ripples crept across the pond, and in return he thought he heard a soft hiss. Was there a word in that hiss? Did it call his name?

Niklas's stomach filled with cold. In his dream, his mother never made it to Sorrowdeep. But he had always believed that if the terror hadn't woken him up, this is where the nightmare would end. His hand found the medallion. A warm pulse surged through his fingers at Secret's response. *Worry.* He gripped the medallion hard.

"Hello? Is anyone there?" He waited. Nothing.

Goose bumps spread all over Niklas's body as he pulled off his boots and dropped his satchel on the beach. He put the Sebastifer figurine in his pocket and tightened the string of the medallion around his neck.

He took another step forward, into the water. Mud oozed up around the stones under his toes. His mother had stood like this on the opposite shore, feet in the water.

Maybe she was down there. Or not her, but a Nightmare version of her, made out of tainted water. Maybe her eyes were black and desperate. He tried to keep the shivers out of his voice. "I need to swim across now. The trolls are going to break the border. I have to stop them."

No one answered.

Sorrowdeep felt cold and silky when he slid into it. A hushed splash sounded every time he kicked his legs. He alone disturbed the water, and in the moonlight it must make him very visible from below. Niklas didn't look down. He kept his eyes trained on the finger of rock on the other side.

Something brushed against his leg.

He thrashed and kicked, whipping around to catch sight of the thing that had touched him. He saw nothing but murky depths, but there was an icy current in the water. It made his arms and legs heavy, like added gravity. He struggled on. His breath came in hurried gasps, and his strokes felt cramped and useless. He made it only halfway before the coldness pulled him down.

When he went under, the moonlight broke into green shards. Hairy lichen drifted up from the bottom. His clothes billowed up as he sank. He couldn't feel his limbs anymore, didn't even know if they tried to swim. His thoughts raced like crazy.

Far below he glimpsed the half-eaten hull of a boat, cradling a rusty square.

The mink cage.

He couldn't see any bones. Only an algae-covered door

that came closer and closer as he dropped toward the bottom.

His chest ached, but the surface seemed so distant now, a glass window to a lost world. Secret's medallion floated up in front of his face, covered in pearls of air. He couldn't lift his arm to catch it. Instead his hand brushed against his pocket and the Sebastifer figurine.

Suddenly he heard the old dog's words, clear as a bell.

That cage carried all her guilt and sadness. You should have seen her that summer, Niklas. All those nightmares. Her head became a cage, too.

This was not just his nightmare. It was also his mother's.

The cage had turned into a keeper of her guilt, a weight of sadness that dragged him down to trap him. *It wasn't her fault,* Uncle Anders had said. He was wrong. It *was* her fault. But she only wanted to help. She had never meant for anyone to die, just like Niklas never meant for Rag to die. Or Secret.

He looked down.

The cage door had opened.

Beside it, his mother hung in the water, tied to the cage with a length of chain. Her nightgown and curls wafted like silver sheets. She had taken the form of her twelve-year-old self, the Erika who had almost drowned here. The one whose statue hid in the chapel crypt with a hollow heart. The one who was too afraid to cross the water.

The Thornghost.

She stared up at him with black eyes.

All this time, Niklas had been so frightened of the dreams and the grave and the secrets, of being left all alone, of having failed her the day she died. But he knew her now. He understood why everything had happened, even why she had tried to erase herself from his life.

He wasn't scared of her anymore. The fear had gone away, and the place it had taken up ached like an old scar that only bothered you when you scratched it. It didn't hurt anymore.

He stretched his arm toward her.

He moved in the water. Not toward the cage, but toward the light above. The current was weakening. Suddenly his body came to life. He needed air. Now.

He kicked his legs. They tingled as the cage let him go. Up and up he swam, until he broke the surface, gasping and coughing. When he got his breath under control, he almost couldn't tread the water anymore. He had to make for land.

As soon as he reached the other side, Niklas looked both in the water and above the water. He scrambled up on the finger rock to see better, leaning out to catch a glimpse of her gown. Sorrowdeep glimmered where water dripped from his hair and body, but of his mother there was no sign.

"I met Sebastifer. He knows why you didn't come."

Niklas paused. He had no idea if she could hear him. "He's sorry. He forgives you."

No whisper, no words, only the distant wailing of the screaming stone far below. Niklas had to go. With shaking fingers he eased the Sebastifer figurine out of his pocket and held it over the pond. "I forgive you, too."

He opened his hand and let go.

Chapter Fifty-one

The wail from the screaming stone filled the Summerhill woods with anguish. Niklas had no doubt what caused the howl. The border was breaking, and if he could not stop it in time, all the bravery he could muster and all the sacrifice Secret had made would not help Summerhill.

He knew all this, yet when he turned the final curve and Summerhill came into view, he still staggered at the sight of it.

The main house slept, the elm tree didn't stir. A clammy, gray mist hung down the hill, stopping abruptly at the screaming stone like foul water lapping at a cliff. There were dark shapes in the fog, stony and tall, with faces of warped and cruel leather that sliced the mist.

Rafsa's army.

There must be a hundred of them gathered on the hill above the Oldmeadow trail, waiting to slash and kill.

Rafsa herself stood in front of the screaming stone, dressed in her scorched bone armor and hundreds of runes. She had fresh burn marks on her skull and shoulders, but when she turned to greet him, she grinned.

"The boy-enemy, come to bleed!"

The trolls all turned to him. Their eyes glowed like fog lights. Niklas stopped well outside the mist, but he had no doubt the trolls would overtake him in seconds if he tried to run. He took a deep breath. "The Sparrow King is gone. The sparrows took him. Broken is Jewelgard again."

Rafsa snickered. "The Sparrow King was always a stupid one, too vain, too certain his mind was the sharpest. The sparrows can have him and the whole realm if they want. They don't concern us anymore."

"The trolls of Broken are dead, too. Petrified by the lighthouse."

She didn't even blink. "I saw. But I have the Summerhill brood. In these woods, it is humans against trolls. Throat against claw. I like that fight better."

A small, crisp noise weaved into the keening of the stone. Niklas knew that sound, too. His first thought was of Kepler, and his frantic warning, *It's my task to ring the bell!* But Kepler wasn't here, and he couldn't place the sound. Not until Rafsa hoisted a white armful off the ground, making it chime with terror.

Edith. Mr. Molyk's bell sheep.

What was she doing out of her pen?

Rafsa had bound her legs with troll rope, but still Edith bucked and tossed her not-so-pretty head, trying desperately to run from the creature that had killed her lamb. But of course she couldn't.

"Don't do it," Niklas cried. "Don't hurt her."

"No?" Rafsa dumped the sheep on the sandy path, where she struggled and kicked but failed to get up. "Maybe I won't. Not if you do as I say." She slid out the scythe claw on her right hand. "I thought I had to cut you to break the stone, but now I think you had a point. You made the border, boy-enemy. You can break it with the magic I gave you. I made the rune on your arm to destroy the stone. Just touch it and make it so."

"How did you catch Edith?" Niklas edged closer, trying to buy some time. "You can't go past the stone."

Rafsa threw her head back. All the bones in her armor clattered. "Easy! Molyk has better things to do than watch over his sheep. I found this one wandering in Oldmeadow. You couldn't have pulled a better prank on him yourself."

Edith rolled her eyes with fear. She had given up trying to run now, but she trembled so hard her bell stuttered. "Please, Edith," Niklas called to her. "Pretty, pretty Edith. Don't be scared. I'll bring you lots of sugar, I promise, sugar and green grass . . ."

Rafsa watched them, heavy-lidded and smug, until Niklas ran out of things to say. Edith was too terrified to hear him anyway.

"That's how it is with you, boy-enemy. You're so eager to sacrifice yourself. But someone else? That's a choice you're too scared to make." Rafsa ran her claw along Edith's side, shearing off a ribbon of tangled wool. "Tonight you will choose. What will it be? Break the border stone or kill your friend?"

Niklas closed his fists. "I won't do it."

"No?" Rafsa clicked her tongue. "For someone who claims to love animals, you leave a lot of dead ones in your wake. Maybe you don't care as much about sheep as you do about dogs or lynxes. But this one . . ." She kicked at Edith, who bleated miserably. "This one you could *save*. If you want to."

Niklas looked around for help, for an idea, for anything that could spare him this decision. He couldn't measure poor Edith's life against his grandmother and uncle and every soul in Willodale, he knew that. But if he let Edith die, it would be Rag all over again. And Secret. Sebastifer. Even poor Marcelius, sinking and so afraid. Worse even, because this time it would be on purpose. It would be his choice. "Pretty Edith," he whispered, more to himself than to her. "Don't be scared."

He rolled up the sleeve of his wet shirt. He had kept the *break* rune hidden for so long that the wound had not fared so well. It rose from his arm in angry welts. Rafsa licked her cracked lips, already tasting the triumph. She held Edith by the scruff and put her claw against the sheep's throat, and Niklas could tell from the troll witch's glittering eyes that she knew she had won.

"I, Niklas Summerhill," he began, but the words got lost in the wail of the screaming stone and the tinkling of Edith's bell. He raised his voice. "I, Niklas Summerhill, made this magic. Now I, too, call this rune to unmake it."

He paused. The troll brood whispered and moaned as they slid their claws out, and the fog gathered and grew behind Rafsa like a wall. She leered at the screaming stone, rattle-boned and hungry.

"All of it."

Rafsa wrenched toward him, forgetting both the stone and Edith, who twisted around and rolled out of reach. Too had not been able to remove the troll rune from his skin, not without cutting it off. But she had improved it.

All Brokeners are thieves, the little cat had said. *I just happen to steal runes.*

The & rune curled through the corner of the rectangle, taking the rune's power away from Rafsa and making it Too's. But hooked onto the end of the &, Too had made an extra mark, an *N* surrounded by swirls and dots. *I made this mark for you,* she had explained. *If I'm right, the rune should now be yours to do with as you will.*

A howl broke from Rafsa as she understood his plan. Niklas screamed at the top of his lungs to drown her out. "All of it! I unmake all the magic in these woods!" His arm seared as if it had caught fire, his legs buckled and he fell to his knees. He dug his nails into the troll rune and yelled, "Break!"

With a tremendous crack, the screaming stone split in half. The pieces toppled. One half fell toward Summerhill, the other toward Sorrowdeep. The first half would have smashed Rafsa into the ground, except she was no longer there.

The troll witch had ceased to be, along with her bone armor and hundreds of runes. Niklas could see no trace of her or of the troll army in the coils of fog that twirled away from the stone, unraveling. Where their giant feet had stood, the moss showed footprints and claw slashes. But already they smoothed out and filled in, erasing Rafsa and all her brood from the memory of the land.

A sigh swept through the woods, ruffling the leaves as it blew up the hill. From the mountains came the sound of distant thunder, except there was no storm coming in. Dust puffed up above the treetops, hiding the face of Buttertop, and Niklas knew in every bone that there would be no going back to the avalanche tunnel. That the troll caves were gone and the gate to Broken locked away forever. He lifted his hand to his medallion. No electric sting. No pulse. Just soft wood against his fingers.

The magic had broken, and with it his stupid cub heart.

But the Summerchild whispered in its dell, clean and no longer tainted, and Edith's bell rang as she dashed down the Molyk trail, free of the troll rope and free to find her lambs. And somewhere under a different moon, in a garden full of jewels, his Secret was probably eating apple cake and telling Kepler he didn't know how to sneak.

"You were right as always, Secret. It had to be done." Niklas slipped the lynx medallion inside his shirt and turned to go home.

Chapter Fifty-two

Just one more thing, he told himself as he latched the Summerhill gate shut behind him. Just to be absolutely sure. Instead of continuing into the yard, he turned left and followed the path down to the stream.

The graveyard slept in its crook of the water. The birds hid in the willows, the raspberries drooped with dew. Erika's grave seemed undisturbed beneath its cover of grass, the headstone untainted by moss. And though the Summerchild filled the meadow with whispers and splashes, Niklas couldn't hear any words in its voice.

The crypt lay dark and silent under the chapel ruins, but Niklas didn't go in. He had seen enough of ruins and crypts for a while. He shoved the hatch into place, to wait for another time and a brighter day.

He was leaving when he saw the new stone, a pretty, flat one with rounded edges and a faint sparkle in the grain. Three lemon-yellow letters had been painted across the top. While Niklas was away, someone had made a gravestone for Rag.

He decided he would put one up for Secret right next to Rag's, and one for Sebastifer, too. He was sure they wouldn't mind one another's company.

The first thing he noticed when he entered the yard was how worn it was. Even in the moonlight he could see the marks of many car tires crisscrossing the dirt. The second thing he noticed was a dark streak that shot out from the barn and headed straight for him. It didn't stop until it had him trapped.

Apart from Secret, Niklas had never heard anyone purr quite so loudly.

"Tobis," he laughed. "That's not very catlike of you." Tobis, being a cat, didn't care. He continued to weave around Niklas's legs, rubbing his head against the damp trousers, sounding like a broken engine. Niklas bent down to scratch his chin. "If you don't stop soon, I'll start to think you missed me."

Tobis reared up on his hind legs to sniff the lynx medallion, then rubbed against that, too, lifting his lip to make sure he left his scent.

"I know," Niklas whispered. "She's quite something."

The door to the main house opened, and Uncle Anders stood in the doorway, hair pointing every which way. The flashlight painted his cheeks hollow. "Niklas," he said. "You stupid, reckless, dear boy. You're home!"

Chapter Fifty-three

When Niklas woke, the strangest sound thrummed up through his bedroom floor. A violin. Uncle Anders was playing in the bird room. Not the sorrowful lullaby of the Summerchild, but a happy, lilting folk tune to stomp around to. By the loud thumps that came with the music, that's exactly what Uncle Anders was doing.

Niklas looked through his windows. To the north, the screaming stone lay broken in half in the moss. To the south, the yard shimmered with sunshine.

He washed his face, found fresh clothes, and rushed downstairs. Underneath the bench in the hallway, the chocolate cake tin felt promisingly heavy.

Still, he waited a moment before he opened the door to the kitchen. They hadn't woken Grandma Alma last night because Uncle Anders said she needed her rest these days. Niklas hadn't said anything, but he worried. The last time he had seen her, she lay tucked into her tiny bed, so frail, it felt like she was gone already. But when he went inside, he found her busy at the kitchen counter, dressed in her splotchy flower apron and smacking her lips. Making tea.

She turned to him. "Well, don't just stand there and gawp. Come over here!"

He crossed the floor and hugged her, and there was certainly nothing frail about the squeeze she gave him. "Grandma!" he said into her white curls. "You look so much better!"

"Well, I feel better." She let him go and returned to the task at hand. "That was some fever. I had the strangest dreams. I dreamt my grandson went into the woods and disappeared."

Niklas waited for some sign that she was joking. He had been gone for five nights, Uncle Anders had told him. If she wasn't going to ask where he had been, he would at least expect some sort of punishment. But as she got the milk jug out of the fridge and set it next to the sugar, she wore her regal face, perfectly pleasant but somehow impish underneath.

He decided to stick to the play.

"Me too. I dreamt Uncle Anders woke all of Summerhill playing the violin."

She snorted as she strained for her mug above the kitchen counter. "More like a nightmare, that."

Not really, Niklas thought. Not even close.

He hadn't dreamt at all last night, but a chill curled down his back, and he supposed it would be that way whenever he heard the word *nightmare* for a very long time. But in the sun-warmed kitchen, dreams were easily shaken off. He fetched the mug down for her, and she dunked it in the big pot of tea simmering on the stove. Judging from the bitter smell, it had been steeping all morning. "Would you like some? I've made extra, from a bottle as per your instructions. Turns out Mr. Molyk has a nose for good, strong tea."

"No, thank you," Niklas said. "Wait, did you say Mr. Molyk?"

"I did." Grandma Alma peered up at him. "Now sit down so I can tower over you when I speak, like a proper queen."

Niklas sat down.

"Mr. Molyk has been here a great deal since you disappeared. He's been searching for you day and night. With the other farmers, with Uncle Anders, and when the others had to rest, alone. Always searching."

"He has?" Niklas picked some sugar cubes out of the bowl and turned them over in his hand. Rafsa had said that Mr. Molyk had other things to do than watch his sheep. "Why?"

Grandma Alma tilted her head. "You know, just because it was someone's secret once doesn't mean you're not allowed to guess." She plucked the sugar out of

Niklas's hand and dropped all of it into her tea. "You've got a passable head on your shoulders, young prince. You figure it out."

Niklas thought of the twelve-year-old Peder Molyk in Oldmeadow and of Mr. Molyk leaning on his shovel by Erika's grave. With the smallest slant, the memory shifted so that Mr. Molyk didn't look angry anymore, just sad and full of regret. Everything had changed after Broken: the stream, the screaming stone, and most of all, his mother.

He had a thousand questions for Uncle Anders, when he stopped playing, and for himself, too. But for now there were just too many muck tricks between him and any sort of sensible reply. So he said, "Can I have some chocolate cake?"

Grandma Alma laughed. "For breakfast? Certainly not. But I may have something else for you." She glanced up at the kitchen wall clock. "Yes, I'd say it's about time. Go outside and wait."

He padded barefoot down the steps. The ground felt cool where the elm tree spread its shade across the yard. He headed for the edge of the netherfield, where Tobis lay basking in the sun on a flat stone, and they sat for a while in companionable silence, watching the butterflies flit across the golden grass.

Of course Tobis heard the noise first. He was too lazy to get up, but he cocked an ear toward the road at the bottom of the field. A plume of dust rose where a dented red car appeared between the trees. As soon as it came into view, it stopped. The passenger door flew open, and a girl hopped out and ducked under the fence, running through the knee-deep grass toward him, grinning like crazy.

Lin.

Niklas felt his breath fasten. *The Greenhood let slip a little secret from the Book of Twistrose,* Secret had told him before they parted. *A name.*

Even across the field, he knew that Lin had changed. Her hair grew as wild as ever, and she still wore the grubby old cardigan. But there was something behind that smile, an inkling of adventures most serious and true.

Niklas walked into the field to meet her.

THE END

ERIKA'S SONG

Wake now, little rose, the night grows dark and old.

your feet must find the trail tonight, to Sorrowdeep the cold.

Your feet must find the trail tonight, to Sorrowdeep the cold.

Wait now, little dog, your voice will carry through. The key lies in her

hand tonight, Se-bastifer the true. Oo ——————————

The key lies in her hand tonight, Se - bastifer the true.

Stay then, ghost of thorns, if you can't play the part.

The key will lead you nowhere when it's locked inside your heart.

The key will lead you nowhere when it is locked inside your heart.

My deepest thanks are owed:

To the most awesome Torbjørn Øverland Amundsen, who read every draft and never got tired. Not even at five a.m. on deadline nights. Not even when I had to be lured across the finish line with candy. (It was caramel, too, because he's that kind of guy.)

To my wonderful editor, Lauri Hornik, for her heart, wisdom, and navigating skills. To Dana Chidiac, for invaluable edits and for paying attention to every little detail. To Kali Ciesemeyer and Jennifer Thermes, for the gorgeous illustrations. To my copy editor Regina Castillo. And to *everyone* at Dial Books for Young Readers who does such a marvelous job of turning stories into stunning, well-published books.

To my agent and dear friend Jane Putch, for being brilliant and a living life vest.

To the luminous Laini Taylor, for inspiration, friendship, advice, and hope. Wells and ropes, forever.

To my fantastic brother, Eivind Almhjell, for Erika's Song and the broken realm. To my beloved sister, Line Almhjell, for the tandem hearts. And to both for the auxiliary brain power.

To my talented friends and colleagues Siri Pettersen, Torbjørn Øverland Amundsen, and Tonje Tornes, for the twenty-four-hour helpline.

To Shanti Irene Gylseth, for lynx advice. To Ina Vassbotten Steinman, for small seeds sown. To Peter Brown, for support and friendship. To Kjeld Hendrik Helland-Hansen and Thomas Ingebrigtsen-Lem, my favorite oddballs.

To everyone who went on a trip with Lin and Rufus and didn't want it to end. To librarians, booksellers, teachers, publishers, bloggers, and everyone who puts books into the hands of readers.

To my fierce little wolf pack, Magnus and Martine, for sharing me with Niklas. To my mother, Unni Ohrvik Almhjell, always. To Madeleine Ryan and Viral Shah, for belonging.

To everyone whose roots stick into the ground below the elm tree on my grandmother's farm. Especially Laila Almhjell, animal whisperer and hero, and Erik and Ivar Almhjell, rascal princes both.

To the beautiful Stine Galtung, whose clever fingers inspired Castine. We'll keep dancing.

To the ferrets of Wild Rumpus in Minneapolis, who absolutely don't know how to sneak.

And last but not least, to Pims, Balthasar, Puskas, Mario, Sputnik, Melinda, Ella, and all you other cats in my life. If I could see you now, I'd squint and look away.